# TO KILL AN ORENTHAL

## The Life and Deaths of the Infamous ORENTHAL JAMES

Written by
Martin S. Freigger

Editor
Greg Freed

URGENCY REYNOLDS PUBLISHING CO.
*New York*

Most Urgency Reynolds Books are available at a special quantity discount for bulk purchases for sales promotions, premiums, fundraising or educational use. Special books or book excerpts can also be created to fit specific needs.

For details, write: Special Markets, Urgency Reynolds Publishing Co., 279 Troy Road Suite 9, Box 301, Rensselaer, New York 12144

Published by Urgency Reynolds Publishing Co.
New York— www.URPublishing.com



To Kill an Orenthal- The Life and Deaths of the Infamous Orenthal James
Urgency Reynolds Publishing Co.
Paperback ISBN 978-0-9792969-0-1

Library of Congress cataloging-in-publication data on file with the Library of Congress.

Control Number: 2007922332

Cover design by UR Publishing.

The text of this book is set in Garamond.

PRINTED IN THE UNITED STATES OF AMERICA

10 9 8 7 6 5 4—ELM—1 2 0 3 7 3— 6 0 6 5

"Despicable"©
"To Kill an Orenthal"
by Martin S. Freigger

"Flabbergasted."©
"To Kill an Orenthal"
by Martin S. Freigger

"Hoodwinked"©
"To Kill an Orenthal"
by Martin S. Freigger

"This is an
Atrocity
of epic proportions"©
"To Kill an Orenthal"
by Martin S. Freigger

"Pulp Fiction of
Murder Fantasy"©
"To Kill an Orenthal"
by Martin S. Freigger

This one's
for you –
all the best –,,
—Martin S. Greiggser

# Dedication

This book is dedicated to the countless men and women of the media who shamelessly provide us an unwelcome abundance of personal heart-ache and misery on a daily basis.

Thank you for bringing us into the private lives of so many unsuspecting victims.

Thank you for acting as judge and jury on so many instances where we did not have the capacity to form our own opinions.

Thank you for hiding behind your misdeeds while pretending to be acting in the best interest of public safety.

Thank you for giving us what we wanted even before we asked. And most importantly, thank you for allowing me to present my contribution.

## Also

This book is dedicated to the countless victims of violent crimes and their families; in hopes that they are able to find peace in the most unsuspecting of places.

# Acknowledgments

I wish to thank my family— for always being there, and for always supporting my projects.

# Fictional Disclaimer

*This is a work of fiction. Names, characters, places and incidents either are the product of the author's imagination or are used fictitiously, and any resemblance to any actual persons, living or dead, events or locales is entirely coincidental.*

# Foreword

This book of short stories is broken down into a series of Hogtales and Murders.

The main character, which is regularly referred to throughout the book as, the infamous Orenthal James, is a complex and difficult character for the normal person to identify with. He is a deviant, and a phony by nature. He is a human predator lurking amongst the innocent, who's every move, is calculated and depraved.

Orenthal James displays blatant disregard for social rules, norms, and cultural codes. His impulsive behaviors and indifference to the rights and feelings of others, proves that he is a dangerous sociopath.

## The Hogtales

The purpose behind each Hogtale is to expose the true nature of the character through stories of embarrassing truths. Orenthal James is a liar; a cheater, a fraud. The magnitude of his manipulation and deceit is immeasurable, but apparent throughout these short stories. After exposing the main characters flaws, each Hogtale is then followed by a story of his untimely death.

## The Murders

Multiple forms of capital and corporal punishment are served upon the infamous Orenthal James throughout the book, without a judge or a jury; without evidence or proof, without due process, civil liberty, or constitutional amendments. The infamous Orenthal James is exposed and executed multiple times without the right of an attorney; without public opinion, political review, or even a speedy trial.

The assassinations; manslaughters, accidents, executions and killings of the main character in this book, give the reader the ultimate satisfaction of being able to read through multiple versions of the characters life and demise, creating a pulp fiction of murder-fantasy.

Simply put, this book is about punishment to the wicked; fast and furious, without an appeal, the way justice was intended to be served.

# Compilation of Short Stories

# Born a Thumb Sucker

## A Murder

Two weeks prior to his birth, Orenthal's momma bragged to anybody who would listen that she just knew she was going to give birth to a little baby girl. Misses James also bragged that she knew her baby girl would be born on *Independence Day*, and that one day, her little baby girl would grow up to be sumbody'.

Exhausted from depression and walking out of the largest room in her beyond modest three-room living space, Misses James at first mistook her labor pains for intestinal fermentation and flatulence. Once Misses James realized her error, she knew she would have to make her way down the stairs in a hurry if she wanted to give birth out in the small shed, the only out-building on the plantation with a water pump and a stove. Misses James had set the shed up much like a delivery room, with a bucket of water and fresh straw for the mud floor. The arrangements were beyond exceptional for the delivery of any farm animal.

Rushing down the dark stairwell clutching her apron, Misses James knew the second she hit the second to last step that there was no chance that she was going to make it out to the shed to do her *grunt-work*. She dropped to her side at the bottom of the dark stairwell, knowing that it was a matter of seconds until she would be clutching hold of her little baby girl.

Misses James had given birth twelve other times before, and this time would be her first little girl. She breathed and pushed, thinking pleasantly of her coming daughter. With blood gushing from her and her body trembling with nature's fury, Misses James pushed one last time, and out popped her little baby onto the dirt floor.

Outside there was a hellacious storm of lightning and thunder, and Misses James ran out towards the shed with her new child in her arms. Covered in mud and blood and rain, she protected her new child from the elements with her apron, entered the shed, and placed her newborn baby gently on the mud floor. Lighting the oil lamp, she rushed back to wash her newborn in the stainless steel bucket.

Excited because she had collected so many hand-me-down girl clothes over the years, she knew that her daughter would be the best-dressed little girl in town. She placed a flower bonnet on her new baby's head, tying it under her chin, as the child sucked its thumb furiously.

Smiling with pride while washing her baby, Misses James tugged gently on what she thought was left over from her baby's umbilical cord. Misses James blood ran cold when she realized her error.

Running out of the shed screaming, still covered in blood and landing on her knees in the mud and the rain. Misses James pounded the earth in great fury with the agonizing reality that her little baby girl had been born an insecure, wobbly little boy.

Abandoning her baby in the shed that evening, she promised herself that she would never, ever feed him and that she would rather her bastard child starve in the cold before she raised another heartache.

Orenthal James was born in Hogsville, Mississippi on July 5, 1949, the bastard child of an illegitimate couple of bastard children.

The next morning at daybreak, Mr. Johnson, the farmer who owned the plantation that Misses James' property was on, was looking all over for his stainless steel bucket. It was time to feed the hogs, and he was furious that that stainless steel bucket had gone missing again. Entering the shed on the outskirts of the field, Farmer Johnson raged when he saw what was in his bucket and screamed, "Who the hell gave birth to a baby in my stainless steel bucket?" Farmer Johnson's yells could be heard for acres.

Standing outside was Misses James' nine-year-old son George. Watching the farmer as he threw the baby out with the bathwater into the mud, George didn't seem too surprised at Farmer Johnson's find.

Pointing his finger and stomping furiously towards George, Farmer Johnson asked, "Did your momma give birth to another baby in my stainless steel bucket?"

"Well, I recon she did, sir," he said proudly.

"Doesn't your momma know I got to feed the pigs with this here bucket?"

"Well, I recon she does sir," he said smiling ignorantly.

"Now, I got to take this bucket, and wash it thoroughly with bleach and hot water," he fumed. "If the pigs ever knew what was in this bucket, they would *never* eat from it again. You tell your momma that if she ever pulls another stunt like this again, I will whoop' her ass."

"Yes, sa'. I tell her," he replied, walking over to pick up his new brother out of the mud who was still sucking furiously on his right thumb.

For the next three months, Misses James would not even look at her new child. George, the seventh of her thirteen boys, took it upon himself to be the sole caretaker of little Orenthal, feeding him leftovers, washing him, and beating him when he cried. George did everything in his power to protect his new brother from the wrath of his mother.

One day, Misses James walked into the second largest room in her three room leased space and announced, "I am going to name him Orenthal."

"What, Mommas?" George asked.

"I'm gonna name my thirteenth son Orenthal. Look at him, this little emaciated thumb sucker. We's gots to get the boy sum' foods or he aint gonna make it." George stood there amazed and relieved that his mother's post partum depression had finally subsided. It seemed now that there was a light at the end of the tunnel for little Orenthal James.

The baby, unaware of his mother's change in mood, sat and sucked his thumb as if it were the only thing that the boy had, which was not far from the truth. In the whole world, besides a dirty cloth diaper, Orenthal had only his thumb.

Orenthal's momma had just about had it with this little boy's thumb sucking. Orenthal would suck so furiously that she could find him anywhere on the plantation just by following the sound of the suck. One day, Misses James walked up to Orenthal and slapped him so hard across the face that it knocked the thumb right out of his mouth with a loud popping sound. Shocked and stunned, Orenthal said "Whus dat foe, Mommas?"

Pointing furiously in a bout of rage, Misses James ordered, "You listen to me, and you listen to me good because I am not going to repeat myself: You have been a menace to me since the day before you were born, and I am sick and tired of hearing you suck that thumb! Day and night, night and day! I am warning you: If I ever see you sucking that thumb or putting any other part of your body in your mouth ever again, I am going to put your ass in a burlap bag and throw you into the Mississippi river. Do you understand me?"

Misses James knew that Orenthal had heard her loud and clear. She had never seen more fear in his eyes before. It almost broke her heart that she had to speak to her son in this manner, but she was at the end of her rope.

"Now, repeats after me," Misses James ordered. "I, Orenthal James."

Orenthal sat there looking at her with a dumb-founded terror on his face.

"Repeat after me, you dummy. Say it!" Misses James screamed in a manic roar.

Orenthal said slowly, "Say what, Momma?"

Misses James, using everything in her power not to drag the boy to the washtub and put him out of his misery, screamed, "Listen to me, you little bastard! Repeat the words that come out of my mouth, or I am going to kill you."

Orenthal stood frozen with his eyes wide open in fear.

"Now, this is your last chance. Repeat after me!" she raged the following single word, "I."

Orenthal, quivering in fear and knowing that his mother was about to end his life, said, "I—"

"Orenthal James." continued his mother.

"Oren-*tall* James," said little Orenthal.

Misses James smacked young Orenthal so hard that he flew off of his feet and landed halfway across the room. She hovered over him like a shadow and screamed, "Orenthal! Orenthal! Not Oren-Tall, you stupid donkey. Say Orenthal!" she screamed.

Orenthal trembled in fear.

"I am not about to raise another illiterate child, and I would much rather drown your ass than have you walking around talking like a stupid jackass!" she continued with certain fury. "Now, say your name correctly, Orenthal, or I'm a gonna do what I gots to do."

Expecting his mother to throw him in a burlap bag at any second, Orenthal clambered, "I can'ts, Momma. I can'ts say Oren-Tall!" He put his thumb in his mouth, his eyes wide open in fear, but he then popped his thumb back out, pulling his arm nervously to his side.

Noticing that Orenthal had the ability to recognize his shortcomings, Misses James raged, screaming, "You had your last chance, boy! Now get into that potato sack!"

Like a good boy, Orenthal crawled over to the burlap potato sack and climbed into it like he was getting ready to go to sleep. Misses James took a roll of hay twine and started wrapping Orenthal like a mummy.

"I's sorry, Mommas!" Orenthal called through the burlap bag. "I's really sorry for all the bad I did in my life."

"Not as sorry as I am," said Misses James. "Believe me, I'm about to save the world a whole lot of pain and sufferin'." She dragged the burlap sack to the top of the stairs and then tossed it carelessly to the bottom.

Following the bag to the bottom of the stairs, Misses James said, "Right here is where you was born, Orenthal."

"I know, mommas," said Orenthal patiently. "Thank you."

Throwing the sack over her shoulder and walking him out to the water well, Misses James said calmly, "You know boy, if all of the pigs hadn't mysteriously died four years ago, I would chop you up into little pieces and feed you to them, but since they're all gone, I guess, I got to do, what I's got's to do."

"Thank you, Mommas," replied Orenthal patiently.

Taking Orenthal and holding his tightly wrapped body by the right foot, Misses James almost had a change of heart. But like a rhinoceros with a sixth sense, Misses James knew that her boy was no good. She knew that she was only doing her part by eliminating this boy from society.

Releasing Orenthal's body into the depths of the well, Misses James heard little Orenthal's final words ("Thank you, Mommas") said patiently as he tumbled to meet his early death in the well. Walking away from the well and staring into the sun, Misses James knew that her boy was no good and that her deed, while criminal, probably saved lives. She knew that she was only doing her part by eliminating her boy from the evils of evolution.

Hitching a ride on a farm tractor into town, Misses James turned herself in to the local magistrate. However, she could not convince the judge to sentence her for the death of her son alone, but the judge was greatly affronted at Misses James callous and reckless behavior of tainting the public water supply. He therefore sentenced her in a court of law to fifteen-days for the crime of murder, and an additional forty-five days in jail on the agricultural violation of threatening a public water source.

Misses James proudly served her sentence in the county jail and was allowed to leave after serving only two-thirds of her sentence (45-days) due to her good behavior. While in jail, Misses James was allowed to go to parenting classes, where she achieved a certificate in child care essentials, which would come in handy for her in the future, because the day that she had left the jail, she realized that she was already three-weeks pregnant.

# DEATH CERTIFICATE

## HOGSVILLE, MISSISSIPPI

File No. 11875

**Dated:** Septemeber 21,1953

**Be it here known** that a young boy by the name of Orenthal James was tossed into the well of the old Johnson Farm by his momma on the 18th day of September,1953.

**Died:**
Orenthal James

**Born:**
July 5th 1949

**Momma:**
Ms. C. C. James

**Poppa:**
Unknown

**Date of Death:**
Reported September 18th 1953

Be it known that these statistics are unverifiable and there is no official record of birth of any person by the name of Orenthal James.

The mother claimed that after four years of child rearing she believed that her son would not ammount to anything in life and that she was "saving the world a whole lotta' trouble."

Be it known that we have no reason to believe that the momma listed above had reason to lie to us.

**-OFFICIAL COPY-**

COOPER G. Jameson
Vital Statistics
Hogsville, Mississippi

# Daddy's Daughter's Friend

## A Hogtale

Orenthal's oldest son Jarmaine walked into the kitchen at around 9:00 P.M. It appeared that he was in a hurry as he walked past his father who looked mischievous.

"What are you doing home tonight?" he asked his father.

"Oh, I'm jus' hanging around," he said, unable to hold back a smile.

"What's so funny?" asked his son.

"Nuthin." Orenthal was smiling even broader now.

"You're never home on a Saturday night, not ever. What's going on?"

Orenthal finally conceded, a little giddy, "What's going on *is* your sister is having a sleepover party with six of her friends." Orenthal raised his eyebrows excitedly. "Tonight!" He rubbed his snout furiously with his right palm. "That's what's going on."

"Dad, I really hope you're kidding me. Please tell me that that is not why you're so excited?"

"Does it look like I am kidding? In fact, I don't know why you isn't hanging around." He looked up at the ceiling and pointed towards upstairs as if he could see through the floor into his daughter's room where the girls were giggling and having a good time. "Why don't you stick around and see if you can help your old man get lucky tonight?" Orenthal asked his son, nudging him with his elbow.

"Yeah, Dad, that's messed up. They are sixteen and seventeen years old. I am out of here," he said disgustedly before walking towards the door.

Completely oblivious to his sons' contempt, Orenthal announced, "One of them is eighteen, I think." He rubbed his hands together. You couldn't smack the grin off of his face with a shovel.

"Don't say I didn't offer you any!"

Heading up the stairs towards his daughter's bedroom, Orenthal knew what he was doing was probably wrong, but there was nothing in the world that was going to stop him.

He watched through the partially opened door for about three minutes, going undetected. He decided to announce his presence by knocking. "A little loud in here girls," he said, moving forward. "Don't you think?" It seemed as if someone had sucked the air completely out of the room. No one spoke; the girls just watched him warily.

His daughter finally said, "What do you want, Dad? Close the door!"

Snapping himself out of an obvious spell, Orenthal realized that this was not the entrance that he had planned. Orenthal knew that he was going to have to change his demeanor and fast if he was going to win these girls over.

Becoming jovial, he laughed, "I was just checking on you girls. I am a little lonely tonight. If anybody wants to keep me company, I will be downstairs," he offered, sticking his tongue out of his mouth and biting down on it, looking all the way to the right.

Walking over and closing the door, his daughter shut him out. "Yeah, okay, Dad. We will keep that in mind."

"Good night!" Orenthal said through the closed door. "If anybody cares, I'll be downstairs all alone!"

One girl said, "Ew! That's creepy!"

"Don't mind him. He is just a loser," his daughter said, completely embarrassed.

Going downstairs into his large office/den, Orenthal sat at a large desk, which had a computer, two televisions, and a large brown leather couch. Surrounded by trophies and autographed pictures, posters, and sports memorabilia, Orenthal looked around his office and asked himself out loud, "What have I become?"

Sitting on his couch, Orenthal felt rejected by the world. Orenthal stared off into oblivion. He barely twitched for almost a half an hour. He was lonely, and he knew *no one* was safe.

Regaining mental consciousness, Orenthal was brought back to reality by the distant sounds of laughter from the girls upstairs. He could hear them running across the kitchen floor and running onto the back deck. Then he heard the splashes of the girls jumping into the pool.

Reaching over, Orenthal grabbed a large remote control and turned on both televisions and the DVD player. On the smaller television, Orenthal put it on and muted the twenty-four-hour porn channel that he had piped into his house through a pirated cable line. On the larger television, whenever Orenthal felt deflated, he was able to find solace in watching replays of his former championship games. He had four hours of highlights on DVD from a special that was run on the sports channel.

Putting the DVD player on repeat, Orenthal would watch them over and over again. Orenthal lay on the couch in despair 'til he finally fell asleep.

At 3:00 A.M., Orenthal was woken by a knock at the door. Orenthal thought he must have been dreaming when he saw a beautiful young lady standing there with an innocent smile, wearing a pink baseball cap on her head.

"Yes, honey?" Orenthal asked, wiping the drool and crust from the side of his face.

"I just wanted to say hi. I couldn't sleep." She giggled. "I think I had too much sugar and caffeine."

For a moment, Orenthal was at a loss for words. "Oh," he said. "I'm sorry; I don't know where my manners is. Come on in and sit down here," he invited, patting on the large leather couch. "What's your name again, honey?"

"Brittany, but my friends call me Britt."

"Well, Brittany, I bet you have a boyfriend, don't you?"

"No, my parents won't let me yet. I am too young, they say."

"Oh, really? Well, I bet the guys just fall all over you at school. You are very beautiful," Orenthal said. "Why are you wearing that hat on your beautiful hair?"

"My hair was wet from swimming, and I thought it might look messy."

"Oh nonsense," Orenthal said, taking off her ball cap and caressing her hair. "You have beautiful hair."

Embarrassed, she pulled away. "No, not really. But thank you, Mr. James. What are you watching?"

"Oh, I don't know, I was flipping through the channels and fell asleep," he replied, shutting the small television off so as to give the impression that he was not watching the porn channel. He diverted her attention towards his championship file footage.

"Oh my God, Mr. James! Is that you when you were young? When you were a star?"

"What do you mean *was* a star? I am still a star."

"Wow, and it's on TV right now?" she asked excitedly.

"*Oh yeah*, they play it once in a while on the sports channel," Orenthal said modestly.

"Wow, I can't believe that I am sitting here with you while it's on television."

Orenthal leaned back on the couch comfortably. He had heard all he needed to hear. "Would you like to watch it with me?" he asked.

"Sure. I will watch it here on the floor," she said, and she began to move off of the couch.

"No, stay right here with me. I don't bite," Orenthal chuckled. "It will help you to fall asleep."

"Okay. Wow, I can't believe this," she said in awe of the clips. Orenthal pulled her closer, putting his arm around her shoulder.

"Now, isn't this nice?" Orenthal asked her.

Looking at him out of the corner of her eyes, Brittany began to feel uncomfortable but thought that she was probably just being uptight. What did she really have to worry about? Mr. James was a semi-celebrity. He wouldn't do anything that might jeopardize his integrity.

The next morning, Jenna tried to get into the bathroom attached to her bedroom, but the door was locked. She pounded on the door.

"I'll be right out," said the quiet voice from behind the door.

"Who's in there? That you, Brittany?"

"Yeah."

"What are you doing?"

Brittany opened the door slowly.

"Oh my God!" Jenna cried in shock. "What happened to you? Oh my God. How did you get a black eye?"

"Oh, I, I got elbowed in the pool while we were horsing around last night." Brittany was crossing her arms insecurely. It looked like she had been crying.

"You look horrible. Are you sick?" asked Jenna, noticing that there was blood on some clothes that had been thrown in the trash can.

"I had my period," Brittany lied. She broke down crying.

Confused and shocked, Jenna asked, "How did your shirt get torn?"

"I don't know. I sleep restlessly. I just want to go home," she cried softly.

"Is everything all right?"

"Yes, I am fine. I just want to go home. I called my mom and she is on her way. I just get emotional when I have my period."

All the girls said good-bye to Brittany as she left. She already looked a little better than she had because she was wearing a new set of clothes and a large pair of dark sunglasses.

As Brittany's mother pulled into the driveway to pick her up, she knew immediately that there was something wrong with her daughter. "Honey, you girls weren't drinking last night, were you?"

"No, Mom. I am just tired. I didn't get much sleep."

As Brittany and her mother drove away, one of the girls said, "I hope she is all right. I have never seen her so upset before."

"Yeah she's usually so innocent and happy," one of the other girls replied.

Later on in the afternoon, Orenthal nonchalantly walked into his daughter's room and leaned up against the door jam. "Hey, honey. How was your night last night?"

"Good," she said.

"Good, you should have your friends sleep over more often. That was nice."

"Yeah," said his daughter, listening to her mp3 player. "It was."

"Did any of your friends have anything to say about me?"

"No, Dad, not a word." The question annoyed her.

Walking out of the room, he said, "Okay, baby. Have a good day. You know your daddy loves you."

"Bye, Dad," she said rolling her eyes. "Love you, too."

# Twim'

## A Murder

It was Orenthal's oldest daughter Jennifer's birthday and the hottest day of the summer.

Knocking on the door of Orenthal's bedroom, Jenny said, "Daddy, can I come in?"

"Come on in, Jenny. Is your friends here yet?" Orenthal was standing in the large bathroom off of the master suite, flossing his teeth furiously in the mirror.

"How can you do that, Daddy?"

"What?" Orenthal asked, looking confused. "Look at myself in the mirror?" He pulled his head back on his shoulders, unable to focus on himself.

"No, how can you floss your teeth so hard without bleeding?"

"A little bit of blood never bothered your ol' pappy," Orenthal said, sniggering to himself. "What's up?"

"Daddy, I would really like to have some of my guy friends come along with us today."

"*Ap-so-loot-lee* not, Jennifer. I will not have this day to be in any way inappropriate," said Orenthal, almost convinced that he would be the voice of reason.

"Well then, I don't want to go," she said. "I told you I wanted money for my birthday, not some stupid boat trip."

"Listen to me, you little selfish bitch," Orenthal said angrily. "I have arranged for you and your friends to hang out on a pontoon boat in Lake Toosak today, and I am your *chap-e-rone.* Now, you girls can hang out in the water, go toobin and water skiing, and you can get some sun. I am not going to have to worry about no boys misbehaving, especially with the girls, and then I have to slap somebody around. I'm not going to have it, Jennifer. Not today, not ever."

"I appreciate it, Daddy, you trying to protect us and all—I really do. But if I can't have *all* of my friends, then I don't want to go."

Rinsing his hands off while gargling and then leaning forward to spit the mouthwash out, he asked in certain anticipation, "So, are the girls here yet?" while wiping his mouth with a washcloth.

"Yeah, five of them. But Daddy, I don't want to go if all of my friends can't go. It won't be fun for us."

"You're going," he said, pointing at her with confidence. "Enough is enough, Jenny. I am not about to lose the deposit I already put down on the boat. We will be leaving here in thirty minutes. There are already five girls here, and you and me make seven. Now how many more people do we need to get on this boat? So please, Jenny, will you stop breaking your daddy's balls? Let's have a nice day for once." Looking over at Jenny, Orenthal realized she was crying. "What's the matter, Jenny?" Orenthal put his arm around her as if to console her,

"I just miss Mom," said Jenny, bursting into tears.

"I know Jenny—we all miss her. But don't you think you're being a little selfish, not wanting to spend anytime with me?"

"I just wish she could be here with us today," Jenny said, choking through tears, "on my birthday."

"What about *me*, Jenny?" Orenthal asked. "What about *my* feelings? You always spent more time with your momma than you did with me. How do you think that made me feel? One day *you's* gonna wish that you had spent a little more time with me. Now let's make the best of this time together today. You never know what tomorrow might bring. Okay?" Orenthal encouraged, looking her straight in the eye.

Jenny was upset when she left her father's bedroom to tell the girls Orenthal's decision on not allowing their male friends to attend the boat ride. They all felt that Orenthal was being unreasonable but vowed for Jenny's sake to make the best of it.

"Let's go anyway!" one girl said in excitement. "It's a day on the lake!" They all screamed in excitement as they readied their stuff for the day.

Watching the girls' line up in a row while getting into the SUV, Orenthal exclaimed, "OOOH-we! I am the luckiest guy in the world." He licked his smackers, raising one eye and then the other. "I am.... I am...."

"Daddy, stop it! You're creeping my friends out."

Snapping out of his fantasy world, he attempted to recover: "C'mon girls, you know I's jus' kiddin'."

"Yeah, well, it's not funny. You sound like a convict. Please stop." The girls chuckled uncomfortably.

"I was just saying how lucky I am to be going on a lake trip with a bunch of beautiful seventeen year old ladies," he offered, smiling innocently.

"Yeah, we heard you, and it's a little weird. Knock it off."

"Hell, I'm nearly three-times all of your ages! I sure hope you don't think I be attracted to y'all? Not that I don't be thinking you aint beautiful, 'cuz you is, but today, I be looking for some girls my own age," he said.

"Enough, Dad. I think you've said enough."

Staring into the rearview mirror with drool dripping from his lips, he wiped his face with his forearm, leaving a crusty white foam on his cheek. Not a word was spoken for five minutes in the car. Jenny felt utterly humiliated.

As the large SUV pulled into the marina where they were going to rent the boat, there was an air of excitement, and the girls looked out over the beautiful lake. They had managed to become comfortable while chitchatting on the way there, since Orenthal had taken his daughter's advice and stopped talking. Now, though, he called out, "Ok, girls! We's here," just before they piled out of the truck.

"Daddy, stop!"

"Stop what?"

"Stop talking like that. It's not cute. It's not funny," she complained, disgusted.

Grabbing Jenny by her by her arm and looking at her maliciously, he chided, "Listen, I didn't go out of my way to be insulted by you in front of your friends all day today. I have spent a lot of money on you, and you'd better appreciate it. Now, I'm tellin' you, Jenny, for the last time: Let's have a good day."

"Ouch, Daddy," Jenny winced, rubbing her arm. "I didn't ask for this trip. I would have much preferred the money." She had to raise her voice as Orenthal walked away. Humiliated again and still rubbing her arm, Jenny said, "I am sorry, guys; he's a fucking asshole." The girls all stood there uncomfortably, pretending they had not witnessed the interaction between Jennifer and her father.

Orenthal walked confidently towards the booth that rented the boats. "Well, well. We's finally here," he said to the young man sitting in the booth reading a newspaper. He felt it necessary to introduce himself: "Orenthal, Orenthal James. Here for my daughter's seventeenth birthday party. We's rentin' the big pontoon for sunbathing and waterskiing." He winked at the kid with a smile that two men couldn't have slapped off of his face.

"Okay, sir," the young man replied, unimpressed. "I need your drivers' license and an accepted form of payment, cash or major credit card. You've already paid your deposit, so I need three-hundred dollars for the boat for the day, and that does not include fuel." The young man continued as if he had said this a thousand times, "It runs about ten to twenty dollars an hour on fuel, depending on how fast you are going and how much weight you have in the boat. You will pay this cost when you return the boat."

Orenthal pulled out a stack of cash from his pocket and counted out three hundred-dollar bills, and then he slapped them onto the counter. "Here you go! Let's get us on the water!" Looking around and stretching his arms out, he called out, "What a beautiful day!"

As the young man prepared the boat and went over the safety rules, the girls all listened in the hot afternoon sun.

"C'mon, girls! Get on some suntan lotion and get some sun," Orenthal hooted, winking maniacally at the kid from the marina. "I'm the luckiest man in the world today."

Interrupting Orenthal's fantasy, the young man cautioned, "The wind is really hustling out there, so you guys need to be very careful with the wakes from the waves. Your life jackets are located under the seats." He lifted one of the seats to show them. "The water temp is about eighty degrees. Make sure you all have enough suntan lotion on. The wind will make it feel cooler, but you will get terrible sunburn if you're not careful."

Orenthal took his seat at the controls of the boat, holding his oversized sunglasses out in front of him and looking at himself, winking and smiling in the reflection. "Yup! We's got plenty of suntan lotion."

"Dad, stop! You sound like a maroon." The girls were laughing to themselves but were all pretty disgusted in Orenthal's nonchalance.

"Okay, let's get out there," said Orenthal. He threw the boat in full-speed reverse, clearing the dock by just a few inches before whipping the boat around. Orenthal threw the throttle forward. *"And full speed ahead!"* he announced.

The terrified girls tried to brace themselves against the violent movement of the boat bouncing from wave to wave. Jenny screamed, "Slow down! Daddy, slow down! Brittany just lost her hat back there! We have to turn around!"

"Nope, hold on to your stuff girls! We's gots places to be!" It was as if Orenthal did not hear or just didn't care about anything in the world. The look on his face showed that he had no intention of slowing down until he got to wherever it was in his mind that he was going.

In a panic, all of the girls were lifting the seats of the boat, scrambling for their life jackets and bucking them up over their sweats. Orenthal switched on the radio and turned the volume up all the way, playing some classic rock.

After fifteen minutes of this mayhem, they were way out in the middle of the lake. The sun was high and hot. Large waves crashed against the boat, making it rock dangerously. "Okay, girls. Jump in. Time to go *twimmin'!* The depth finder says it 123 feet deep here!" All of the girls just sat there, looking at each other. They all felt as if they were in the middle of an out of control roller coaster ride.

"Daddy, this is not fun. Can we find a beach?"

"What do you mean this aint fun? We came to get sun; we came to go twimmin'."

"This sucks. I want to go home," said Brittany, picking up her cell phone. "I'm calling my father."

"What's the problem?" Orenthal asked.

"She's pissed that you didn't turn around to get her hat. And you're not listening to what *we* want to do, and you're driving like a maniac. We want to go home."

Desperately, Orenthal pleaded, "Oh girls, I am sorry. Please, no need to get upset. I swear you won't hear another word out of me. Act like I'm not even here for the rest of the day. We will go where you want to go, and do what you want to do. Now, let's try and enjoy Jenny's birfday. She's been really looking forward to doing this."

One of the girls—out of frustration, sick of the heat, and trying to make the best of an uncomfortable situation—said, "Okay, I'm going swimming. We're here, and I am hot." She took off her lifejacket, sweatpants, and sweatshirt, revealing a bikini bathing suit. She jumped into the water, carefree as ever. Everyone watched as she flopped around in the water, splashing and kicking. "C'mon!" she screamed. This is awesome!"

One after the other finally got undressed—Orenthal pretended not to be admiring their fine young bodies—

and they all screamed as they jumped into the water. One by one they climbed back up the ladder onto the platform of the boat and jumped back into the water.

"That's what I'm talkin' 'bout," said Orenthal, licking his chops. Orenthal snorted, cocking his head in the direction of the girls climbing in and out of the boat. Orenthal rocked back and forth in a trance as he watched the girls. All of his actions made the girls feel very uncomfortable.

Wrapped in a beach towel, Brittany approached Orenthal. "Mr. James, I am sorry about making an issue out of losing my hat. You see, it was my new hat," she offered as a truce.

In a high-pitched voice Orenthal said, *"Noooo problem-o!* This is your girls' day!" Standing up and attaching the towrope onto the water tube, Orenthal threw the tube into the lake. "Who's gonna be the first to go toobin?"

The next two hours passed by quickly. Everyone was having a great time. One after another, the girls took turns riding the water tube, and Orenthal was successful in maneuvering the boat into sharp turns, launching the girls off into the water. It seemed after the horrible start they had had, everyone was now enjoying the day. One of the girls asked, "Mr. James, why don't you get in?"

"Oh no, girls. I can't twim," he responded. He was sweating profusely.

"Well, at least you can take off that heavy sweat suit. You're sweating!"

"Oh no! Don't yous all worry 'bout me. I can't twim, and this day is for you." Taking out a digital camera and licking the foam away from his lips, he said, "Okay, girls. Let's all pose for a group picture!" The girls all rolled their eyes as they lined up for the picture. "Say cheese!" Orenthal took his time, snapping about forty-five pictures.

"C'mon, Mr. James! Jump in with us!

"I told you, I's can't twim," he said convincingly.

"Daddy, stop saying twim! You sound like a degenerate. Say swim."

"Respect yo' daddy!" Orenthal retorted. "I'm spending lots of money on you today." He winked at the girls and said jokingly, "That always gets her. She's worse than her *mudder.*" He said choking on his chortle.

"Cut your dad a break," said Dina. "He's just having a little fun."

"Let's go into the island to get some food," another girl suggested, pointing into the direction of a large island.

"Okay, girls! Batten down the hatches! We be full speed ahead to the island. I's hungry, too, and parched." The girls all dove quickly to their positions for another wild ride inland.

Once they arrived at the island, Orenthal directed the girls to a deli-style convenience store. "You girls get what you want. I'm buying," said Orenthal, walking over to the beer cooler. He pulled out a twenty-four pack of beer, shouting, "$7.99? That's a deal!"

The girls ordered submarine sandwiches with potato chips and bottled water. "Daddy, I am going to get a case of water."

"9.99 for water? It's cheaper for beer," Orenthal laughed. Pulling the tab open on his first beer, Orenthal downed the twelve-ounce can in two gulps. "Boy, I's thirsty!" Going cross-eyed and belching, he wiped his nose and said, "I needs another one! Why don't you girls go outside and grab a picnic table while I pay?" He downed his second beer, throwing the empty one into the trash can behind the cash register.

Walking outside, Orenthal said, "Isn't this nice?" as he popped his third beer in five minutes, gulping it like a madman and throwing the empty can across the picnic area into a garbage can.

"Daddy, maybe you shouldn't drink so much if we are going to be boating?"

Orenthal belched loudly. "Maybe you ought to worry about yourself and stop worrying about what your daddy does." He grabbed another beer. "Besides, I's thirsty. Watch, I can down this in three seconds!" Orenthal lived up to his word for the first time in years. "Boy, that sun's got me overheated, and that beer sure tastes good on my tongue," he panted.

"Daddy, you're going to get drunk."

"Oh, hogwash," he said. "Do you know how much beer it takes to get a man my size drunk?" he asked proudly. He popped the next can and took three more huge gulps before it too was gone. A belch followed.

The girls were all now very concerned. "Hey, Jen, we are not getting on that boat with your dad if he keeps drinking," said one of the girls.

"Daddy, stop drinking. You're scaring us."

Orenthal locked onto his daughter with a hideous glare. "I told you, shut ya mouf, or I'll give ya sumthin' to bitch about." Opening his sixth can in less than ten minutes, Orenthal downed it faster than the last. Throwing the can into a pile across the picnic area in front of the trash receptacle, a sign read; "NO CANS-NO GLASS."

The girls finished up their lunches and got up from the picnic table. Heading towards the beach area, one of the girls said, "Jen, I am calling my dad. I am not getting on that boat with your father. He is drunk."

"I know, Liz," Jenny said. "I don't know what to do."

"My dad has a boat at the other marina, and he can come and get us. I'm sorry, but I'm just too uncomfortable," Liz suggested as they watched Orenthal drink one beer after the next, throwing the cans across the picnic area. Understanding her friends' concern, Jenny was so embarrassed and ashamed that she started to cry.

"My phone isn't working out here: no signal," she said desperately.

Standing up, Orenthal stumbled in the direction of the girls, announcing, "Okay, ladies! *ALL-ABOARD!*" The girls all stood there stunned at Orenthal's casual manner and lack of concern for their safety. They stood on the shoreline, looking at each other and shaking their heads back and forth.

"Before we get on the boat," Orenthal began, but he had to stop as he belched loudly without excusing himself, "Let's get another group picture girls!"

Like any good predator, Orenthal came to his senses when he sensed their fear and realized that he had again lost the girls confidence. He did some quick talking, trying to recover: "Oh, yeah. You know what, Jenny? I did have a few drinks. Do you want to drive the boat the rest of the day?"

The girls were caught off guard by Orenthal's sudden clarity; further, they had never suspected this lummox would yield the controls of the boat.

"Yeah, Dad! That sounds good. One of us will drive."

Orenthal appeared completely sober and in the clearest of voices said, "You're going to have to be *real* careful. It's not a toy." He stumbled towards the front of the boat, mumbling, "You know, I was getting tired of driving anyway."

All of the girls now appeared to be a little more relaxed. "Thank God," one of them said.

Getting in the boat and heading right to the front to the largest seat, Orenthal sat down and kicked his feet up. "Boy, I was parched! I was *de-hy-drated!* If I could twim, I would jump right in to cool off."

"Dad, it's swim. Stop talking like a vulgar dumbass."

"Yous a little feisty, aint-cha? Jus' like yo momma!" Orenthal taunted, putting his head back onto a towel.

"Does anybody know how to drive a boat?" asked Jenny.

"My dad has a boat," Liz reminded her.

"Well, can you get us back to the car safely?"

"Yeah, definitely. I just hope we can find our way back."

One at a time, each of the girls mustered the confidence to get into the boat. Before, when Orenthal was in the back of the boat at the controls, all of the girls were in the front of the boat. Now that Orenthal was sitting in the front of the boat, all of the girls made room for each other in the back.

"What do you want me to do with these?" asked the last girl to get into the boat. "There are five beers left."

"Just leave them on the dock," Jenny replied, turning her head away in shame.

As the engine started, Orenthal raised his head off of the towel as if he had no idea where he was for a second. "Be careful girls," he said. "Be careful."

Backing the boat away from the dock slowly, they proceeded cautiously towards the other side of the lake at a slow pace that was comfortable for the girls. No one said a word until one of the girls picked up Orenthal's digital camera.

"Let's take a picture of that pig asleep with his mouth wide open. He looks like a bum on a park bench," one of the girls mused. Everyone laughed.

"Jen, I'm really sorry. I know he's your dad, but he has some real issues."

"I know," she said, looking into the distance. "I am not proud of him."

One of the girls stood over Orenthal to take a picture of him drooling as he slept at the front of the boat. All of the girls laughed. The girls passed the camera around to each other to show how silly Orenthal looked.

As they began to cycle through the pictures that Orenthal had taken, the girls were sick to discover that half of the pictures were intimate close-ups of the girls in their bikinis. There were no headshots, just unsuspecting shots of their bikini areas.

"What a scumbag!" one of the girls said. "Hey look, it's your ass, Jen. Your dad took a picture of *your* ass. That's disgusting!"

They deleted the inappropriate pictures one after the other. Jenny was beyond humiliated. How could she ever look at her friends the same way again? Crying, she said, "I—am—so—sorry, guys! I didn't want to have this stupid boat trip, but he made me!" She burst into tears.

Consoling Jen, Liz said, "It's not your fault your dad is a scumbag, Jen. When I said earlier that your dad has issues, I mean it. He has little or no impulse control. He's manipulative and lacks any sort of empathy for you or anybody around him. He is completely a-social. He is a textbook psychopath. I am serious! This is what I want to go to college for. That man is a threat to everyone around him." Liz shook her head sadly and convincingly.

All of the girls gathered around Jenny to console her as her father slept. Liz ended up saying the most relieving tidbit: "It is not your fault."

Cruising along at about ten knots, the girls enjoyed a nice breeze that cooled their skin. The trip was beginning to feel rather leisurely. Then Orenthal lifted his head from the towel and looked out into the horizon. Sitting up, he announced, "Okay, girls! Crank up the speed! Daddy's gotta drain the snake, if you know what I mean."

All at once the girls pulled their heads back in disgust. "Ew…What a pervert!" one of the girls said.

"This is as fast as we are going, Mr. James," Liz replied.

"Well, I gotta pee off the boat," he said, standing up and walking towards the back of the boat. All at once, all of the girls lunged towards the front of the boat, pushing each other to get out of the way of Orenthal as he stood at the back of the boat.

"Stop the boat!" he yelled. "Stop the boat." Liz put the boat into neutral and crossed her arms. The boat coasted to a complete stop and bobbed in the waves.

Orenthal was now standing on the back deck with his legs apart, looking like a drunk outside a baseball stadium in an alley. As Orenthal stood there about to relieve himself, he looked back at the girls and said, "Now don't anybody look—unless you want to."

"Dad!" Jenny screamed, appalled. The other girls groaned.

"Keep quiet. I got stage fright! I can't go," Orenthal whined. Just as the flow of urine began to hit the clean lake water, Jenny leaned over and pushed the boat's throttle into forward, which launched Orenthal into the deep blue lake.

Chaos ensued on the boat: some girls laughed; others screamed. Jenny said, "Let me drive," as she grabbed a hold of the boat's controls. Spinning the boat around, she pushed the throttle into full speed, heading right towards Orenthal as he bobbed, flopping his arms in terror. She kept the boat fifteen feet from him and passed by him quickly, washing a huge wave right over his head.

All of the girls laughed now. Their mirth drowned out Orenthal's as he screamed, "I can't twim! I can't twim!" He flapped his arms as the boat made a second pass by him.

One of the girls threw out a life preserver to Orenthal, but the wind blew it about twenty feet from him. "He's treading water like a pro," Liz said. "He can swim!" They all laughed again.

Bringing the boat around again, they passed right by him at top speed. Orenthal screamed, "Help!"

"Okay," Jenny thought out loud. "I've had enough fun." Spinning the boat around and pulling up along side of him, Orenthal was still screaming for help like a child. Jenny could hear him choking on water and gasping large snorts of air.

The boat in all of its momentum went right past Orenthal. The girls were still enjoying Jenny punishing her father.

"Shit, we got to go around again." Jenny gunned the boat to make a quick wide circle to come back and pick her father up, but as she made the turn, she realized that Orenthal had disappeared. "Where is he?" she cried out. "Oh my God! Where is he?"

All of the girls leaned over the boat to see if they could spot Orenthal. The waves were very deceiving, and every twenty-yard section appeared to be the same. "Where is he?" she screamed. "Oh my God!"

All out panic broke out on the boat. Smiles turned to stunned grimaces. "There's the life preserver over there!" One girl pointed frantically. Jenny launched the boat in the direction of the life preserver. "I don't see him! Call 911." She stopped the boat to look out over the waves. No one could believe what was happening.

Silence grew over the boat. Was this a joke? How could he have just disappeared?

*[Oh where, oh where, did the Orenthal go? Oh where, oh where could he be?]*

Fifteen minutes passed before the first Coast Guard boat arrived at the scene. As the marine patrol pulled up alongside the rented pontoon boat, all of the girls were waving their arms in a panic. When the Coast Guard officers climbed onto the boat, they were trying to calm the young hysterical crowd of girls. Helping one girl at a time, the crewmen transferred each girl onto the safety of the Coast Guard boat.

Jenny was hysterical and shaking. "He can't swim. He drowned! Oh my God!"

"We will take it from here. We're going to find your father!" said the officer.

"He just fell off the boat. He had to go to the bathroom, and he fell off!" Jenny cried.

"Did he have anything to drink?"

"Yes! Oh my God," Jenny bawled as she boarded the Coast Guard boat. "It's all my fault!"

The girls stood on the Coast Guard boat in a daze. A crowd of boaters and jet skiers had surrounded the area searching for the body. Jenny looked out over the chaos; her eyes wide open in fear. Her father's digital camera was still in her hands. "He's gone," she admitted, leaning over the boat, she began to sob.

The reality of the situation was beginning to set in. Opening her right hand, she dropped the digital camera into the water and watched as it is swished and swayed out of sight into the darkness below. All of the girls were surrounding Jenny, consoling her.

Standing in a straight line, the girls explained their stories to the police officer that had arrived on the scene. The girls nodded their heads in agreement with each statement that was made to the officer. The police officer understood the trauma of an incident like this and paid no attention to the inconsistencies of their accounts of the event.

"Jen, this situation is not your fault. It is a terrible tragedy," said the officer. The Coast Guard boat headed back to shore, but none of the girls could take their eyes off of the water until they got to shore. At the marina, they watched the flashing lights of the rescue boats out in the distance.

Well over an hour had passed when a radio transmission screeched across the airwaves: "We got him!" A calm voice over the radio announced, "EMS, be advised we are trying CPR and will do so until instructed otherwise."

"Received," the radio screeched.

"We have an ambulance here standing by at the marina."

"Received. We are en-route on the red!"

The rescue boat pulled up to the shore and quickly loaded a heavy stretcher into the back of the ambulance. Pulling away slowly, the ambulance had only its flashing lights on and did not use sirens.

Two police officers walked over to Jenny. One was carrying a large black bag. She stood there in shock. Two of her friends were still consoling her.

"Jennifer," the officer said empathetically, "these are your father's clothes. We found his wallet and his car keys. This sweat suit soaked with water and his shoes weighs over seventy-five pounds," the officer said, discouraged.

"Oh my God," said Jenny. "Seventy-five pounds!"

"He might as well have just tied an anchor to himself, especially if he couldn't swim," said the coast guard officer aloofly. "Just a tragedy. This was nobody's fault."

Jenny became emotional and hugged the officers, thanking them for their help as they loaded the heavy bag into the back of the SUV.

Just as the girls were about to drive away, the young man from the booth at the marina ran over and said, "I'm really sorry about your dad." Handing her an envelope, he said, "Here is the deposit he gave me for the boat."

"Oh, thank you so much," said Jenny.

He scratched his head. "Again, I am really sorry."

"Thank you!"

"Well, for what its worth," he said, "happy birthday!"

Jenny looked out over the horizon to see a gorgeous sunset. Taking the envelope with the cash in it and putting it in her small purse, Jenny felt guilty since she had told her father that she would rather have money for her birthday. Driving away, one of the girls looked back at Jenny and said, "It's going to be alright, Jennifer. Everything is going to be okay."

She couldn't help but agree.

## Three Days Later

Standing at her father's funeral, Jen was surrounded by her family and friends, who all gave her more support now then ever. "Yeah, I think we are going to throw his ashes into the lake," Jenny said smiling gently.

For the first time in many years, Jennifer felt that she was going to be alright.

# Lake County

Lake Toosak Police Department

## MISSING PERSON REPORT / DROWNING

Page 2 of 5

**DATE:** August 15th **TIME:** 15:35
**Victim:** Orenthal James/ Deceased **Race:** W **Sex:** M

**NARRATIVE:**
On the above date and time I received a 911 call for missing Person in water...50+ year old male. Cannot swim. Arrived at scene at 15:40. Multiple female witnesses report man was intoxicated when he went to the deck of the boat to urinate, falling in. Witness 3 states that she threw the Victim a life preserver but he could not get to it. All witnesses state that Victim fell below the surface when they lost sight of him. Coast Guard on the scene at 16:00 Hrs, multiple rescue boats and volunteers at scene. At 17:05 Hrs the dive rescue team from Lake T. recovered the body. Along with the body we received a sweat suit. Placed separately from the body, the wet sweat suit weighed approximately 80LBS causing the man to fall below surface to bottom of the lake.

**Cause of Death:** Accident

***NOTE: Victim is on State's Sex Offender Registry***

No further information available at this time.
End of Report EOR:

**#6016554**

List of witnessed see page 2 of 5

# Chop Liftin'

## A Hogtale

The average person would not have suspected Mr. Orenthal James to be a petty perpetrator. He was well dressed, drove a nice car, and had the appearance of an average person. Most would believe that Orenthal was at the very least upper middle class—maybe not extremely wealthy—and no one would ever suspect that he would lower himself to the level of an ignoble shoplifter.

The security cameras of the local superstore were affixed at the front door. Mike, the nineteen-year-old security supervisor, expected that this would be a regular day in which he would follow the usual degenerates through the aisles and watch them as they tried to get away with shoplifting any and all items.

Shoplifting is a major problem for these large chain stores and costs them billions in lost revenues over the course of a year. The average person bears the weight of this degeneracy through the markets' higher prices.

Shoplifters believe that they are entitled to whatever they want, and they believe that they deserve the items they steal. They apply this mindset to every aspect of their lives, sneaking around and pretending to be someone that they are not. These people are manipulative, greedy, and unconscionable. The deviance of a shoplifter is immeasurable.

This story starts off with the infamous Orenthal James doing what he does best: destroying anyone's faith in society and then making himself out to be the victim.

Staring into the monitors in the security control room, Mike was working with three other loss-prevention specialists, monitoring any suspicious activities in the store.

Mike said, "Hey, isn't that Orenthal James?" He brought up the screen on a large monitor so that everyone could see, and they all watched the large male walking casually through the aisles. No one said anything.

Mike exclaimed, "Orenthal James! You know, the infamous sports star!" He hit a button and moved another camera from a small screen onto the large screen.

"Oh yeah, that is Orenthal James," one of his co-workers confirmed.

"Wow, you wouldn't think he would shop here, would you?"

"No, and at the very least, you would think if he did, he would have someone shop for him."

Using the cameras to follow him down the aisles and to watch the very nicely dressed Orenthal go along his way, Mike admitted, "I wonder what he is here for."

"Who knows," replied one of the other guys. "Probably duct tape, a shovel, and a tarp." Everyone laughed at the innocent joke.

"Maybe he's here filling out an application for the door-greeter position." As they laughed and cracked more jokes, Orenthal walked up to the photo counter. The security personnel couldn't hear the conversation Orenthal was enjoying with the beautiful seventeen-year-old cashier with long blonde hair; while another young, but not so cute, female employee sat eavesdropping.

Walking past her coworker to the pile of finished film, the girl grabbed two envelopes with the name O. James on them. "I got it right here, Mr. James," she said, smiling innocently.

Orenthal was leaning on the counter with a big smile on his face. "What's a beautiful girl like you doing working in a place like this?" he asked. "I thought only losers worked here."

She didn't take offence but smiled back and said proudly, "Oh, my mom works here. She's a front-end cashier, and she got me the job."

"Well," said Orenthal, "a beautiful girl like you needs a job working in a restaurant where you can make *big* tips," he said, winking at her. "You are modeling material," he continued shamelessly. "You need to get an agent."

Blushing and embarrassed, the girl smiled and asked, "Do you really think so?"

In a high pitch voice, Orenthal replied, *"OH YEAH!"*

He held the *yeah* for at least three seconds.

"Well, I was thinking about getting another job."

"Well then, if you give me your number, I know I can hook you up with an agent," said Orenthal. "Now, I'm not saying your going to start out in some glossy rag or anything, but I know I can get you into a couple of exotic clubs." He raised his eyebrows and put his tongue between his teeth.

Pulling her head back in disgust, the girl laughed uncomfortably and replied, "Oh no, I would never model like that. That's nasty."

"Let me tell you," he said casually, leaning in, "that's where all of the models get their starts. Give me your cell phone number, and I will have someone get in contact with you."

"I don't have a cell phone," she said.

"What kind of girl doesn't have a cell phone? How do you keep up with your friends?" Orenthal asked arrogantly.

"I use my home phone," she said.

"Oh, then give me your home number," said Orenthal, persisting.

"Well, I really can't, It's not my number. It's my mom's, and she would kill me if—"

"Melissa, give him your number!" interrupted the other girl. "Girls dream about getting an offer like this everyday!"

"Not me. I'm going to college."

"That's what all girls say, but they don't really mean it," Orenthal interrupted with a giant stupefied grin on his face.

"Well, I am sorry, Mr. James. I am just not able to give you my number."

"Here," the other girl blurted, scribbling quickly on a piece of paper. "This is the number to the store. She works all the time. Ask for the photo counter and for Melissa." She handed Orenthal the piece of paper.

Melissa stood there with her mouth wide open, too shocked to react.

"Ok, girls. Well, thank you for your time," said Orenthal, walking away with the pictures in the envelopes.

"Mr. James," called Melissa.

Spinning around on his stylish black dress shoes in hopes that she had had a change in heart, he asked her, "Yes?" as if playing hard to get.

"You have to pay for your film here, sir," she said.

"Oh," said Orenthal, losing his smile. "No, I am still shopping. I am going to pick up a few more items, and I am going to pay for this up front," he said.

"Oh, ok! Have a nice day, Mr. James," said Melissa as he walked away. The phone rang immediately, and she answered it: "Good afternoon! Thank you for calling the photo counter. This is Melissa. How can I—"

"Missy, it's Michael, in Loss Prevention."

"Oh, what's up?" looking up towards the cameras and waving.

"Did you get his autograph?" he asked, and she could hear all the security personnel laughing.

"No, he's a dirt bag."

"Why? What happened?"

"Nothing really. He was hitting on me and telling me that I could be a *model*, and he wanted my number. I told him no, so he walked away."

"Did he pay for the pictures?"

"No, he said that he was still shopping."

"Oh, ok," said Michael, still laughing. He hung up the phone.

Michael announced to his co-workers in the monitoring room, "He was hitting on Melissa, and she shot him down."

"Ohhh, another one shot down by Missy!" joked Joe. All three continued laughing, as they scanned the aisles for criminal activity.

Following Orenthal into the greeting card aisle, Mike joked, "Hey, look! I think he fell in love. He's going to get her a sappy love card."

He watched Orenthal thumb through a few cards, and he noticed Orenthal suddenly look left and then right before putting a greeting card over the top of the two envelopes of pictures and sliding them into the front of his pants.

"Whoa! This has to be a joke. There is no way this is real. He just put the pictures in his pants!" All of the guards watched Orenthal as he now started towards the front of the store. "No way!" exclaimed Michael. He keyed the microphone on the two-way radio. "Hey, Jeff! We just got a high profile customer putting two envelopes of pictures from the photo counter in his pants. Large frame, well-dressed male, walking your way. Orenthal James. You know, the infamous athlete."

"Received," said Jeff. "I'll keep an eye out for him."

Walking right past Jeff, Orenthal said, "Hello there!" as he walked out the front door.

Jeff, caught off guard by the circumstances, did not have the courage to confront the large man as he walked past.

Yelling over the radio, Michael said "Jeff, stop him! We have video evidence plain as day. I will be right out!"

"Are you sure?" asked Jeff. "What do you want me to tell him?"

Excited, Michael yelled, "Get him, Jeff, before he drives away!"

Jeff ran into the parking lot and spotted Orenthal standing near his vehicle; a police officer was parked behind Orenthal, placing a ticket on the windshield of his SUV.

"Excuse me, Mr. James!" called Jeff. Orenthal did not hear him as he was taking the ticket off of his windshield.

"Hey, buddy!" Orenthal called rudely to the cop who was about to get into his car. "What the fuck is this?"

"It's a ticket for parking your car in an unauthorized spot," said the officer.

"Whoa now, wait a minute!" said Orenthal dramatically. "I have chronic arthritis! I can barely walk."

"Well, it looks like your getting along just fine to me," said the officer, pointing to Orenthal's black shoes and looking up at him. "Mr. James… I'm sorry…" said the officer. "Is that you?"

"Damn right it is," said Orenthal, irritated.

"Oh…. My bad, sir," said the officer apologetically. "I didn't realize it was you. You know, you have some of these wealthy people who think they are so entitled that they can park their car anywhere," he said, walking towards Orenthal, taking the ticket out of his hand. "Mr. James, you really ought to get one of the placards or license plates that will authorize you to park in one of these spots," the officer suggested.

"Yeah," said Orenthal, depressed. "I guess I just got a problem with my pride, you know…. I just can't say I'm an invalid."

Laughing, but not amused at the derogatory term towards persons with disabilities, the officer took the parking ticket and pulled it in half. "I'll gladly take care of this for you, sir."

"I appreciate it," Orenthal said.

Arriving at the parked vehicles, Michael was surprised at the coincidence of their already being a police officer on the scene.

"Excuse me, officer!" Michael said.

"Yes?" asked the officer, looking disinterestedly.

"We are glad you're here because we have a little problem with Mr. James."

"Wow. You *yahoos* really take this parking thing pretty seriously," he mocked.

"That's not why we're here, Mr. James," said Michael, speaking to Orenthal but looking right at the police officer. "We have video surveillance of Mr. James stuffing his pants with merchandise and walking out of the store. And we have more than reasonable suspicion to hold him for questioning."

The officer pulled his head back, squinting in disbelief at Orenthal.

"What?" asked Orenthal, looking confused. You gots the wrong person!" Opening the door to his SUV, about to get into the vehicle, Orenthal continued, "Unless I am under arrest, I am leaving."

The police officer, recognizing the potential for disaster in the event that this was a misunderstanding, said cautiously to Michael, "Hey, this is a serious allegation to be making against a model citizen. I think it would be in the best interest of everyone here to let Mr. James go on his way." The officer raised his eyes wide open, using body language to suggest that this would be the best course of action.

"Thank you, thank you very much," said Orenthal to the police officer. "And you can be sure that I will be calling my attorney—"

"But we have it on video!" argued Michael.

"You aint got shit on video," said Orenthal, "and you heard the officer. I am leaving. And I am calling my attorney." As Orenthal raised his leg to enter his vehicle, an envelope full of pictures fell out of his pants at the ankle, pouring photos onto the pavement.

"There, that's the merchandise he stole!" pressed Michael, looking at the officer.

"I didn't steal it!" argued Orenthal. "I paid for them!"

"Mr. James, could you provide us with a receipt for the transaction? Then you can be on your way," requested Michael confidently.

"Sure I can," said Orenthal, reaching for his wallet and opening it up. There was no money inside. Orenthal was rifling through a bunch of wrinkled receipts. Getting out of the car angrily, Orenthal continued, "And when I find it, I want every one of your jobs. I want names and badge numbers! You are all going down." The second envelope of pictures fell out of his pants along with a greeting card.

"We have you on video, Mr. James, stuffing your pants and walking out. You were talking with the girl at the register, and then you walked away without paying. You then entered the gift section where you thumbed through a few cards. You placed the merchandise in your pants, and we watched you walk out of the store." Michael looked at the police officer, concluding, "He never paid for those items, and if he had, why would he put them in his pants?"

"Yes, I did pay for them," Orenthal insisted. "Ask the girl in the back, her name is Melissa… Here is her phone number…She gave it to me… She said she wants to be a dancer… I don't know, maybe I forgot to pay for them, but I never *intended* to."

The police officer interrupted, "Is it possible, Mr. James, that you didn't pay for them?"

"No! Ab-so-lute-ly NOT! I paid!" Looking annoyed, Orenthal said to the police officer, "You know, I have diabetes, and my sugar is low, so maybe I did leave.... I forgot.... The girls were talking to me and asking all kinds of questions. I must have forgotten."

"Well then, why did you put them in your pants?" asked Michael.

"I don't know. I guess I just didn't want anyone to know that I shopped here. I don't know. It was an accident."

"Well, Mr. James," said the police officer, looking at the loss prevention specialists in order to lead them, "I am sure that these gentlemen would be happy to ring up your merchandise and allow you to pay for it and let you go on your way—"

"No," interrupted Michael. "This man stole merchandise from our store, and I don't care who he thinks he is, I want him prosecuted just like any other nickel and dime thief. Otherwise, what kind of a precedent would we be setting for the hard working people who come here and legitimately spend their money? I want him placed under arrest for shoplifting."

"Listen, I got distracted. I know it might look bad, but I aint never been choplifted before," Orenthal pleaded innocently.

"Can I speak with you privately?" asked the officer, pulling Michael aside. "Hey, he may be telling the truth. Why don't you give him the benefit of the doubt? You know, this is petty, and the last thing you need is his lawyer here making a huge case out of this. Let's bring him inside, let him pay for his merchandise, and let him go. Trust me, it won't be worth the hassle."

"Yeah, but, we have him on video stuffing his pants! He knew exactly what he was—"

"Listen, Michael," the officer interrupted. "Even if you're right and you know you're one-hundred percent right, you have to look at the big picture. Believe me, I know it's frustrating, but an incident like this can end up blowing up in your face, and *you* will look like the bad guy. Do you understand what I am saying?"

Michael shook his head up and down slowly without saying a word to show that he understood the officer.

"Ok, let him pay for his merchandise, and we will send him on his way," said the officer.

They walked back towards Orenthal, who was standing there with both of his arms out as if he were being crucified and was beginning to rant: "Officers, I aint never been chopliftin! I aint never choplifted in my life."

"I understand, Mr. James. I have spoken with Michael here, and he has agreed that it would be in everybody's best interest to allow you to go back inside and pay for your merchandise. How does that sound?"

"OK, but I really never been choplifted in my life," said Orenthal desperately.

"It's shoplifting," said Michael annoyed.

"Yeah, choplifted," Orenthal said.

"No, you're saying choplifted, and it is shoplifting."

"See, I don't even know how to say it," said Orenthal defiantly as they walked back into the store.

"Mr. James, we will take you into the back where we can ring up your merchandise, and you can be on your way."

Walking past the young girls at the photo counter, Orenthal said, "Hi Melissa! You let me walk out of here without paying!" Melissa turned her back on him.

"Mr. James," Michael said as he scanned the items, "$6.77, one hour photo. $6.77 for the second batch, and the card, $2.88. Who's this for?" asked Michael.

"Oh, it's for my wife. You know, you can never be too appreciated," he said.

"Ok, it comes to $17.73 with tax, sir."

Looking through his wallet, Orenthal said, "Shit, I aint got any cash on me." He snorted loudly. "Here, take the credit card."

As Michael swiped the credit card, Orenthal tried not to appear uneasy. "Wow, I bet you guys run into some real shit birds in this business," he joked, trying to divert attention from the credit card machine.

"Yeah," said Michael sarcastically. "You wouldn't believe it." Pulling a receipt from the credit card machine, Michael said "Mr. James; it's saying that this card is not valid."

"Oh, it must be my pin number," he said.

"No, I don't think so. It didn't ask for the pin," said Michael.

"Well, here. Here is my ATM card. This will work," giving him the second card.

Swiping the second card but shaking his head in disgust, Michael looked at the police officer, waiting for Orenthal to enter his pin number.

"Funds unavailable, it says."

"Are you kidding me? Just my luck, the banks must be down," Orenthal tried.

"No, it says here funds unavailable, Mr. James"

"Well, I am really sorry for this, but I can go get some cash, and come back in a few minutes to pay for it," Orenthal offered.

Looking at Michael, the police officer asked, "Is that okay with you, sir?"

Looking amazed and shaking his head in half nods, he responded, "I guess it's going to have to be."

"I am sorry, but you have to believe me when I say to you that I aint never been chopliftin before. Hell, I got more money than *God.* That's why you never see me chopping in a store like this," said Orenthal as he began walking towards the exit. "I will be right back."

"We will hold your items here until you come back and pay for them sir," said Michael, holding the small bag of goods.

The police officer and Michael followed Orenthal to the parking lot and stood on the sidewalk as Orenthal got into his SUV and pulled away quickly, driving the wrong way down a one-way lane. He bumped a curb, and his tires screeched into the intersection, almost causing an accident. The officer and Michael could hear horns blowing.

Michael said, "Wow, he is such a—" Unable to finish his sentence he just stared out in disbelief.

"You know, I believe he didn't mean to do it," said the officer. "I believe he's lost his mind."

"No, he is guilty as hell," said Michael. "He didn't even have any cash on him to pay, and his credit cards were either invalid or funds unavailable."

"Yeah, well, he must have money," said the police officer, walking towards his cruiser.

"We'll see," said Michael, turning around and heading back into the store, repeating to himself loudly, "He is *guilty as hell.*"

A week later, Michael was not surprised that Orenthal never returned to pay for his items. Sitting at his desk, he began to curiously sift through the pictures that Orenthal had left behind. Surprised, he found that most of the pictures were inappropriate snap-shots of multiple young women—nude or in bathing suits—standing in different poses. One of the pictures looked like a picture of a bath tub full of blood with a young girl who appeared to be sleeping in it. Realizing that he did not want to open Pandora's Box any further, he put the pictures back in the envelope.

Faxing a confidential memo about the incident to the other local stores, Michael taped a copy of the letter to his filing cabinet.

Taking the bag containing the pictures and the greeting card, Michael attached a large note to the bag before throwing it on top of the filing cabinet.

Shutting off the lights and walking out of his office, he shook his head in disbelief, thinking to himself that this is just another example of how screwed up society is.

Illuminated by the light of black and white surveillance monitors, the note attached to the bag displayed the words, *Orenthal James—Must Pay!*

## World Mart Ltd.

*ATTENTION ALL SECURITY PERSONNEL*

**Confidential Memo:** **August 21st**

In an apparent attempt to shop lift merchandise from our West Haven store, Mr. Orenthal James was apprehended by our security staff. Mr. James was given the opportunity to pay for the items that he stuffed in his pants and in turn did not have the funds available to pay for his alleged stolen merchandise. Mr. James advised us that he was going to return within a few minutes to pay for his items, and has not yet done so. In the event that you see Mr. James in one of your stores, please make sure that you keep an eye on him and if another incident of this type should occur, please contact the local police department and have him arrested for the appropriate charge. Thank you for your anticipated cooperation in this matter.

*William B. Madison*
*Security Chief*
*West Haven Store*

The Greeting card that Orenthal got for his wife, but never paid for said:

FRONT

*To My Wife.*

*When they said that*
*you only hurt*
*the ones you love...*
*I never knew how*
*true this could be.*

BACK

*I am sorry for*
*the awful things*
*that I have done*
*to you, to us,*
*to your friends,*
*To our family*
*and I can only*
*beg of you, and the lord*
*for forgiveness...*

# Pig Roast'

## A Murder

Outside of being one of the most despicable beings on the face of the planet, Orenthal James is also a thief. He would take anything right under your nose and wouldn't care who saw it. It's not because of a mental issue or kleptomania; Orenthal steals because no one has ever called him on it. He feels entitled to take whatever he wants, when he wants, and—up until this point—no one has ever challenged this sentiment.

Orenthal had been stealing since he was born, and no one had ever taught him a lesson until here…

In the city where Orenthal lives, there is an organized group of Middle Eastern men who came to America to earn an honest living peddling fuel out of once American-owned gas stations. The price of fuel sky rocketed shortly after they finished seizing the pumps, and once fuel became an ultra commodity, hitting well over two dollars per gallon, Orenthal began to simply steal it. Once he realized how easy it was, he became brazen and often wondered why he hadn't stolen it before.

The theft became a game to him. He would pull into a gas station, usually when it was very busy, and just get out of his SUV, fill it up, get back in, and drive away. By the time the attendant realized he had been robbed, it was too late.

Because of criminal mentalities like Orenthal's, most gas stations have caught onto this degenerative behavior. Most stations now insist that people pay cash before fueling or pay with a credit card at the pump. This inconvenience can be blamed on people like Orenthal who cannot be trusted to do anything.

Orenthal robbed these gas stations for over a year and never once paid a penny for fuel. Besides getting away with stealing gas, Orenthal would also walk brazenly into the convenience store and grab oil, candy, windshield washer fluid, coffee, and a newspaper and walk right out while his SUV was filling. Orenthal never paid for a single item. He would just simply drive away without paying, and he never looked back.

Orenthal began to get greedy at this game and would sometimes hit the same station twice in one week. Finally, one attendant recognized the SUV and refused to allow Orenthal to fill his vehicle unless he paid first. Orenthal simply got back into his truck and drove down the street to rob the next station.

The art with which Orenthal stole gas became so advanced that he would actually swipe his invalid credit card upside down so that, just in case a camera was watching, he could easily say, "Oh! See, there I thought I swiped my card, my bad." He had it all figured out in his head. All he needed to do was give reasonable doubt, and he figured he could talk his way out of murder.

Swiping his credit card upside down at the fuel pump, as if by paranoid ritual, Orenthal began to fill his gas tank up. Standing there whistling the tune "Dixie," he was surprised when suddenly the pump stopped. Over the loud speaker Orenthal heard, "Sir, I need to see you. Your card did not go through."

Orenthal stood there with his arms open wide, staring at the attendant in the gas station. He yelled out, "Hey! The pump stopped. What the fuck?"

The attendant repeated, "Sir, I need to see you inside. Your card did not go through."

Orenthal snidely commented, "That's your problem, buddy," and he put the cap on his tank, got in his vehicle, and drove away with $11.19 worth of gas.

When a police officer arrived to review the tape, there was nothing he could do because the tape showed Orenthal swiping his card. The officer argued with the attendant that Orenthal did not commit a crime but was confused and frustrated by the system.

"Does it look like this guy is a thief?" he asked the attendant. "This is Orenthal James! There was no crime here. He thought he paid. We have bigger problems than this to deal with." The officer appeared aggravated as he walked out of the gas station.

The next week, early in the evening, just before it was about to get dark outside, Orenthal pulled into another gas station for his free fill-up. Orenthal knew it might be a little trickier this time to steal because the station was not busy. When a station is busy with customers the attendant is usually too busy to pay any one customer much attention.

Confident in his ability to pump and run, Orenthal pulled into the gas station. The attendant, who was now very wise to Orenthal's tricks and the owner of several stations in town, walked right out to Orenthal and said in a

Middle Eastern accent, "You pay first. You owe me. You drive off last time. You owe me seventy-five dollars."

Orenthal said, "Fuck you, buddy. Learn how to speak English. I never drove off wiff $75 worf of gas,"

"Worf?" asked the attendant. "I speak excellent English, sir, and at least I say worth, not worf, you jackass. Now pay me, or get off my property."

Orenthal retorted, with a large smile on his face, "You listen to me, ha-bibe. You got the wrong guy. I never drove off without paying. If you don't need my business, I will go elsewhere."

"You owe me seventy-five dollars! I have you on tape, you son of a bitch!"

Laughing, Orenthal said, "Maybe if your people hadn't blown up nine-eleven, I would give a fuck. But I don't." Inhaling and clearing his throat, Orenthal spit a large wad of phlegm right onto the face of the man and said, "Go fuck yourself," as he got into his SUV and drove away.

Running inside the station, the man used a paper towel to wipe his face before calling his brother who was working the gas station two blocks down. As he was explaining what happened, Orenthal pulled into the station. "Yes, he is here now. I will take care of it," said the attendant of the second station. He stopped the tape on the surveillance camera and ejected it before walking outside to greet the unsuspecting Orenthal.

Getting out of his car, unaware that the brothers had just spoken to each other, Orenthal began to fill his tank.

"Good evening, sir," said the attendant. "Sure is a nice night," he offered coyly.

"Yeah," Orenthal said, aggravated.

"You must pay before you leave."

"Yeah, were all set. I swiped my card."

"There must be something wrong with your card, sir. It didn't go through."

"Well, that's just too bad, isn't it? You ought to get your system fixed. The last time I was here, I swiped my card twice, and I got charged twice.

"No, sir. That is not possible."

"You fucking guys got to learn how to run a business! You come to this country and rip us off with high gas prices and hassle us when we try to pay." Just as he said that, Orenthal's cell phone rang. He nearly yelled into his cell phone when he said, "Yeah, I am at the fucking gas station, and this fucking ha-bibe is trying to rip me off again."

Looking at the attendant, Orenthal failed to realize that the tank was overflowing onto the cement. "I'll be in to pay for it," Orenthal said to the attendant loudly.

Now focusing his attention back to the cell phone, he continued, "Yeah, you would think that gas is expensive enough! Haven't these fucking people done enough to ruin the economy?" he said, hanging the pump back up.

As he was standing there talking on the phone, Orenthal believed that the attendant had walked away, but suddenly it felt to him like someone was dousing him with a hose. "What the fu—?" he began, twisting the cap back onto the gas tank. As quick as that happened, Orenthal realized that the owner of the gas station was standing there soaking him with gasoline from another pump. "What the fuck are you doing?" Orenthal screamed.

With the taste of petroleum choking him and fuel dripping into his eyes, Orenthal stood there dumbfounded and could not calculate what was happening. He stood there frozen as the attendant continued to douse him with fuel.

"This is a brand new jacket, you mother fu—"

Before he could finish his sentence, he realized that the attendant had a lit butane lighter in his other hand.

Stunned, Orenthal dropped his cell phone and stood there with his eyes and his mouth opened wide.

Orenthal looked left and then right and realized that he had nowhere to run. Now focusing all attention on the lit lighter in the man's hand, Orenthal watched as the attendant tossed the Zippo towards his petroleum soaked body. Out of instinct and pure stupidity, Orenthal caught the lighter in his right hand as he looked up in complete terror.

As the reality of Orenthal's nightmare reached full climax, the attendant calmly watched the blinding explosion. Orenthal did not scream at first, but he hollered unintelligibly as he was pounding his hands onto his burning body.

The attendant reached into Orenthal's vehicle, looking for anything of value before he doused the interior with fuel. In the ashtray was a single syringe with dried blood in the tube and a wad of cash. Taking the cash out of the ashtray, he soaked the driver's seat with fuel and walked away towards the building, unsympathetically oblivious to the screeching hog.

Had Orenthal ever paid attention in school, or had he the capacity to recall even the most elementary of all lessons, he would have remembered the stop, drop, and roll drill; he instead ran in circles, attempting to pound the fire out of his flesh. He pounded on his head, and the flesh came off like burnt bacon slices. Screaming but trying to tear off his clothes, he peeled off whole chunks of his skin. His SUV burst into flames.

Realizing that this was so heinous an injury that he wouldn't even want to live through it, Orenthal charged into the store looking for revenge. Choking and burning, Orenthal fell onto the welcome mat in front of the check-out counter an exhausted and burnt mess.

Picking up the phone and dialing 911, the attendant said, "Yes, come quick, I have man who is on fire. He has his cell phone on. Come quick! Come quick!"

The synthetic material of Orenthal's clothes had melted right into his soft tissue. The smell of petroleum and burnt flesh, hair, and clothes were too much for the attendant, and he vomited right onto Orenthal's charred body.

Orenthal laid there. The owner could still see the whites of Orenthal's eyes turned yellow through his over-cooked eyelids. He watched the life leaving Orenthal's body. Each breath became more and more labored, and each exhalation contained white smoke. It appeared that Orenthal went into a coma

Looking out onto the gas station while Orenthal laid there dying, the attendant pushed and then pulled the fire-extinguisher lever which activated a series of powder extinguishers outdoors that covered the entire ground with a white dust but did nothing to put out the burning SUV.

Arriving on the scene, a group of firemen worked furiously to put out the vehicle, which was now fully engulfed in flames. The thousands of gallons of gas below the ground in reserve tanks and the possibility of the car exploding made for a few very tense moments.

"Come quick, come quick!" said the owner of the gas station bringing attention to the smoldering corpse lying in the entrance of the building. A young fireman panicked at the sight of Orenthal's smoldering remains, and blasted him with a stream of high-pressure water.

*"NO, NO , NO!"* an older fireman yelled as the flesh was being washed from Orenthal's body "Less pressure, less pressure!"

The flesh hissed as it cooled. On many parts of his arms and face, the bones, muscles, and ligaments were apparent.

A police officer approached the owner cautiously and asked, "What happened?"

"He was on his cell phone, and there must have been a spark. I don't know," offered the attendant as an ambulance arrived on the scene.

Not one emergency personnel could figure out the first thing to do for the suffering Orenthal. Everyone was stunned at the sight of the man that had been cooked alive.

"Yes, and then he ran into here. I call 911," said the attendant looking out at a parade of fire, rescue, and police vehicles.

The fire marshal walked into the gas station with a helmet on his head and exclaimed, "Static electricity!"

Interrupting the scene of the brutal death, Orenthal let out a most disgusting series of noises and grunts as he lay there, tended to by EMS.

The paramedics, knowing that Orenthal's entire body was covered with burns, carefully lifted his charred remains. A high-pitch scream escaped Orenthal. The only thing more disturbing than the sight and the screech was the sound of the burnt flesh crunching under the paramedics' fingers like the carbon on the outside of burnt toast.

The paramedics rushed Orenthal to the ambulance. One of them vomited in the parking lot after the task was finished, and she wasn't alone. No one could believe their eyes. The owner of the gas station asked seriously, "Could he have committed suicide?"

"No, it was static electricity," said the Fire Chief confidently. "It's a phenomenon that is happening all over the country. Either that or it was his cell phone," he concluded, as if either answer was good enough.

Walking out to the powder covered cement with the police and firemen, the attendant pointed to a sign on the pump that read NO CELL PHONES. "See? No cell phones. He didn't read."

The fire marshal asked him, "Do you want us to hose down the parking lot to get rid of all of this powder?

"Sure, you can," he said. "Good, yes!"

The police officer asked, "Do you have a surveillance tape of the accident?"

"Oh, yes. In here," he said, walking back into the store as the officer followed him. "But it is not on."

"You didn't have it running?"

"No," he replied. "Not always."

The officer said, "Well, that's no good to us."

"I'm sorry," said the attendant.

The firemen were hosing down the entire parking lot, washing the powder into a drain ditch. More police, firemen, and paramedics arrived at the scene, hoping to get a sight of the burnt corpse. A news crew had arrived on the scene and was shooting a live broadcast of the tragic accident. Out at the police perimeter, a man of Middle Eastern descent was heard saying, "Yes, this is a family business. My brother—I need to see if he is okay." A police officer let him through the crowd. Walking up to his brother, he hugged him and said in Arabic, "Are you okay?"

Handing his brother the handful of cash that he took from Orenthal's car, the man winked at his brother and said, "Let him burn in *hell*, too."

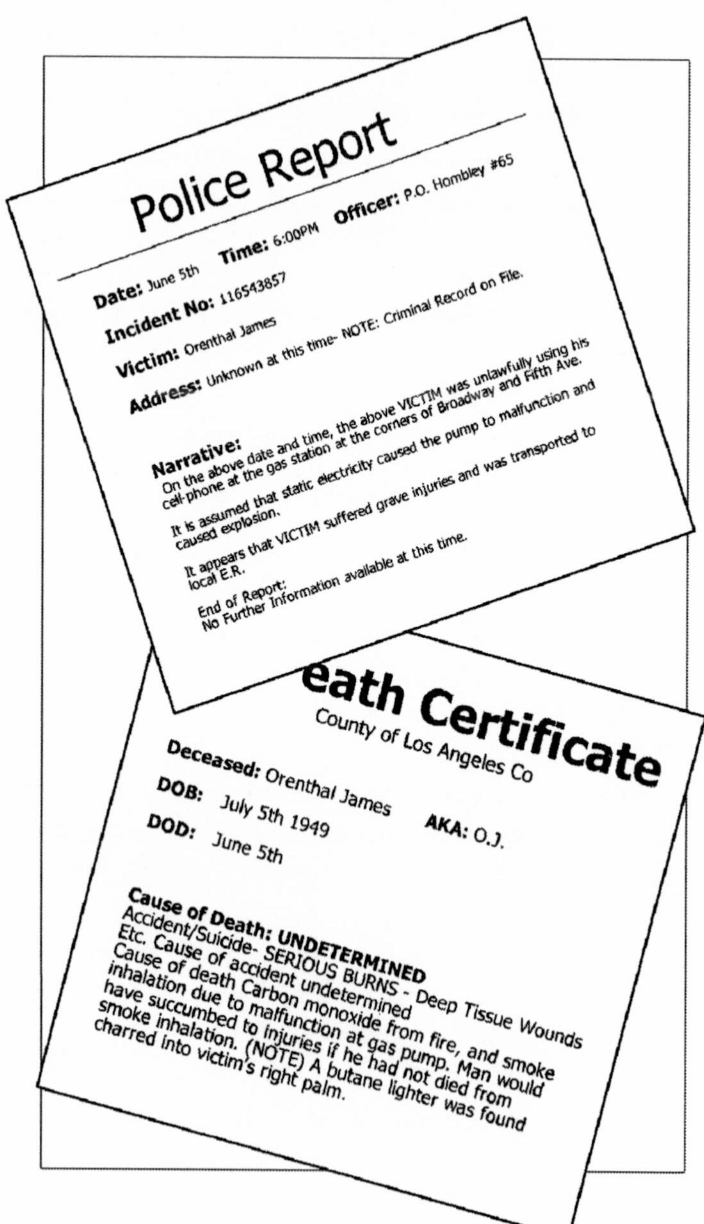

Police Report

Date: June 5th Time: 6:00PM Officer: P.O. Hombley #65

Incident No: 116543857

Victim: Orenthal James

Address: Unknown at this time- NOTE: Criminal Record on File.

Narrative:
On the above date and time, the above VICTIM was unlawfully using his cell-phone at the gas station at the corners of Broadway and Fifth Ave.

It is assumed that static electricity caused the pump to malfunction and caused explosion.

It appears that VICTIM suffered grave injuries and was transported to local E.R.

End of Report:
No Further Information available at this time.

eath Certificate
County of Los Angeles Co

Deceased: Orenthal James AKA: O.J.

DOB: July 5th 1949

DOD: June 5th

Cause of Death: UNDETERMINED
Accident/Suicide- SERIOUS BURNS - Deep Tissue Wounds Etc. Cause of accident undetermined Cause of death Carbon monoxide from fire, and smoke inhalation due to malfunction at gas pump. Man would have succumbed to injuries if he had not died from smoke inhalation. (NOTE) A butane lighter was found charred into victim's right palm.

# Self Help'

## A Hogtale

Standing in line at a local bookstore, Orenthal was waiting to check out a new self help book that he hoped would be able to give him advice on how to control his anger. Thumbing through the pages and minding his own business, Orenthal didn't seem to mind that there were fifteen other people in front of him.

No book in the world could have prepared him for when a four year old child pushing a baby stroller, slammed it right into the back of Orenthal's heel. "God damn it woman!" Orenthal screamed at the mother, "I got the *gout* in both heels." His outburst had startled everyone who had heard it.

"I am so... sorry," said the woman fashionably, picking up her infant baby from the stroller who was now crying. "Michael, say your sorry to that man," she said to the young boy who just stood there with a smirk on his face.

"Why don't you watch where the hell you are going?" Orenthal demanded.

Every person who was in line in front of him was now looking back to see who was making such a disturbance.

"What am I, a fucking side show?" Orenthal barked forward. "Mind your own goddamn business!" he said.

The woman who was standing directly in front of Orenthal appeared scared as she looked over her shoulder and then cautiously stepped out of line. Everyone felt uncomfortable.

Thumbing through the pages, still clearly fuming from the accident, it appeared that Orenthal was talking to himself.

"Michael!" the mother screamed with a shriek. The child had grabbed the stroller and again rammed it purposely right into the back of Orenthal's heel.

The pain launched Orenthal forward and to the ground, landing him on his side knocking a display of miniature books and novelties over. Orenthal screamed a bout of obscenities that was so inappropriate that not a single person in the line felt sorry for him.

An elderly man who was standing in the line walked over and helped Orenthal up. "Get your hands off me old timer," Orenthal said rudely, "I don't need any help from some ole' geezer."

Raising both of his hands and appearing unslighted, the older gentleman simply stepped back into line.

"Sir, I am so sorry," said the woman, "I can't explain why he would--"

Stomping his foot into the baby's stroller which was holding a stuffed animal, a baby blanket and a baby's bottle, the stroller collapsed, and the wheels broke clean off of the front of it. The woman was now standing there stunned.

"I *tole'* you to watch where you were going," Orenthal said in a possessed tone, his eyes were fixed in rage. Orenthal reached forward trying to take the baby out of the woman's arms as she backed away quickly protecting her child from this predator. Every person in the store was now looking right at Orenthal.

"The cop's are on their way," one woman screamed.

Huffing and puffing furiously, looking sharply left, and then right Orenthal pointed at the woman and said, "You're *goddamn* lucky you got so many witnesses," still pointing he repeated louder, "goddamn lucky."

Stepping in between Orenthal and the woman was the elderly man who had helped him moments ago, "You dropped your book," he said holding it patiently in front of Orenthal.

Slapping the book out of the old mans hands Orenthal said "I don't need no goddamn anger management book." The old man stood his ground while the woman stood protecting her children. Pushing the old man out of the way Orenthal pointed at the woman and said loudly "I'll be waiting for you in the parking lot," and then walked furiously towards the exit. Orenthal had managed to terrorize every person in the store.

Walking out to his SUV that was parked on the curb, Orenthal got into his vehicle appearing very angry. Driving away, he was satisfied that his threat of violence was enough to stay in the back of the woman's mind every time that she was getting into her car for the rest of her life.

Watching from the window as Orenthal drove out of the parking lot, the cashier said to the large crowd of concerned patrons, "He's gone," repeating it as if to assure everyone that the threat was no longer there, *"he's gone!"*

# Unfortunate Series of Events

## Part One- A Murder

The infamous Orenthal James was involved in a horrible accident. And like all ignorant baboons before him, their own actions eventually cause them a bit of personal grief in the game of trial and error.

Orenthal entered the emergency room on a stretcher, yelling loudly enough to let every person in the emergency room know that he had arrived.

Because Orenthal believed himself to be entitled to special treatment in the first place, and was also in a bit of pain, he believed that his injury should take precedence over all other people before him at the emergency room of Mother of Mercy hospital.

Screaming in absolute agony, Orenthal demanded to see a doctor and ordered any person he saw in a pair of scrubs to get him some pain medication. "Doc, I need pain meds! Doc, it's killing me! Hurry!"

Earlier in the day, Orenthal had been watching the two-man team that was installing a professionally built doghouse in his back yard. Orenthal needed the doghouse to cover up a large hole that he had recently dug. He didn't have a dog, but he joked that the dog house was so big that he could rent the space out to a vagabond or perhaps a sycophant, or even eventually live in there himself if the opportunity or need ever presented itself.

Orenthal was not paying cash for the installation of his new doghouse, instead he convinced the contractors to accept payment for their work in sports memorabilia. Here was a grown man who was shamelessly trading baseball cards and trophies, as if they were legal tender for all debts public or private. This sad reality proves the child like mentality of the infamous Orenthal James. He was a man with a very large head; but a very small mind.

As the contractors were putting the frame up for the elaborate doghouse, Orenthal asked, "Hey, fellas, when do you think you will be done with this dog house?"

"You can't rush perfection," said the contractor, using a high-powered nail gun to drive 3½-inch nails into the wooden frame in a rapid fashion.

Like a child, Orenthal was mesmerized by the nail gun. "Hey, buddy, you got a permit for that?" Orenthal asked, intrigued.

"Just another tool of the trade, Mr. James," said the man proudly. "Moves a job twice as fast when you have the right equipment!" He showed off the tool, sending three nails securely into place on the wooden frame.

"Wow, can I see it?" Orenthal asked inquisitively.

"Well, I really shouldn't, but I guess you can," he said, handing it over to Orenthal.

Caught off guard by the weight of the gun, Orenthal carelessly lowered the nail gun to get a better grip on the tool and accidentally activated two quick jabs, sending two 3½-inch nails directly into the bone of his knee cap.

More startled by the sound than the pain, Orenthal didn't realize for a moment that he had just crippled himself permanently. When he tried to offset his weight on the injured knee, he crashed shoulder-first into the earth in a pain too impossible to describe.

Adding his ignorance to Orenthal's injury, the contractor pulled out another indispensable tool of the trade: a pry bar. In a panic, the contractor stood on Orenthal's lower leg, using all of his force on the lever, pulling with violent jerking action in an attempt to remove the nails from Orenthal's kneecap. He only succeeded in tearing the rounded flat tops clean off of both galvanized nails.

The nails had locked themselves into Orenthal's knee cap as if they had grown in the steely knot of a firm *Elm* tree. This was not a good day for the infamous Orenthal James.

Orenthal had passed out from the pain and was awaken in the back of an ambulance by the strong smell of ammonia smelling salts. This would prove to be a very demanding trip to the emergency room—physically and mentally—for both Orenthal and the staff at the local emergency room.

Screaming at the top of his lungs, Orenthal got the attention of every person in the emergency room. A young girl who had fallen while ice-skating who was in need of stitches in her chin even stopped crying out of empathy for the large man in the stretcher as he was pushed by.

Every slight movement of the leg gave Orenthal a sharp raw pain. Every breath he took emphasized the pressure on the wound. Every heartbeat attempted to push blood through the two gnarled nails sticking out of his knee. Orenthal was screaming as if he had just witnessed a bloody murder.

Orenthal's language was filthy. His attempt at being outrageous was not winning him favors with the staff in the emergency room. Passing by mostly female nurses, Orenthal was even heard saying, "Bunch of incompetent bitches," on more than one occasion. In Orenthal's defense, the pain must have been horrifying.

Responding to the unacceptable commotion, a doctor entered hurriedly behind the curtain where Orenthal was waiting and said, "Mr. James, you must keep your voice down. You are disturbing the other people here, and that is not fair to them."

The words that Orenthal used to belittle and berate this female doctor were so callous, so disgusting, that no one would ever believe it. As a professional and understanding Orenthal's trauma, the doctor tried to reason with him, ignoring his bold, cruel, and sexist words.

"Mr. James, I am Dr. Pinochet, and I am the head doctor, in charge of trauma in this hospital. Please, try and compose yourself."

He screamed even louder, "As soon as you get me some fucking meds, I will shut the fuck up!" Orenthal continued to scream in agony while the head doctor examined his knee.

Looking concernedly at the wound, Dr. Pinochet said to the nurse calmly, "We need an X-ray."

She turned back to Orenthal, saying patiently, "Mr. James, I know this must be terribly painful, but please watch your language. There are *kids* here and people trying to rest."

"I don't give a fuck about anybody else!" bawled Orenthal. "I want some pain meds, and I want a competent doctor, preferably a man, not some incompetent bitch who is worried about my emergency room etiquette." Orenthal continued to rage out of control. "Put me to sleep and fix my fucking leg! It hurts!"

Disgusted, Dr. Pinochet nodded her head confidently and said to the nurse who was examining Orenthal's wound, "Give him sedation with pain protocol level three."

Looking at Orenthal, she continued, "Mr. James, unfortunately there are patients with life and death situations right now in this OR that are going to have to take precedence over your injury. I am very sorry, but a helicopter just landed, carrying two young men who were gravely injured in an automobile accident. This, plus all of the other unexpected influx here at the hospital has put us understaffed, and we must prioritize each patient by the severity of their trauma."

"Do you know who I am?" Orenthal asked, grimacing in pain.

"Yes, Mr. James, I know exactly who you are," said the unimpressed doctor. "We have treated your wife here on numerous occasions," she offered with a curt grin on her face.

This was not the notoriety that Orenthal had hoped to be remembered for, and he raged into another series of belittling comments. Orenthal threw a can of diet soda across the OR that a young nurse offered to him as an attempt to calm him down, saying, "I'm not on a diet, you stupid bitch! Bring me a Hawaiian Punch!"

Disgusted at Orenthal's behavior, Dr. Pinochet said, "We just paged a doctor from another facility to come and help us with our caseload. In the meantime, I will have the nurse administer a relaxant that will help you with your anxiety and some pain medication, and I will get back to you as soon as I can." She smiled at him as if that were enough explanation for the moment.

Enraged, Orenthal yelled, "Anxiety? You don't know what pain is! Get this fucking nail out of my leg," he said, pausing to take a deep breath through his nose and snorting with a mad look on his face, "before I *kill* someone!" He raged with blood in his eyes and on his hands.

A security guard entered the room. Looking very calm, he said, "Mr. James, I am going to have to ask you to calm down or I—"

"Or I what, mother fucker? What the fuck is you gonna to do to me?" Continuing with his vulgar tirade, Orenthal swore that he would sue every person working in the hospital, from the head doctor all the way down to the orderly that was moping up the diet soda from the floor.

Finishing off this series of threats and insults, Orenthal challenged, " I be callin' my *law-yah!* Yous don't know whose yous be messin' wit'! "

A woman who had just entered the room called out, "Doctor Pinochet!" The critical care nurse rushed towards her. "OR-3 is ready. We need you, stat!"

"You're number three on my list, Mr. James. Three out of thirteen. I can only ask that you please be patient," Doctor Pinochet pleaded, as she ran down the hallway with three other nurses.

Entering OR-3, Dr. Pinochet wasted no time tending to and analyzing the multiple grave injuries that the teenage boy had sustained in the car accident. Judging by the appearance of his injuries and analyzing the heart and brain monitor, Dr. Pinochet knew that she and her team were in a battle against the odds.

Dr. Pinochet had been working for the last twenty-eight hours, and this was supposed to be her day off. She chose to stay and help because of short staffing and the unexpected influx of patients.

Working furiously with her trauma team for over thirty-five minutes, the whole trauma team understood that hoping and praying for a miracle was the only option left, but each individual continued to work desperately to save this young man's life.

The young man reminded the doctor of her own son. Dr. Pinochet has always followed the rule that most doctors should in a situation like this one. And that is to act as if the patient were a member of your own family. This rule was one that she had hoped that every doctor in every emergency room in the country would follow in the event that they might one day, god forbid; have to work on a member of her family.

In this horrible incident Dr. Pinochet acted as if it were her own son laying on the gurney. Dr. Pinochet was faced with the sad reality that the task was impossible and that every excruciating, exhausting move she and her team had made had been in vain. Staring over the young body full of tubes and covered in electrical patches, the doctor knew by the lack of response on the heart and brain monitors that there was no life left in this young boy.

Over come with emotion, Dr. Pinochet let out a wail of uncontrolled emotion. "Shit! Shit!" she exhaled furiously, holding her hand over her facemask. She looked around the room, knowing that she had the added burden of being the person with the most credentials and the duty to end the valiant struggle to save this boy's life.

Speaking in a cracking voice and looking over her exhausted staff, Dr. Pinochet announced, "We have done all we can do. Thank you for your heroic efforts. Note the chart: this boy was pronounced dead at 15:37 hours."

Bowing her head and closing her eyes as if saying a quiet prayer, Dr. Pinochet was interrupted by the words, "I will notify his parents. They are in the waiting room."

Realizing that this young nurse was way too eager and green to face the grueling task of notifying the next of kin with the appropriate dignity, Dr. Pinochet said, "Young lady, please." She paused, attempting to find the appropriate words. "I will take care of notifying next of kin. Take a quick break and get washed up. I am going to need you in OR-2 in five minutes."

Walking out of the operating room, Dr. Pinochet was holding the file of the young man that she had just pronounced dead and was on her way to speak to the boys' parents. Interrupting her train of thought as she walked down the hall, Dr. Pinochet was reminded of the nightmare of her third most crucial patient. "I need a fucking doctor. Now!" she heard Orenthal scream.

There was the sound of clanging, like someone had thrown or dropped metal pans. Listening curiously through a closed door, Dr. Pinochet could hear the familiar voice of the hospital's security officer.

"Mr. James, please! Please! The doctor will be in shortly."

"I need pain meds now! You don't know who I am or who I know! I will have this hospital shut down!" Orenthal clamored.

Walking towards and opening the door to the urgent care waiting room, Dr. Pinochet found a young couple in their early forties holding onto each other for dear life. There they were doing the only thing possible in a time like this: holding onto each other and waiting. It was as if they believed that the harder they held onto each other, the better the chance that their son would survive this accident.

This was never easy.

Dr. Pinochet tried everything in her power to remain composed and professional as she offered politely, "Mr. and Mrs. Eckle," smiling gently. "I am sorry, but...."

Dr. Pinochet stumbled for words. What could she possibly say to soften the blow?

Holding back, she looked into the eyes of this young couple and kept the reality of their son's death from escaping. She knew that the parents up to this point were still clinging onto hope.

Falling to her knees she wrapped her arms around the young frantic couple. Not wanting to take away any dignity from the boy, as if she were protecting his honor, Dr. Pinochet let these parents down most graciously.

"The trauma," she offered holding tighter. "Was too much..." holding even tighter as the mother began to wail. "For *any* body to take... And we tried everything we could," she said, sobbing with the young couple. "I am so, so sorry..."

Holding the young couple, a series of screams of emotion followed the truth, and no other words were spoken. A silence grew in the room, overpowering the mother's quiet sob and occasional gasp for air. The mother continued to repeat the word <u>no</u> over and over again. The loss of their son was too much to take.

Regaining her composure Dr. Pinochet knew that her expertise was needed throughout the hospital and that her time here was done. She could again hear the sounds of a madman screaming obscenities.

Standing up from the young couple, Dr. Pinochet wished that she could hold them until all of their pain would go away, but she knew that that was just not possible. There is just not enough time in the world, and she must get back to work.

"Thank you, doctor, for all that you did for our son. Thank you for caring," the young father said, tears pouring from his eyes with the utmost sincerity.

"It is my pleasure," said Dr. Pinochet. "I am only sorry that I couldn't have done more. But I have to get back to work. I am very sorry for your loss."

"Yes, you sound very busy, doctor. Can I get your name?" asked the young father dazedly, smiling graciously through tears.

"It is Dr. Pinochet," she said, returning the smile. "I must go. There will be someone out in a little while to help you with the necessary paperwork and arrangements. Again, I am very sorry." She backed out of the room, turned, and walked away slowly.

Opening the door to the ER, Dr. Pinochet heard smashing glass as an anxious nurse ran up to Dr. Pinochet and said, "We gave him three times the shot of volume, and he is still raging! We can't stop him. And the kid in OR-2 is losing vitals! We're having a melt down here," she exclaimed.

"I will take care of it," said Dr. Pinochet, walking towards Orenthal's stall. Pulling the gate aside, she saw a member of housekeeping and a nurse picking up broken glass that had been smashed out of a metal cabinet with glass doors. She turned to Orenthal, who looked both in misery and very pleased with himself. "Mr. James, I will give you—"

"You fucking whore!" he screamed, interrupting her. "Get me a male doctor that knows what the fuck he is doing," he shouted, completely out of control.

Turning her key and reaching into a locked cabinet, Dr. Pinochet pulled the plastic sleeve off of a large syringe. Picking up a bottle of medication, Dr. Pinochet lifted her chin towards the fluorescent lights and watched as she filled the syringe full of the clear solution.

Walking over to Orenthal, she said, "Mr. James, I need you to remain quiet, please!" Taking an alcohol swab, she rubbed his left bicep circling a bull's-eye with the moisture. She inserted the needle.

"Whoa, wait! Shouldn't you put that in the IV?" he asked her.

"Oh, yes, Mr. James. I am sorry, I am just a female doctor. Sometimes I get confused," she said sarcastically.

"You incompetent bitch," Orenthal said. "You don't even know what the fuck you are doing." Orenthal was too ignorant and self absorbed to pick up on the good doctors satire.

"I am trying to save lives Mr. James. That's what I am doing," as she pushed the clear solution from the syringe into Orenthal's intravenous tube patiently.

"You couldn't save your own life, if your life depended on it." he said coldly. "Stupid Bitch…"

Dr. Pinochet turned her back to Orenthal and inhaled while tightening her lips, holding her breath for just a second; she reached into the unlocked medical box and grabbed another small bottle.

Lifting her chin again and watching the clear solution fill the syringe; Dr. Pinochet appeared as if she were carefully measuring the contents of the controlled substance.

Walking back over to Orenthal, she looked at him and half smiled, and as she was just about to insert the syringe again into Orenthal's IV, she bowed her head in shame.

"What the fuck are you waiting for, a reprieve from the governor?" Orenthal screamed. "Can't you see I am in pain here?"

Injecting the lethal dose into Orenthal's IV, Dr. Pinochet said, "Now, Mr. James, I will be back in a few minutes. I am going to see if I can get you a male doctor." She extended him a comfortable smile as she walked around the room, raising the cold metal bars on both sides of his hospital bed.

"That sounds more like it," said Orenthal, smiling from his crib.

It seemed that Mr. James was already a little more relaxed. Finally, he was quiet for more than thirty seconds.

The orderly seemed a little less timid.

The nurses seemed to breathe a sigh of relief.

The young girl waiting to get stitches smiled as she held a piece of gauze to her chin patiently and watched a cartoon on the television.

All efforts were now underway in OR-2 for the other seventeen-year-old boy that was fighting for his life.

After forty-five minutes of trauma work, the young man had been raised from critical to stable condition. There was serious bleeding which was stopped and a blood transfusion had brought him back from critical. Walking out of the operating room, Dr. Pinochet told her team that she would notify the parents of the boy's improving condition.

Walking into the critical care waiting room with a lighter burden than before, Dr. Pinochet said, "Mr. and Mrs. Milstein, your son was in critical condition due to femoral arterial bleeding, which we were able to stop, and he is now in stable condition after a series of blood transfusions. I assure you that we are working hard here and doing everything in our power to help your son. I don't want to give you false hopes, but I will tell you that he is doing much better now than he was twenty minutes ago."

The parents were nodding their heads gratefully, holding on to each other afraid to breath, knowing that if they exhaled, it could tip the scale in the other direction for their son, and they did not want to take that chance.

"I must get back into the OR. I will keep you notified of his condition. Right now, it's touch and go. Barring anything out of the ordinary, your son has a good chance of making it through the night." Excusing herself, Dr. Pinochet said, "I am sorry for the informality, but I must go."

Walking back into the ER, Dr. Pinochet heard the words, *"Code blue!"* being called over the intercom. A strobe light flashed over the bed that Orenthal James was in.

Watching from a distance, Dr. Pinochet admired the courage and organization of her young emergency room staff. Watching as they worked diligently on the infamous Orenthal James, she observed their emergency room reflexes.

Seven minutes had passed, and her opinion that she was working with one of the finest groups of emergency room professionals in her career was confirmed.

Walking over to the corpse, the doctor interrupted the controlled flow of emergency protocol and announced,

"We have tried all we can. This corpse is pronounced dead at 16:45 hours."

All of the nurses seemed shocked that Dr. Pinochet was calling it quits on a quasi-celebrity that seemed to have died from a horrible knee injury.

"We should try more," said the nurse that had administered the three doses of painkiller to Orenthal earlier. "We can't stop!" Suddenly, a look of terror came over her face. "I gave him too much volume!"

"No, honey, I did it. It is on me, not you." Dr. Pinochet shook her head sympathetically, admitting blame. "Now, please, you have done all that you can do. I am ordering you all to take a break and regain your composure. I need you to focus. We have more patients to see."

Looking paralyzed, the young nurse could barley nod her head up and down when she said, "Yes, doctor," and slowly walked away.

Addressing the other staff, Dr. Pinochet said simply, "This corpse has almost achieved room temperature… He has been dead for at least a half-an-hour. There is nothing we can do for him."

Repeating, as if she was just stating a plain cold fact, "This corpse is pronounced at 16:47 hours." Holding her stethoscope to the jugular vein of the corpse of the infamous Orenthal James, searching for any signs of life and looking into his glazed eyes… "Make it 16:45 hours. This corpse is pronounced dead at 16:45," she said comparing her time to the watch on Orenthal's wrist. Dropping Orenthal's arm onto his abdomen and pulling the white sheet over his face, Dr. Pinochet said, "Okay, folks, let's go!"

"Momma said there'd be days like this," she said softly before focusing her attention onto the other patients. "We've got lives to save, worth saving!" she encouraged her team.

"Here, young lady, notify the next of kin," she offered to the eager nurse handing her Orenthal's chart.

Amazed at Dr. Pinochet's leadership abilities, everyone went about their duties, confident that they had done all that they could.

# Unfortunate Series of Events

## Part Two- A Doctor

The sign on the closing door read Confidential Meeting—Authorized Personnel Only. The head of all of the hospital's staff had gathered behind it.

Mr. Joseph Betterford, the hospital's chief executive officer, had called the emergency meeting to discuss the death of the infamous Orenthal James, which had occurred a week before in their emergency room.

This was to be an informal exploratory meeting to search for facts before moving to resolve any of the issues formally.

Looking around the room, Mr. Betterford said, "Thank you, gentlemen, for meeting here this afternoon on such short notice. Dr. Pinochet should be arriving here any moment."

In the room were three of the hospital's attorneys, the chief financial officer, the executive vice president, and Dr. James Pritchard, who—in the event of Dr. Pinochet's termination or resignation—was ready to take on the new role as acting head of the hospital's emergency department.

Shuffling through papers nervously and looking at his watch, Dr. Pritchard did not realize that he was speaking out of line when he addressed the room by saying, "And when *she* gets here, gentlemen, I have a list of eighteen clear violations that she seems to have dismissed, and we know for a fact that she has falsified her timesheet."

Looking around the room, it was apparent that no one was impressed with Dr. Pritchard's findings.

"She falsified her timesheet, Jim?" Mr. Betterford asked him.

"Yes, and she has been for years."

"Are you saying that she is stealing from us?"

"Well, no. For instance, on the date in question, she put down on her time sheet that she worked from 12 A.M. until 12 P.M., twelve hours, when in fact, we know that she worked for well over thirty hours in the span of two days."

"That's a win for us," said Mr. Betterford. "I don't understand your point?"

"The point is, Dr. Pinochet seems to make her own schedule and likes to come and go as she pleases around here; and I think it is just another example of how lax she is in her approach to working here, and her carelessness is going to cost us big." Dr. Pritchard looked around the room to see if anyone was biting on his slanderous bait.

Everyone in the room now realized that Dr. Pritchard's presence at this meeting was probably not in the best interest of the hospital, especially since he was the next in line to take over for Dr. Pinochet as the head of the emergency department.

Charles Lipscomb, the hospital's head accountant, said, "Gentlemen, for the record, Dr. Pinochet has worked for us for the past sixteen years, and she has worked under the same contract for the past eight. She routinely signs in for four twelve-hour shifts per week, no matter how many hours she works, and has never once put in for overtime, which she is entitled to do." He glanced quickly around the room, nodding his head confidently. "Also, for the record, it is estimated that Dr. Pinochet works, on average, between an extra twenty-four to forty-eight hours per week without any additional compensation whatsoever."

Everyone in the room appeared to be astonished at this fact.

"So you're saying she works for free?" asked one of the attorneys.

"I am saying that she takes her Hippocratic Oath to an extent that no other doctor has ever done before in this hospital and her dedication is second to none. She is one of the reasons we have been able to keep the ER running in the black," said Mr. Lipscomb. "Without question, Dr. Pinochet would receive two to three times what we are paying her if she were actually compensated for her time."

Entering the room with a quiet, "Good afternoon, gentlemen," Dr. Pinochet took her seat. Dr. Pritchard showed his disappointment by looking down at his watch. She continued, "I apologize for my tardiness. I had a patient in the ER that needed my attention before I came up here."

Mr. Betterford responded, "Good afternoon, doctor. Of course, we understand," he added before taking his seat at the head of the table.

"Now, I don't have to remind any of you that this meeting is off the record. I want all cell phones, tape recorders, and any means of electronic communication including pagers shut off. Nothing that we discuss here today is on the record," he repeated, looking around the room seriously. "This is an exploratory meeting to help us decide our course of action, and I will give everyone a moment right now to double-check their possessions to ensure that all electronics are *off*. Does everyone understand?" Mr. Betterford asked.

Sitting quietly, everyone nodded in agreement.

"Now, Marty, what do we have here, legally? Where do we stand in this case?

Leaning back in his chair and holding his pen to his chin, the senior staff attorney said bluntly, "I don't want you to take this the wrong way, but I will put it as simply as I can. It appears that this is gross negligence." He stated it as if it were a matter of fact. "It was wanton and reckless. This is classic open and shut malpractice involving a very famous patient that we were responsible for." The men grimaced at the bad news.

"Dr. Pinochet, how do you explain the situation?" Mr. Betterford asked her.

There was a brief pause before she answered. "Joe, as I have said, this was an error. We had much confusion in the ER that day, and we were acting in the best interest of *all* patients at the time of the incident; somehow, we erred."

Raising his eyebrows while lowering his chin towards his chest, he nodded his head up and down looking over his glasses. "You did a lot more than err, Mary. It appears that your team killed this guy with a lethal overdose of painkillers," he said nervously with a raised voice.

Looking around the room, it was clear that he was not the only person surprised by his sharp tone, but he continued. "And we're not going to be able to just offer the family some meager sum hoping that they will walk away. This is the infamous Orenthal James! This could cost us millions! Do you have any idea of what that is going to do to our malpractice insurance?"

Relaxed, Dr. Pinochet interjected, "Mr. Betterford, I have worked here for over sixteen years, and I have not so much as caused you to have to answer even a simple grievance on my behalf. Never one complaint of being unprofessional. Not one. And in case you've forgotten, I have a wall full of meritorious service plaques from you as well as hundreds of letters from patients and family members of patients for the outstanding service to the community that I provide." Mr. Betterford flushed furiously and began to respond, but Dr. Pinochet refused to be interrupted, continuing, "We have had doctors come and go from this hospital who have cost you millions in damages. Now, I agree, this is an unfortunate series of events, and I am taking full responsibility for it. If you wish to suspend me, then please do so; otherwise, I would like to get back to my job, we have patients waiting."

"No, Dr. Pinochet, you don't have to remind me of your impeccable record, but the autopsy and toxicology report shows here that there was over *ten-times* the lethal amount of pain killers in his body. This is not defendable in a court of law!" Mr. Betterford sat there as if expecting a reasonable answer from someone in the room.

"Take a look at the toxicology report gentlemen," said Pinochet. "This man had street drugs in his system. Cocaine! Heroin! PCP's! All of which would explain why he raged. This would explain why the pain meds had no effect on his system. In my opinion the culpability is as much on the deceased as it is on me and my staff," Dr. Pinochet stated plainly.

Sitting forward, and again speaking out of turn, Dr. Pritchard said, "It's indefensible. It sounds more like *murder* than malpractice." He raised his right hand, palm up, arrogantly pointing his hand in the direction of all members in the room, challenging someone to disagree with him.

"As, I have said, Mr. Betterford, there was an unfortunate series of events which led to the death of the infamous Orenthal James." She rolled her eyes, disinterested. "And I regret that I must take some responsibility, but I have paid my fair share of malpractice insurance in my career, and now, it seems, it is my time to collect. The law of averages has kicked in here, gentlemen. I can't be expected to maintain a perfect record. I am doctor, but I am also human. You cannot expect perfection, even if perfection is what you have received from me for the past sixteen years."

No one could believe how simply Dr. Pinochet had said it. "Have we gotten a letter of intent from a law office yet?" asked one of the other board members.

"Nothing yet. We are expecting one within the week, but they have a full year to file a lawsuit for wrongful death, and you know how these fucking lawyers are. No offense, Marty," he added, smiling towards the hospital's lead attorney. "But you know these guys will be crawling up Mrs. James ass for the next three hundred and sixty-five days reminding her just what a role model he was and what a loss it has been on her and her family."

Marty winked back at Mr. Betterford. "I agree with Joe. This is a mess. If I were on the other end of this lawsuit, I would wait at least six months to file and not specify for any damages, and I would wait for the first offer from the hospital's insurance. And I have to say, on a low figure, we should offer the family…." He paused, performing a delicate math equation that could only be learned in a law school and weighing the expected reactions of the people around the room. "We should offer the family, at the very least, six-million dollars, as a respectable sum."

"Oh my god," said Mr. Betterford, shaking his head looking towards the ceiling tiles.

Unaffected by the news, Dr. Pinochet asked, "So, does this mean I am suspended, or shall I continue as usual?"

Interrupting the flow of the meeting, and out of line for the third time, Dr. Pritchard said, "Well, doctor, as soon as it hits the papers that you are taking responsibility for this man's death, I expect that your career here will definitely be on hold."

Interrupting nervously, Mr. Betterford said, "I disagree. Dr. Pinochet has been an indispensable member of this hospital for sixteen years and has amassed an impeccable record, and as long as she feels comfortable maintaining her position as the head of our ER, then I recommend that she continue. You all might feel differently, but in the meantime, I say that we just sit back and wait for the lawsuit to come in, and we will go on from there." Mr. Betterford paused tentatively before asking, "Does everyone agree?"

Everyone nodded in agreement except Dr. Pritchard.

"Very good," said Dr. Pinochet, standing up to leave the room. "Then I will continue as the head of the ER under my same schedule, and we will see what the public sentiment is."

"Wait a minute, Dr. Pinochet. We are far from done with this meeting," announced Dr. Pritchard.

"Oh, really, James?" she asked shortly, sitting back down. "I didn't realize that I answered to you," she said smoothly, scolding her insubordinate underling. "The fact that you are next in line for my job doesn't take away from the fact that I trained you here. And I don't think anybody here is quite ready for you to take over in my place just yet, so please, hold your horses, Jimmy, and get back to work, and leave the litigation to the men that handle litigation."

Turning her head to address the other men in the room, she said in a much more respectful tone, "You fellows have a lot to discuss; this issue was out of my hands the moment that I pronounced Mr. James dead. My expertise is with the living, and saving lives, your expertise is litigation, and defending the dead…Since I have agreed to take full responsibility for my actions, I see no purpose for me to sit here while you men figure out a defense." She waited briefly for an objection. When none was forthcoming, she continued, "So, if you will, please excuse me. We are short-staffed, and my expertise is far better suited for the ER than this situation." Standing up, Dr. Pinochet walked towards the exit, and without hesitating or looking back, she unlocked the door and walked out of the room.

Stunned at her nonchalance, Dr. Pritchard looked at Mr. Betterford and said, "I trust that you will have a word with her in private?"

"Honestly, men," said Mr. Betterford, "I have to agree with her. What more could she say? Let's not beat a dead mule here. When the lawsuit comes in, we'll move forward. Until then, let's not drive each other crazy with what-ifs."

"Well, I assume that you will be monitoring Dr. Pinochet's performance, and—"

"Jim, there's not a doctor in three counties—including yourself—that could walk *two-feet* in her shoes on any given day. Like she said, this was an unfortunate series of events."

Standing up from the table, all but Dr. Pritchard filed out of the meeting room, as the other men agreed that it was only a matter of time that they would be required to answer any legal correspondence in this case, and they chose to allow the process to take its course, and hoped for the best.

# Unfortunate Series of Events

## Part Three- A Lawyer

An attorney by the name of Luis Cobbler was ringing the doorbell of the James' home. He had represented Mr. James in a number of criminal and legal battles before. Now, uninvited, he stood there in a crisp new suit as Mrs. James answered the door. "Good morning, Mrs. James. I am sorry to bother you, but I have the results of Orenthal's autopsy, and I would like to go over the paperwork in preparation of the lawsuit that we discussed at the funeral last week."— It was an awkward moment before he realized that he was an unwelcome guest. "If you will just sign a few documents, I'll be on my way."

"No, Mr. Cobbler. I am not at all interested in filing a wrongful death lawsuit for the death of my husband. As I told you, I do not see any purpose."

"Well, Mrs. James, I know this is a bad time for you, but since your husband was a man of stature and status in the community, you would be entitled to quite a significant amount of money, in the millions. And—between you and I—a doctor that works in the ER told me that the doctor who committed this atrocity has already admitted that she is willing to take full responsibility for the death."

"Yes, I am well aware of the situation," said Mrs. James. "I already spoke with Dr. Pinochet at the funeral.

She explained to me that they were overworked and understaffed, I am not about to add to their workload by means of a court system that is already fraught with frivolous lawsuits by incompetent lawyers."

"See, they have already admitted guilt. This is huge," said the lawyer unable to control his excitement.

"It is very easy for a lawyer to point blame onto an overworked doctor in a crowded emergency room. I have been in that emergency room before. Unfortunately, a bunch of times, a few at the hands of my late husband, and I know Dr. Pinochet personally. She is a beautiful person and an exceptional doctor, and she has helped me many times. I know how busy it can get. I am just glad that I can now put this all behind me."

Seeing that it did not appear to be registering in actual numbers in her head, the lawyer offered, "We are looking in the ten to twenty million dollar range." When even this failed to get a response out of her, the lawyer continued most despicably, "And of course it would be for your kids, for their future!" He wore a half-cocked grin that could only be learned in a law school. "You know, you have to think about the children. They would never have to work a day in their lives."

Disgusted at the notion, Mrs. James said coolly, "I want my kids to work. I want them to grow up and earn their way. Look, Mr. Cobbler, do you think these kids even understand or even miss their father? I hate to burst your bubble, but he was never here for my children, and when he was, it was never fatherly."

She opened the door further to display three young kids all, less than four years of age, playing on the floor with a few toys. A nanny was picking up the youngest child to feed him a bottle.

"Is that Jesse?" asked Mr. Cobbler, pointing at a young boy who was pushing a plastic dump truck over the carpet. "He was so strong at the funeral."

"Yes, Luis, he is very strong. And I have to tell you that I didn't appreciate you telling my four-year-old son that he would have to be the man of the house now. He is a boy, not a man, but as far as I am concerned, he is more of a man now than his father ever was."

Looking at Luis right in the eyes, she noticed that he was red with shame. She pressed on, "I will not allow my kids to grow up as victims, and I will certainly not enter a courtroom and lie under oath when asked if I miss my husband."

Very shocked at Mrs. James words, he had never thought that he would have to sell himself, especially in a case like this. Normally, even in the most serious cases, the person would usually hide their greed behind the façade of being in the best interest of their children.

Perhaps he had come too soon.

"Well, Mrs. James, obviously you are still in shock, and you're not thinking clearly. I want to give you my card, and I will follow up with you in a few weeks," he said flatly, handing her his card. "How does that sound?"

"Well, Mr. Cobbler, I would appreciate it if you would not contact me," she replied, folding his card in half and handing it back to him. "I have no intention of filing a lawsuit, now or ever."

"Well, you have up to a year to file, and I want to represent you, on behalf of your husband, who I did consider a friend of mine—"

"Well, that's nice Luis, because my husband didn't have any *real* friends. I would appreciate it if you would leave. Your attempt at sincerity is making me nauseous."

"Yeah but Misses James," he said desperately. "What about your kid's future?" he asked again.

"Honestly Luis, I consider this a blessing. All things happen for a reason, and my kids will grow up strong. And if you think for a second, that I believe that you are standing at my front door, looking out for the best interest of my three children, then you are only fooling yourself." Looking at him straight in the eyes Misses James pressed the attorney "You don't care about me, or my kids. The only thing that you will ever care about is the thirty-five percent commission plus fees that will total in the millions of dollars for you, and I am not about to make your career… So if you want to help me by acting in the best interest of me and my children then you will leave and never return... Any questions?"

Mr. Cobbler backed away, amazed at her unreasonable spite. Had he said something wrong? What in the hell just happened?

Out of desperation Mr. Cobbler issued one more plea, convinced that he now understood, "Do you already have an attorney, Mrs. James? Because we could change all that or work together."

"Mr. Cobbler, I had retained an attorney, who was helping me to prepare my divorce with Orenthal, which I guess is now final, even in the eyes of God… Orenthal was a horrible husband and a horrible father, and I will not be using any lawyer to file a wrongful death lawsuit. This outcome has saved me a lot of heartache. And, as impossible as that may seem to you, I can't put a price tag on my peace of mind or my children's."

"Well, if you ever reconsider, could you please give me a call?"

"No, I wont," she said bluntly. "I won't reconsider. And if you ever step foot on my property or call on me or a member of my family again, I will sue you for harassment, and I am sure that I will find a lawyer that will help me. Now, please, get off of my property."

Getting into his sports coupe and looking into the rear view mirror, he shook his head involuntarily, as if shaking off a heavy-handed slap. He felt so ashamed. He could not believe it. His ears and cheeks were bright red, and he wondered if he would ever meet a woman of such character again.

Was she serious? Driving away, he couldn't help but feel ashamed for his behavior. He picked up his cell phone and called his office. "Yeah, it's me. You're never going to believe this."

# House of Ill Repute

## A Hogtale

Believing that what happens in Las Vegas actually manages to stay there, Orenthal James also believed that all persons, much like him, go to Vegas to smoke crack and beat prostitutes. All of the rumors about world-class dining, shows and attractions are merely a cover-up for his degenerate behavior, which had become more and more risqué with each trip that he took.

Every time Orenthal saw a commercial for Las Vegas, he imagined that it was calling him personally. This will be his third trip in two months, and he had traveled alone each time, having told his family that he was going away on business.

Checking into his room and doing a line of coke off of the nightstand, Orenthal was sure that this was the beginning of what was going to be a great night. Taking a large knife out of his black carryon bag and putting it in his pants pocket, Orenthal was now prepared for the evening.

Orenthal entered the hotel bar, and anyone watching him meeting a young, newly married couple would have thought that Orenthal had reunited with a couple of old friends. After about an hour of buying this new couple drinks, telling jokes, and giving the appearance of being an all-around normal and jovial guy, Orenthal decided to test his luck with his new found friends.

Looking right past the young bride to her new husband, Orenthal said "So, Mark, what do you say you and me go out and hit a few clubs tonight? You can leave the misses here at the hotel, and I will show you what Vegas is all about."

"No, sir, Mr. James," said the young man. "We are on our honeymoon," he answered politely. "I can't leave my new wife here, or I'll be divorced by Wednesday," he said, laughing. "I'm sure you understand." His wife was laughing and seemed embarrassed.

"Divorced Wednesday next week or Wednesday ten- years from now: what's the difference?" Orenthal jeered. "Save yourself the decade of misery and come out with me, and I will show you how to *really* enjoy Vegas."

Orenthal continued on in his manic rant: "Talk about Vegas odds!" He pretended to shake an imaginary pair of dice, blowing into his hands before tossing the dice out into nowhere. "Fifty-fifty chance you'll be divorced in less than ten years. Those are real statistics, my friend, so I say enjoy Vegas while you're here." Getting a kick out of himself, Orenthal laughed out loud alone for a few seconds as the young couple looked at each other, repulsed by this man's change in behavior.

Turning his face slowly towards the young couple, Orenthal said in the most disrespectful of tones, "Well then, how about I get one of the whores from the casino to come up and we can share bitches and party in my room tonight?" He smacked his gums and licked his lips and mouth, scratching his face and head with a crazed, psychotic look in his eyes.

The young couple looked appalled and was definitely shocked by Orenthal's twisted demeanor. "Hey, buddy," said the young man seriously, "I think you had a little too much to drink tonight. Why don't you get lost?" He nodded once confidently before turning his back on Orenthal.

"Ok," said Orenthal, shaking his head boldly and turning his body so that he could now look the young wife in her eyes, looking like a crazed murderer slithering his tongue at her like a snake, "but yous' all don't know what yous' be missin'!" he said, laughing as he walked away from them, leaving behind his large unpaid bar tab.

Walking into the lobby of the casino, Orenthal said to the bellhop, "Get me a cab, boy."

"Right here, sir," said the bellhop, escorting him out to the first available taxi.

Once Orenthal had gotten into the cab, the Middle Eastern driver asked, "Yes, where can I bring you, sir?"

"I want to kill a whore tonight," said Orenthal, crossing his legs awkwardly in the back of the cab as if to appear sophisticated. "I need some crack, or coke, or heroin; my buzz is crashing," he said.

"No, sir, we do not promote drugs here. It is illegal—you can get arrested," said the taxi driver quite seriously.

"How 'bout, you do what you're told," Orenthal sneered maliciously. "Shut your fucking mouth and do as I tell you: I want whores, I want blood, and I want drugs. It's that simple." Smiling, Orenthal could see his own face in the rear view mirror. He was always impressed at his acting abilities. "Jesus Christ, I come to the city of sin and I get Gandhi for a taxi driver," he said as the driver threw the car in park.

"You get out of my car," said the taxi driver.

"Fuck you," said Orenthal nonchalantly. "I aint getting out 'til I get what I ordered: drugs and hookers! Either that or the only other thing that is going to *quench my thirst tonight:* is me getting a little *blood* on my hands," Orenthal threatened, methodically raising his loosely clenched fists, still staring at himself in the rear view mirror, now with his eyebrows raised. "And your family won't like that option. Now, drive me to a whore house before things get real messy for ya," Orenthal ordered.

Parked at the exit of the casino, the driver picked up his cell phone and said, "I call you a new ride. You get out!"

"Are you serious?" asked Orenthal sounding concerned. "I didn't want to have to kill anybody just yet tonight," Orenthal said reaching into his right pants pocket, "but since you asked for it, I guess I gots to do…"

Just then another taxi pulled up alongside of the cab and rolled down the window. The driver, a Spanish man with long hair wearing a New York Yankees hat, said, "Señor, you want some ladies and drugs?"

Like Pavlov's dog responding to a dinner bell, Orenthal snapped out of his trance, smiled and quickly stepped out of the first cab accidentally leaving his knife behind on the seat. Grabbing the door handle to the second cab and sitting in the front seat, Orenthal enthusiastically shook the driver's hand and said, "Hey, Maestro! Take me home!"

The driver knew exactly what Orenthal was looking for and said in a Spanish dialect, "I got a place; it's just on the outskirts of the desert, about thirty miles from here. There you can get anything you want." He winked once at Orenthal.

Snorting and rubbing his nose with his palm furiously, Orenthal said, "Take me, hombre! You just saved that mans life!"

"Si, señor," said the taxi driver, stepping on the gas pedal.

As the first Taxi driver cleared his meter, he watched as the other taxi took off. He though to himself how glad he was to not have to deal with that bloodthirsty-cutthroat another second. Just then, almost by instinct, he looked into the back seat of the cab, which is customary for taxi drivers to see if the previous customer may have left anything of value behind before picking up another fare. Stunned, the driver found a fearsome looking Stiletto switch blade that appeared to be razor sharp sitting on the back seat. Reaching into the back of the cab and grabbing the knife carefully and closing it, he noticed that there was dried blood on the handle of the weapon. Looking into the rear view mirror at himself, his face went pale. He had just stared death in the eye. Little did this man know how close he came to cheating death tonight? Vegas odds makers would have lost their money on that bet.

20 Minutes Later

Orenthal woke to the announcement "Okay, señor, we are here! The best whorehouse in the desert! You get whatever you want in there! That will be twenty-six dollars, please," he said, tapping the meter.

Orenthal took thirty dollars out of his pocket and said, "Keep the change, Taco!"

"Gracias, señor," said the taxi driver as Orenthal left the cab. It seemed like Orenthal was on remote control, or even floating instead of walking, as he entered the house-of-ill-repute.

The smell of cigarettes and stale beer and the loud music were all very welcoming to this immoral sloth as he looked around the dimly lit room with his tongue hanging out of his mouth. There were three men who appeared to be locals scattered around the stage area with their eyes glued to a young woman who was naked and dancing around a bronze pole. Behind her was a bright neon sign reading OPEN 24-Hours. To the left, at the end of the bar, there was a large Asian man dressed in a meticulous gray suit. Sitting in front of him was a stack of paperwork, so he appeared to be the owner.

Orenthal walked up to the stage holding a five-dollar bill in his mouth. The young dancer responded with a smile. Walking seductively towards Orenthal, she took the money from his mouth using only her breasts. Orenthal grabbed a hold of her, giving her a tight squeeze. The young girl enjoyed the attention of a man who was willing to pay for what he wanted. Walking back to her pole, the young girl would not take her eyes off of the infamous Orenthal James.

As Orenthal was taking his seat at a table near the stage, a young Asian woman came up and purred seductively into Orenthal's ear, "I'm Leah, and I take good care of you," and then kissed him lightly on the cheek before licking her lips.

"That's what I'm *talkin'* 'bout," said Orenthal excitedly. He did not notice another small woman who had just rushed to the side of the large Asian man at the bar to whisper in his ear. Waving furiously but discreetly, the large man shouted something quickly in a foreign language into the direction of the back room, and then got the attention of the barmaid. He whispered something in her direction.

The barmaid "Linda" was an older heavy set woman who appeared that she had done her time as a prostitute for far too many years, and has realized that her earning potential as a barmaid is far more appropriate and financially feasible than going up against the younger girls for the hustle of men looking for a good time. Her time and years of being a prostitute, as with most prostitutes had rendered her pretty much obsolete. Because benefits and retirement do not come with this line of work, Linda makes a pretty decent living at this club, acting as a consultant to the new girls in the industry, and helping the owner keep track of the girls and keep them in line. Experience like this, of an old time hooker is indispensable for a place like this. Linda was honest, and loyal, and together, Chichi and Linda run a reputable whore house, and they know how to handle potential trouble.

What Orenthal didn't know is that one of the girls recognized him from one of the other clubs he visited a few weeks ago, and she had just warned Chichi that Orenthal is pretty much banned from every whore house in Vegas.

Getting the attention of the young Asian girl who was dancing for Orenthal and calling her over, Linda winked exaggeratedly and said "Chichi says that drinks are on the house for this gentleman," handing her a scotch on the rocks. Leah knew that there was more than just generosity laced in this beverage and that this was a sign that Orenthal was an unwelcome guest. Leah's eyes broadened with curiosity, but she didn't get an answer. Linda turned her head quickly and walked away so as not to raise any suspicion.

Walking over to give Orenthal his drink, Leah was hesitant because she knew that Orenthal had brought with him a roll of cash, and she did not want to miss out on the economic opportunity of a loaded quasi-celebrity. "Sorry to keep you waiting, big boy," Leah cooed, handing Orenthal the drink. She thought up a quick lie: "You know, we're getting ready to close up for the night."

"That's O.K.," Orenthal said through a broad smile. "I just need a little bit of pussy and some smack, or crack, or coke, and I will be on my way." He arrogantly held out a hand full of cash, knowing that in a whorehouse his money would get him anything he asked for.

"I will take good care of you," said Leah, kissing Orenthal on his cheek. "I will be right back." Orenthal smacked her hard on the ass as she walked in the direction of Chichi, who was now standing at the end of the bar.

"That's what I'm talking about," said Orenthal as if he were in a trance. "I like this place."

"What's going on, Chichi?" Leah asked.

"What's going on is, that man is no fucking good," said Chichi cautiously.

"Why? What happened?"

"Two weeks ago, that man beat the shit out of a girl at the Cowboy Saloon. He left her for dead, he didn't pay, and he tangled with two of the bouncers on the way out." Pointing his finger towards the exit, he commanded, "Get him out of here."

"That was him?" Leah asked, having heard the story. "But he has a handful of cash!"

"I don't care if he has a million dollars on him; I want him out of here! So, if you want to follow him and take your chances, then sayonara, my little *bishoujo*'. I want him out of my business."

Taking her orders from Chichi, the young girl went over and sat on Orenthal's lap, kissing his cheeks and ear, nibbling at his neck. She knew that the drink they had given him would knock him out within a few minutes, and she wanted to be there when he crashed so that she could grab any cash on him before the bouncers did.

"You're a big man," said Leah. I bet you need a couple of women, don't you?" Orenthal just sat there, shaking his head up and down. "You're a high roller, I can tell. Let me get you another drink," she said, looking at Linda.

The next drink that Leah gave Orenthal was again laced heavily with a powerful animal tranquilizer used by veterinarians who need to perform emergency surgery on large animals. Every other time she had seen this used, it had knocked the unsuspecting target out cold within two minutes. After more than five minutes had passed, Leah, Linda, and Chichi watched in anticipation as Orenthal just sat there with a stupid degenerate look on his face. Sweating, he stared out at the empty stage, watching the flashing lights as Linda prepared another drink for their special guest.

Walking over and handing Orenthal his drink, Leah winked and said "On the house, big fella." Orenthal slugged it down in one large gulp.

"Here," said Linda dumping a dust pan with cigarette butts and spent matches into a bowl of popcorn. "Give this man something to munch on," she said handing Leah a dog bowl that was filled with popcorn, mixing it up, she smiled.

"Now this is my kind of place!" shouted an amused Orenthal. All eyes in the place were now on him. Everyone was waiting in anticipation for Orenthal to fall out of consciousness. Once this happened, the bouncers were prepared to take him out back, beat him within an inch of his life, load him in the back of a truck, and drop him off somewhere out in the middle of the desert.

Wrapping his arms around Leah like a pair of vice grips, Orenthal said, "I am ready when you are." He winked and sneered. His breath reeked of poison.

"Oh, yeah," said Leah nervously. "I get back from my break in five minutes. Then I will dance on stage for you. And then you and I can go in the back," she said.

Releasing his clutch on her, Orenthal said, "I'll wait right here for you." Drool ran out of his mouth. "When you go, tell the ugly bitch behind the bar that I am ready for another drink." he said reaching into the bowl with his large hoof and then stuffing his face with popcorn.

When Leah left for the back room, all of the staff huddled around Chichi, who told everyone that this was unprecedented. He had never seen someone like Orenthal take two doses of the tranquilizer and not crash. "He must be so drugged up that it has no effect on him. I am just afraid he might rage," offered Chichi, clearly concerned for the safety of his staff.

"What do you want me to do?" asked Leah.

"I can spike him another drink," shrugged Linda as she looked out and seen Orenthal who was still in his seat devouring the popcorn.

"Do you want me to give him another one Chichi," asked Linda smiling.

"No way," he said, shaking his head. "I am not going to chance killing this guy. Every time a body ends up missing or is found in the desert, it is bad for business for months. It's a matter of economics."

Here they were out in the desert, where even the hookers and the bouncers have more scruples and standards than this hog who was sitting alone at the bar, now licking the salt out of the bottom of the empty dog bowl. Sitting alone was a sexual predator whose money wasn't even good in one of seediest whore houses in Nevada, and he didn't even have a clue that the whole world was aware of his despicable high jinx.

"Leah, I want you to go out and tell him that you get six-hundred per hour and see how he responds. If he doesn't have the money, we will ask him to leave. If he refuses to leave, then we will call the police. I hope, in the meantime, the tranquilizers will kick in."

Walking back out with a big smile on her face, Leah said, "Sorry to keep you waiting."

"There you are," said Orenthal. "I was beginning to think you had run out on me. Where is my drink, little girl?" he asked snidely.

"What else can I get for you tonight, besides a drink?"

"You know what I want," he said, licking his chops and biting down hard on his bottom lip. "I want to kill you tonight," said Orenthal maniacally.

Shocked, Leah backed away saying, "Oh no, you are crazy!"

Seeing the look of fear on her young face, Orenthal realized his choice of words were dark and telling. Snapping out of his trance, Orenthal said, "Oh, no, honey.... I meant that I want to give it to you like you never had it before," he offered, trying to recover. He turned his head counterclockwise, smiling embarrassedly. "You know what I'm sayin'."

"I get six-hundred dollars per hour," said Leah, hoping and praying for the tranquilizers to kick in.

Reaching into his shirt pocket Orenthal pulled out a wad of hundred dollar bills. Counting out twelve one-hundred-dollar bills, he said, "Grab a friend, and let's blow the roof off the place." He was grinding his teeth like a mad man and sweating through his shirt.

Grabbing the money by instinct, Leah turned around quickly and said, "I will be right back."

Licking his chops unmercifully, Orenthal said, "I will be right here."

Walking over to Chichi at the end of the bar, Leah handed him the money and asked, "What do I do?" Still, she was excited; she had never gotten more than three-hundred per hour from any customer, and you could get any two women in the house for five-hundred per hour. "He wants two," she added, holding up her index and middle finger of her right hand.

"It is not worth the risk. I will take care of it," said Chichi. "I want everybody to go in the back," he said shutting the power off to the neon sign that reads "Open-24-Hours."

Now this was a signal to all of the locals who knew better than to ask questions, as they took their change off of the bar, and excused themselves quietly from the establishment. One of the men offered a quick, "Good-night sir," as he walked past Orenthal and then out the front door.

Orenthal did not seem to notice that the room cleared out as he sat there waiting for his girl to return, then suddenly all of the lights came on and the music went dead, which snapped him out of his fantasy. Squinting through the bright lights, Orenthal made out the large frame of Chichi who was walking towards him.

"What happened, boss?" Orenthal asked, evidently troubled.

"I am sorry, Mr. James. We are closed."

"What?" asked Orenthal. "I already paid."

Chichi handed him back the twelve-hundred dollars, saying, "Here is your money back. The girls all went home. There is nothing here for you. I arranged for a car and a girl from another agency to accompany you back to Vegas. I am going to have to ask you to wait outside."

Orenthal looked around, and the only person in sight was a small older man who was cleaning up bottles and sweeping. He wondered if he had actually fallen asleep, dreaming instead of daydreaming. No one was there; it didn't make sense. It seemed to Orenthal that seconds ago there were at least ten girls, a few bouncers, a DJ, and an ugly barmaid, but they were all gone. "Wow," he said. "I must be going crazy."

"We called you a car, and here is some cash for the fare back to Vegas. We sure are sorry, Mr. James," Chichi said, walking Orenthal to the door. Looking back, Orenthal noticed the dark neon sign that said OPEN-24-Hours. Confused, he stood outside with Chichi, waiting for the taxi to pull up.

"I have a confession," Orenthal blurted out into the cool night's air.

"What's that?" Chichi asked.

"I am a murderer," said Orenthal choking up with tears. It seemed as if his words were releasing pressure from his conscience as he stared out into the dark desert.

"Only God can forgive you," said Chichi, raising his left arm to look at his wristwatch unwilling to pass judgment.

The awkward silence between the two men was broken with the sound and headlights of a large white limousine pulling into the mostly empty parking lot. The driver walked around the car and opened up the back door and announced, "Mr. James, your ride back to Vegas awaits you." When Orenthal got in the back of the limo, he was even more confused when he saw what appeared to be a blonde model waiting for him with a smile.

"I must be going crazy," said Orenthal. "I must be dreaming."

"This is your dream come true," said the blonde.

Closing the back door to the limo, the driver waved to Chichi, and then got in the car and drove away slowly.

Turning the music up and lowering the lights back to dim, Chichi held both of his hands together, smiling. He then held the index and middle finger of his right hand out as a sign of victory. Chichi didn't believe that he could have handled this situation any more perfectly.

"You gave him the old Royal Treatment, and it worked," Linda said proudly. Everyone in the house laughed.

"I just hope that transvestite doesn't get six-hundred bucks out of him," he chuckled. He's going to need his money for STD treatments."

"Yeah, I hear that AZT isn't cheap," said one of the working girls.

"Okay, everybody back to work," Chichi said smiling as he turned the power back on to the neon sign. Just then two cars pulled into the parking lot.

# Crack Heads are Unpredictable

## A Murder

Coming home after an entire week of debauchery, Orenthal was cleaned up and feeling guilty that he had left his wife and kids alone for an entire week without calling to let them know where he was or that he was okay.

Looking around the room at his wife and kids and realizing that he seemed to be more of a stranger than the man of the house, he leaned in to give his wife a hug. "Honey, I missed you so much. Doesn't anybody care where I have been?"

Standing there with her arms crossed, Orenthal's wife answered for the family: "No, Orenthal. We don't care what you do."

"I have been away on business. I am trying to make the family money!" he exclaimed, trying to put his arms around his wife. Putting her hand up into Orenthal's chest, she pushed him away. "I would have called, but I was just so busy. I never know when to call! Somebody might be sleeping," he said unconvincingly.

Looking around the room for any bit of affection, Orenthal said, "Hey kids, aren't you glad to see your daddy home after a long week of work?" Standing there, Orenthal had his arms opened wide, hoping that one of them would run and jump up into them like he had seen so many times in the movies. "Hello! Doesn't anybody care about me?" he asked.

The three kids just walked out of the kitchen into the living room, completely ignoring Orenthal. "Come here, little Jessa," Orenthal said.

Like a predator would pick out the weakest link in a herd of prey, he ordered his youngest daughter, Jessa Bell, to come to him. Picking her up with a disgusting crack crash beam on his face, Orenthal said, "I knows you missed me da' most, didn't you, Jessa?"

"Ouch! You're hurting me!" the young girl cried as Orenthal squeezed her tight, unaware of his mule strength.

"I's not hurting you, baby. I's just huggin you," Orenthal said, releasing his monster grip. "Didn't you miss yo daddy when he was gone?"

Afraid to say no, she was unaware that her head was shaking left and right; her chin quivered, and her lips became tight. Her eyes squinted, the lines in her forehead grew, and she began to cry. Her body language was enough to tell the truth.

"Why you cryin?" asked Orenthal.

Exhaling in fear, the first thing that came out of her mouth was, "Your breath stinks, Daddy."

Completely taken aback by his little girl's observation, Orenthal asked, "What?" He looked at her confusedly. "My breath stinks? Like what? I just brushed," he offered in disbelief.

"Like dookie," said the little girl with a frown.

Shaking her in his arms and putting his face right into hers, Orenthal said with a violent scowl and his hot breath "You best respect yo daddy. You hear me, little girl?" She burst into tears and screamed, "Mommy!"

"Put her down, Orenthal!" demanded his wife.

As Orenthal put the young girl down slowly, she ran desperately to her mothers arms.

"Sure, run to your mommy, little girl," Orenthal taunted. "Just remember one thing: your mommy aint going to be there for you forever," he remarked, licking his lips maniacally.

Looking around the room, Orenthal felt completely rejected. He knew that his behavior warranted this reception and that he was going to have to do some major damage control if he wanted to get his family back.

"Well, I'm sorry I was gone so long. I am sorry I didn't call. I was out on *bidness'* trying to make money for my family. I am trying to make lots of money so that I can afford expensive things for you all."

Looking around the room desperately, Orenthal said to his wife, "Let me make it up to yous. I *will like* to make dinner here tonight for us. How's *dis'* sound? We can all be together as a family."

Thinking to herself, "It sounds like you need a lesson or two in proper grammar and sentence structure, you donkey," she just sat there with her arms crossed.

There was no response. Looking at his son, Orenthal asked, "Hey, boy, what do you think? Daddy's gonna make dinner tonight. Hows d'is sound?" His son looked at him in complete disgust. No one had anything to say.

"Look!" Orenthal exclaimed. "You got these kids brainwashed!"

"No, Orenthal. They are treating you like a stranger because you are a stranger to them. Try being a father for once."

"I am the man of the house," said Orenthal. "I don't have to be the father." Walking towards the door, he was announcing the meal that he would make when he returned, saying the items out loud. "We's gonna have a leg of lamb and some pork chops, a nice green salad, some baked potatoes…." Walking out of the house he continued… "And for desserts, I's gonna get some strawberries, and we's gonna have strawberry shortcakes! Yous' all love strawberry shortcakes. With whipped cream on top!" he said excitedly as he shut the door behind him. Orenthal said, "I be home real soon."

Getting into his car, Orenthal looked at himself in the rearview mirror and said out loud, "No one appreciates anything I do!" Grabbing a hold of the steering wheel tightly, he couldn't pretend not to understand why his family didn't love him. "I don't deserve to live," he blubbered. Tears welled up in his eyes as he drove out of the driveway. On the way to the market, he was thinking about where he had been for the last week. He should have been out looking for a job, but instead he had taken money out of the savings account that his wife had set up for the children's college fund.

Using this money recklessly, Orenthal had gone on a drug and hooker spree. In the past few days he had smoked enough crack to kill two men. He knew that there was no excuse for his behavior. Orenthal knew he had to be a better person if he wanted to get his family back. To make it up to his family, the least he could do today, he thought, was make them a nice home-cooked meal.

The path to the local market put the sun in his eyes, and the pores of his skin were swelling and espousing a noxious blend of alcohol and illicit drugs. He knew that he had let his entire family down again, and he just couldn't help himself. He knew that he had to change his life around before it was too late.

Pulling up to an intersection at a red light, what appeared to be a street person walked in front of Orenthal's vehicle and stopped. Feeling humble, Orenthal rolled down the window and flashed a five-dollar bill at the bum.

Orenthal had always had a knack for commingling with the lower forms of life that the streets had to offer and making them feel special. Handing the bum the five-dollar bill, Orenthal said, "Hey, things will get better." Looking the bum in the eyes, Orenthal could tell that this man was a good person. It seemed that he was just down on his luck.

"Hey, buddy, can you help me?" the bum asked.

"What do you need?" Orenthal responded.

"I need a ride to the bus station."

Knowing that this was the beginning of a new him, Orenthal said, "I am heading a few miles down to the market, which will get you closer. How's that sound?" He reached over to open the passenger door. "I's gots to get home to my family," he said proudly.

"I really appreciate it," said the man as he hurried over to the other side of the car. He did appear very grateful for Orenthal's generosity.

This kind of charity work was exactly the vote of confidence that Orenthal needed. A moment ago he was just about convinced that he no longer served a purpose, and now it seemed that he was helping this vagrant get his life back on track.

Orenthal thought to himself that he must have a face that even a stranger knew meant goodness. Otherwise, people like this would not feel so comfortable getting a ride from him. Another boost to Orenthal's ego was the fact that there were people out there that were actually less fortunate than he was. This was turning out to be a very good day for the infamous Orenthal James.

"Where you headed?" asked Orenthal.

"I am heading to the other side of the state," the bum said, pointing out towards the horizon. "I just got out of rehab and fell off the wagon last night," he continued. "But I guess you wouldn't know what I am talking about."

"Sure I would," said Orenthal. "I smoked crack for a week straight, ending yesterday." Orenthal looked at the man with a confidence and pride that only a crack head could have. "Isn't that something?" Orenthal asked. "I stopped smoking crack last night, just when you started smoking it, probably." Looking out at an imaginary circle, Orenthal said, "The wheel in the sky keeps on burning."

"Turning," said the crack head, correcting Orenthal. "It's the wheel in the sky keeps on turning."

"No it aint," said Orenthal. "It's burning." If there is one thing I know, it's my music, buddy." Turning his head confidently to look at the bum, "It was Journey, released in 1976. I would bet my life on it. I grew up listening to that music."

"Why would a wheel burn in the sky?" asked the street bum, looking for clarity.

"It's metaphysical," explained Orenthal. "The wheel represents the sun in the sky, and it keeps on burning, see?"

"Oh, maybe you're right," conceded the bum, seeing no point in two crack heads arguing further. "Do you have any crack on you?"

"No, sir, I don't," said Orenthal proudly. Remembering his new role as the shepherd, he felt obliged to help the weak. "And you should really try to stop smoking that stuff. It is not good for you," Orenthal said convincingly, giving the bum advice that he knew he couldn't keep himself.

Pulling up to the next intersection, Orenthal realized that a cop was following him. "Fuck," he announced. "I got the po-lice on my tail," he said as he drove right through the red light.

Looking into his rearview mirror, he continued through another red light. The police car followed cautiously through the intersections. "This fucking cop aint gonna let off on me," Orenthal complained.

Looking amazed at Orenthal's blatant disrespect for the law, the crack head said, "What the fuck would possess you to go through two red lights knowing that a cop was following you? What the fuck is wrong with you?"

"Well sometimes, if they thinks I's brazen, they too scared to pull me over," said Orenthal, studying the rear view mirror.

"That's bullshit," said the crack head. "I have never seen no junkie just blow through red lights before. You are just begging for trouble. Is this car stolen?" the crack head asked Orenthal.

Noticing that two cop cars were now behind him, Orenthal said, "He thinks I'm riddin dirty. You aint riddin dirty, is you?" asked Orenthal, looking at the crack head nervously.

The bum just looked forward, scared for his life.

"No use in running," Orenthal said. "They's got me. Fuck!" Orenthal pulled his car over to the side of the road before the cops put on their lights and sirens.

Looking back, the crack head said, "What the fuck? They didn't even pull us over yet!"

Orenthal fastened his own seatbelt and said, "Put your seatbelt on. It may pay to be a little courteous here." Looking into the rearview mirror, Orenthal now saw three cop cars, and all of them turned on their flashing red lights at the same time.

Coming over the loud speaker, the police officer in the front car announced, "Take your keys out of the ignition and place them on the roof of the car."

"Here we go," said Orenthal. "Felony stop." He took the keys out of the ignition.

"Keep your hands where we can see them."

Placing the keys outside of the car on the roof above his head, Orenthal stuck his head outside of the window, looked back at the officers and waved as if to say, "Everything is okay here, officers."

The crack head looked at Orenthal and said coldly, "Thanks for the ride," before jumping out of the passenger side of the vehicle.

Orenthal, confused, said, "Hey, no problem. Stay out of trouble," as the crack head jumped out of the car. It was as if Orenthal had forgotten where he was for the moment. He then realized that things had the potential to get really ugly, really fast.

Watching in disbelief, the crack head was now pointing what appeared to be a loaded .45 caliber handgun towards the police officers. "He's got a gun!" screamed one of the officers, backing away for cover.

The crack head pointed the gun towards the cops, and let three bullets fly. Each of the bullets punctured a hole in the first car, smashing its windshield. There was silence for about five seconds.

Orenthal looked into his rearview mirror at the scene that was taking place behind him and screamed in desperation, "Wait—WAIT! I'M INNOCENT!" Holding his hands up in the air, Orenthal fumbled to get out of the car as quickly as he could so that he could explain this to the officers, only to get tangled up in the seatbelt that he had just fastened.

Finally getting out of the car, and hoping to be recognized, Orenthal still had his hands in the air as he cracked a smile to break the tension between himself and the officers. Just then he met a flurry of bullets. He was hit once in the chest, once in the leg, once in the right hand, and once in the side of the ear, leaving a high pitch ringing sound in his head. Orenthal was in shock as he dropped to the ground, not knowing which way was up.

Each one of the bullets that hit him felt like hot bee stings. "Could this possibly be?" he thought to himself, unable to speak. Another series of shots were fired, but Orenthal didn't feel any other bullets enter his skin. Terrified, he rolled towards the car for cover.

On the other side of the car, Orenthal could see the crack head was now laying in a pool of his own blood, and he was still shooting back at the police.

Orenthal screamed at the bum, "WHAT THE FUCK ARE YOU DOING, CRACK HEAD?"

The crack head turned to look at Orenthal. "YOU'RE THE FUCKING CRACK HEAD THAT WENT THROUGH THE RED-LIGHT- ASSHOLE!" he screamed back as if pointing blame. Pulling the gun up, the bum now aimed it in Orenthal's direction. The look in the crack head's eyes was the same look he gave Orenthal at the intersection before getting into the car. The look was a connection. His eyes told a story of a lost soul looking for guidance.

He pulled the trigger. The first bullet bounced and ricocheted off of the tire one inch away from Orenthal's head. Orenthal could not believe his dumb luck as he tried to roll away from the vehicle towards safety.

As he rolled, Orenthal felt another series of bullets. One hit his back and traveled up his spine and into his shoulder; another went through his black dress-shoe, hitting the bottom of his right foot. At least two bullets bounced off of the pavement, throwing sharp shards of asphalt into his face. Another bullet entered his right side as he rolled himself towards the curb. It felt as if he was having a muscle spasm in his side as he rolled up into the fetal position facing the car, unable to do anything but wait to explain his side of the story.

The crack head continued to shoot at him from under the car, but the pain was too much for Orenthal to move or to do anything but lay there. This was a terrible misunderstanding. How did he get himself in such a peculiar predicament? He wondered, "Don't these cops have protocol that they must follow in order to prevent these instances from occurring?"

Screaming out again, Orenthal shrieked, "I'M INNOCENT!"

"Shut the fuck up!" yelled the crack head. "You made your bed. Now lay in it! Shut the fuck up!"

Just then another shot came from the crack head and hit Orenthal right in his lower jaw. Orenthal thought he could feel gravel in his mouth, but it turned out to be chunks of his own teeth.

Orenthal couldn't hear anything now. He was losing blood from multiple gunshot wounds. It was like he was living a scene in a movie, where the character was being ambushed at war, and everything was quiet and in slow motion. Trying to scream out again, Orenthal had no control of his mouth or face, and he just gargled a horrible snort.

Orenthal thought quietly that this scene must end soon. He saw another flash coming from under the vehicle, and it was as if he could see the bullet leaving the gun. It took the same exact path as the last bullet, entering his lower jaw. Orenthal began to choke and spit up blood and bones and teeth.

Orenthal's eyes were wide open in terror; he was dazed, and confused. This all seemed like a horrible nightmare to him as he lay there helplessly. Within minutes, a police officer was standing over him with a very serious look on his face, pointing a gun right at his head. The police officer appeared to be screaming something. Orenthal looked up in horror and tried to scream for help and the only sound that came out of his broken face was the sound of a hog that had just had its throat cut in a slaughterhouse. Orenthal turned his face towards the earth in submission. The police officer put the gun right to the back of Orenthal's head at a forty-five degree angle and pulled the trigger.

## Three Hours Later

Back home, Orenthal's family was still unaware of the gruesome episode that took place a few hours ago. Looking up at the clock, Orenthal's wife sat down at the dinner table with her children. They had Chinese food delivered. Shaking her head, Orenthal's wife was sure that he had again been pulled off the wagon by someone, something.

Interrupting the silence at the dinner table, Jessa Belle asked, "Mom, are we going to have strawberry shortcakes with whipped cream on top tonight?"

Disgusted but trying not to let the kids down, Orenthal's wife went to the refrigerator and opened up the freezer and said, "How does ice cream sound for dessert?"

"Yeah, ice cream!" shouted the children in harmony.

Opening up the refrigerator door, Orenthal's wife said, "With whipped cream on top." She shook the can of whipped cream, smiling for the kids.

Making the sundaes in little dishes, Orenthal's wife put whipped cream on each. She also placed a single birthday candle in each of the desserts as her way of diverting the kids' minds from their absent father. Setting a dish down in front of each child and one for herself, Misses James lit each candle and said, "Okay, kids. Everybody, close your eyes and make a wish, and then blow out your candles!"

It seemed that life was already getting better at the James' household this evening. Once again Orenthal went missing, and everyone secretly hoped that he would not be returning. Little did they know, was that they all got their wish.

# Internal Affairs Bureau

CASE # 1897524885985

Police report: After following a vehicle that has been seen before in drug areas, the officer had witnessed the driver of vehicle pick up a known drug addict/dealer- following the vehicle and running the license plate... the vehicle came back to Orenthal James... The vehicle was unregistered, and uninsured... Having probable cause to pull vehicle over, the officer waited for back-up to arrive. The driver of the vehicle blatantly ran three red lights as we pursued without lights... Upon felony stop, known crack head stepped out of the vehicle brandishing a loaded weapon, shooting multiple shots at officers, we in returned fired at the passenger. In the confusion, it appeared that the Driver had a weapon, and he jumped out of the car... multiple shots were fired. The known crack head shot Mr. James multiple times..- A total of at least 81 shots were fired. EMS was on the scene and pronounced both suspects DOA-
Investigation to follow.
End of report

**DISPOSITION/STATUS: CASE CLOSED**

**NO WRONG DOING FOUND ON BEHALF OF ANY DEPARTMENT MEMBERS-
ALL DEPARTMENTAL RULES AND REGULATIONS WERE FOLLOWED.**

Investigator Mark Trueman # 1212
PUBLIC INTEGRITY UNIT
Page 2 of 2

# Probable Cause of Death

**VICTIM: ORENTHAL JAMES File # 16498448 -**

Cause of death is 18 miscellaneous gunshot wounds. 15 Shots were from a 9MM weapon. And two shots were from a 45 caliber handgun. Severing multiple organs and hitting face- one unidentified gunshot wound to the right temple is believed to be actual cause of immediate death.
In his blood there were traces of crack, cocaine, methamphetamine, heroin, steroids, anti-depressants, a multi-vitamin, alcohol, and pcp's
EOR

CLASSIFIED

# Role Model'

## A Hogtale

Orenthal walked confidently into the main office of the high school, finding a pleasant secretary at the desk. "Hello," Orenthal said. "I am here to see Principal LaCosta."

"Yes, sir. And your name?"

A little perturbed that he must state the obvious, Orenthal looked left; then right, and then up, as if he were thinking about it or arguing with himself internally, before saying, "My name is Orenthal, Orenthal James. I am here to be a mentor for the next week for troubled students."

"Oh yes, Mr. James. Please have a seat and Principal LaCosta will be right with you."

"Thank you, ma'am," said Orenthal politely. He stood in place, looking around the office at the pictures on the walls.

"Sir, you may have a seat if you wish," said the secretary, pointing towards a row of chairs.

"Thank you, ma'am. I prefer to stand," replied Orenthal, smiling intently and completely self-absorbed.

Orenthal was reflecting on the fact that he was actually sentenced by a judge to perform a week of community service for an undisclosed drug possession charge that he had pleaded *no contest* to after dragging it through the court system for nearly a year.

The judge gave him an option: do forty hours of the sheriff's work order, raking cemeteries and sweeping public parking lots, or do the same time as a mentor at a local school for troubled youths. Orenthal thought he chose the easy way out.

Moments later, a slim woman standing only about five feet tall and wearing a gray suit walked quickly into the office, passing by Orenthal as if he weren't there. "Excuse me, Suzanne. There is an SUV parked on the curb, and I would like you to have it towed. It is a large white SUV, and it is right in the bus-loading zone. The license place is N-T-I-T-L-E-D."

"Oh, hello, miss," said Orenthal. "I believes that that may be my SUV you are talking about. I parked it there because I pulled my hamstring, and I am having some real trouble walking." He rubbed his right knee.

"Oh, hello, Mr. James," she said. "I need you to move your car right away. I need you to park in visitor parking and then report back to me immediately for your week's assignment."

Feeling as if he was back in grade school, Orenthal said sarcastically, "Yes, ma'am. Right away." He walked towards his SUV reminded of just how tough a high school principal could be.

Holding his head up, he pulled his car into the visitor parking lot and parked in the first available handicapped parking space.

"Good morning Ms. LaCosta," Orenthal interrupted when he made it to her office. "Sorry about parking my car on the curb. You see, I's got a bad back."

Unsympathetic, Principal LaCosta sat up straight and looked Orenthal right in the eyes. "Mr. James, it is quite unusual that we have the opportunity to have someone of your notoriety here in our school. I am going to have to ask you that while you are here on school grounds, you remain as professional as possible while interacting with our student and staff population." She nodded her head once confidently. "Especially with the students that you will be working with one-on-one, the most fragile of our student population. You must keep in mind that our students will observe every action you make here. As a role model, Mr. James," she said clearing her throat as if she had just swallowed something bitter, "You are affecting the lives of these young people, and you must make sure that you leave a lasting, positive impression. Do you understand?"

"Oh, yes, ma'am. Yes, I do," he said, looking down to wipe something off of his shirt.

Continuing her orientation, she said, "Okay, the students that you will be working with are either developmentally delayed or high-risk students. These students come from all backgrounds and either are on the verge of dropping out of school or have already dropped out and since returned. Our job, Mr. James, is to encourage them to stay in school and to emphasize just how important an education is and how a high school diploma will lead them to college or give them the foundation to be able to build a career that will help them to become productive members of society."

Looking at Orenthal, Principal LaCosta noticed that he seemed to be completely distracted by whatever it was on his shirt. "Mr. James, can you tell me what it is that you plan to do to help our students? Mr. James?"

"Oh, yes, ma'am," Orenthal said, looking up from his shirt. "I am here to help the students to receive an *edge-*

*a-ma-kay-shun*," he said, smiling as if he had just gotten away with something juvenile.

"Excuse me?" asked Ms. LaCosta, looking very serious.

"I said I am here to see that these kids take getting their edge-a-ma-kay-shun seriously," he said, turning his head cockeyed and smiling with one eye closed.

"Mr. James, I don't think you're funny. In fact, I think your attempt at humor is despicable. If this is going to be your approach to helping my students, then I am going to have to ask you to leave now. We need role models—not buffoons—to encourage these kids. And I do not need you making light of our work here in any fashion. I need to know that you are going to be serious, that you are here to help, and that you will not hinder our process. Now please, I have to request that while you are here you speak in relative, non-degenerative terms to my students; otherwise, your help here is not needed. Do I make myself clear? Do you understand me, Mr. James?

"Yes, ma'am, I do," said Orenthal. "I apoli-gize. I jus' be foolin' witch-yah."

"Now, Mr. James, it says here that you graduated from college with a bachelors in Sports Management."

"Yes, ma'am."

"But it also says here that you received your GED from a local boys and girls club."

"Yes, ma'am."

"Now, Orenthal, please show our students the hurdles that you have jumped through to get to where you are in your career now. Please, in your interaction with the students, make it apparent to them that anything is possible."

"Yes, ma'am. I will do my part."

"Okay. Now, I am going to have to request that you show up early and park in the designated area." She handed Orenthal a parking pass. "I would like you to write a brief narrative of your day, listing the names of each student that you worked with, and before you leave for the day, I would like you to hand it in to me. Is that clear?"

"You're takings this pretty seriously, aren't you?" Orenthal asked.

"Mr. James, this is as serious as life and death. These students' lives depend on the example that we set for them on a daily basis. We are their only chance. If you don't take this seriously, then they won't."

"Yes, miss. I understand," said Orenthal. "But, this is pretty demanding for someone who is volunteering their time, don't you think?" he asked with half of a grin on his face; the other half held a snide look.

"Yes, Mr. James, it is quite demanding. But let's realize that this is a court-ordered sentence that you agreed to for a minor crime that you plead no contest to. What that crime was is of no consequence and has no bearing with me, Mr. James. I am not interested at all in what you do with your personal life," she said, holding up a folder from the court with Orenthal's name on it. "I have to report your progress and attendance to the judge, so please, don't think that I am going to cut you any slack because of your fame, real or imagined. I am doing this as a favor to the Superintendent. So, don't think for a moment that I would have you volunteering here otherwise. Let's get that straight right now Mr. James."

Taken aback at the principal's nerve, Orenthal did everything in his power to resist the urge to jump over the desk and pummel the small woman of principal.

Leaning forward with a large smile and his eyes wide open, Orenthal nodded his head up and down slowly, a testament to his surrender. "Yes, ma'am. I understand you completely," he said.

She stood up and said, "If you will follow me."

Walking down the clean hallway, Principal LaCosta evidenced her pride in her school. "Here is the main hallway where most classes are held for the eighth-graders." They crossed a hallway near the library entrance. "And over here is the gym, where most athletics take place." They walked down the hallway, passing a second gymnasium. "This is the gym where the students are preparing for a basketball game to be played here tonight. And over here is the In-School-Suspension room, better known as ISS," she said quietly. "This is where the high risk students are assigned and where you will remain for the next week." She opened the door and walked in.

All of the students could not help but notice Orenthal and the principal walk into the room. Principal LaCosta said, "Good morning, students. This is Orenthal James. He will be here this week to help you understand the importance of school and of getting your high school diploma."

The students all looked up at Orenthal and seemed very surprised to see that he was there to help them. "Wow," one kid said.

The teacher assigned to the classroom stood up to greet Orenthal and the principal. "It's a pleasure to meet you, sir," said the young man. "My name is Matt… Matthew Martin. You can call me Matt or Mr. Martin, whichever you prefer, sir," he said nervously. "If you wish, you can introduce yourself to the students."

Clearing his throat while walking to the front of the room, Orenthal began, "Good afternoon students. As some of you may know, my name is Orenthal, Orenthal James. I am a former professional athlete, and I am here for the next week to help you students realize just how important it is for you to stay in school to receive your education. This is very important to me, and each and every one of you must take me seriously." Orenthal looked at Principal LaCosta who appeared a bit nervous. He continued, "And I am here to make sure that at the very least, all of you leave this school with a GED. I received my GED, and I went on to graduate from a great college and had a great career as a professional bowler, amongst other things. And had I not achieved my GED, none of that would have been possible."

Principal LaCosta seemed impressed at Orenthal's natural ability to capture the attention of the students. His sincerity caught her off guard. It was apparent to her for the first time that this could be one of the best experiences that these kids would have under her tutelage.

Principal LaCosta said quietly, "Excuse me, Mr. James. I will leave you to do your thing with these kids. Good luck," she said, winking with a smile.

"Thank you, Principal LaCosta. I appreciate the opportunity," Orenthal replied.

After a thirty-minute lecture, Orenthal received a round of applause from the eleven students in the classroom.

"Mr. James, that was very impressive," said Matt Martin, standing up in front of the class. "And I am sure that each of these students feels a little differently about their education and how important it is."

Matt turned to address the class. "Today, each of you will take the GED pretest on one of the computers. This pretest will show each of you your strengths and weaknesses. Then, I will take each of you individually and help you to achieve your GED by the end of the school year." He nodded his head in excitement.

"So now, if each of you could take your seat at a computer and sign on, you can begin your GED prep exam, and we can get an idea of where you will need help."

All of the students stood up to take their positions at a computer.

"Thank you again, Mr. James. If you wish to sit at a terminal, you can surf the Internet and do your email, or whatever you wish. When the students are done, we will go over the results."

"Certainly. Thank you," Orenthal said, sitting down at a computer.

Signing on the computer as GUEST, Orenthal clicked on the short cut that said GED PRE-TEST. The program began.

The program prompted:

(Please enter your first name) "O" he entered.

The next field asked for his last name, and he accidentally typed "K". Realizing his error, he pushed the backspace key and then re-entered "J".

"Welcome O J," the computer screen read.

Snorting in excitement, Orenthal was amused that the computer already knew his nickname.

(Let's Begin Your Test)

It had been a while since Orenthal had taken any test, and the last test Orenthal took involving a computer, was court ordered and required his DNA.

As Orenthal sat in front of the computer, he decided that he would take the GED test, just to see how well he would do. Being a graduate from a prestigious university, he was convinced that he would receive at least a 100% on this test.

Going through each multiple choice question, Orenthal breezed through the test, especially on the math questions. Most of the students had finished before him, but Orenthal attributed this to the fact that the kids were much better at using the computer than he was.

One young kid approached Orenthal and said proudly, "Mr. James, I got a seventy-two! I would pass my GED if I took it today."

"That's great!" said Orenthal. The student walked off while Orenthal finished up his test.

Finally, Orenthal's computer screen read, (Click Here To Receive Your Score). Looking around the room to make sure no one was watching, Orenthal clicked the button. The screen flashed a small ticking clock and the words:

(Calculating Your Score)

Sitting in anticipation Orenthal gasped when he read the results: Orenthal had received a score of fifty-three.

(We're sorry, O J; you did not pass your GED prep exam.) The computer screen read;

This is how you rated in the following areas:

Reading – Below Average

Writing– Below Average

Arithmetic– Poor

Comprehension– Poor

Logic– Poor

Interpreting Written Material– Below Average

(Please click on the above area's for a tutorial on these subjects.)

Reviewing the above information carefully, Orenthal was relieved to see that he did not need any help in math. "Sure," Orenthal said to himself. "The one subject that I'm really good at, they don't even mention." He shook his head unconvinced, not realizing that the word arithmetic meant math. "This is the exact reason why I have very little faith in standardized testing. They don't look at the whole picture."

Clicking out of the screen before anyone could see that he had failed the GED test; Orenthal continued to ponder his failure. How could this be possible? How could he, a college graduate, have possibly failed a GED test?

Amazed at this and ashamed, he clicked on the next test on the computers desktop: (U.S. Citizenship Test, a pretest for non-citizen students looking for immigration status within the US.)

Clicking on this test, he thought to himself, "Now here is a test that I am sure to pass!"

Orenthal needed to feel like he had accomplished something today. Being a competitive person, Orenthal was not going to walk away without proving his stellar intellect to this computer one way or another. He began the immigration test.

(Please enter your first name) "O" he entered.

(Please enter your last name) "J" he entered.

"Welcome *A H,*" the computer screen read.

"This exam will test your readiness for a pre-citizenship exam for non US citizens looking to become a legal US immigrant into the United States."

(Click Here to Begin:)

"There," Orenthal though to himself "This must be the easiest test in the world," clicking on the (BEGIN HERE) button.

Question 1. How many colors are there on the US flag?

"Well, that was easy," he thought. "Two." Laughing out loud, he was proud that he had caught this trick question. Thinking to himself, "The answer is, red, white and blue, but not everyone realizes that white is not a *recognized* color in the United States. Most immigrants would probably get this wrong," he thought to himself.

Question 2. How many stars are there on the US flag?

"Huh," cake he thought. This would be a simple exam. He was sure to get a 100% as he breezed through the questions like a *real* U.S. citizen should.

Question 32. Who elects the president of the United States?

Looking up into the lights and squinting, this was the first question that Orenthal would guess on:

B. Congress…It must be congress, right…?

Moving on to the next question, Orenthal was starting to feel the pressure from the harder questions.

Question 33. What is the executive branch of our government?

"Hell, that's easy," he thought

D. The Managerial branch…

Answering all of the questions, Orenthal was sure that he had passed, not exactly a hundred percent, but he knew that there were a couple of questions on the test that were there to trick everyone up.

Clicking on the (Click Here to Receive Your Score) button:

The screen flashed again with a small ticking clock and the words:

(Calculating Your Score)

The following message came up on the screen:

"O J – you received a total score 44% out of a possible 100%.You need to receive at least an 80% to become a U.S. Citizen."

"It is likely that you are having trouble reading and comprehending the test questions in English, and this may be affecting your total score. Please consult your teacher or immigration tutor to go over the answers to the test. All of the answers can be found in the accompanying booklet-How to Become an American Citizen".

If you need help in Spanish: (Click here)

If you need help in French: (Click Here)

If you need help in any other Language, please (Click Here)

http://www.homestead.com/prosites-prs/index.html

"What?" Orenthal nearly asked aloud at the end of the exam. How could he have possibly failed a citizenship test? He was born a citizen, and he failed?

As a kid approached the desk that Orenthal was sitting at, he tried furiously to block the screen from the student's view. Orenthal panicked. Forgetting how to clear the screen, he reached under the desk and yanked the cord out of the outlet.

"There!" Orenthal said convincingly. "I think I was downloading a computer virus or something," he explained as the computer screen went blank.

Getting up from the table, Orenthal went over to observe another student as he worked at a computer. Orenthal just stood there and hovered in the background as if he were seriously observing the student's progress. In all actuality, he was bored out of his mind and thought he must look productive standing there in a stance of authority as time passed by.

"Mr. James, could you please help me with this math question?" The young man almost startled Orenthal.

"Hmmm. Let me see." Orenthal looked down at the question, which read 8 ÷ 2.

As Orenthal studied the screen, for the life of him he could not recall the meaning behind the division symbol. He knew that it had something to do with the energy; times the mass of the object, multiplied by the speed of light, but he was just not sure if the formula was supposed to start with the first or the second number of this very hard equation?

"What, do I look like Einstein?" Orenthal asked himself.

Looking over this very tough algebra, Orenthal refused to be defeated by this question, but he knew that he could not come up with the answer.

"Now, son," Orenthal said seriously, "if I was to tell you the answer, then you wouldn't be learning. I am not here to give you the answer." Orenthal raised his eyebrows as if he were genuinely concerned.

The student said, "No, no. I am not looking for the answer. I am asking you what I must do to figure out the answer."

Orenthal again said, "No, I am not here to give you the answer, that's why you have math-matic books, so they can teach you. If I showed you, then you wouldn't be learning." He walked away from the kid. Orenthal decided that it was time for him to take a break.

Walking out of the classroom and out into the hallway, Orenthal felt that he was in a daze. He still wondered how he could have possibly failed the GED test earlier today.

Could it be true that he was just an uneducated imbecile that never really learned anything in his life and had just skated by on his sports career by means of inadequate supervision and intimidation?

The moment humbled him. He was a true disappointment to himself and his family. He was a born loser; a boner, a legendary failure. He realized that everything he had ever achieved had been unearned or ill gotten. His life was a sham; a gaffe, a boo-boo, an oversight, a complete indiscretion.

Orenthal had a hard time inhaling with all of these new words and thoughts bombarding his thick skull. The rest of the day was a haze, but when he left, the kids said they were excited that he'd be back tomorrow. Driving away from the school, he had wondered how he had ever gotten this far in life?

Orenthal went home that night and fell right to sleep, even skipping his dinner. He was completely depressed at life's sad reality's. The next morning, Orenthal even had a hard time pulling himself out of bed. How could he possibly go on feeling so low?

Showing up late at the school the next day, Orenthal parked in the first available handicapped parking space. Walking quickly into the main entrance of the school, Orenthal met Principal LaCosta in the hallway.

"Mr. James, you are late," she snapped. "And you did not sign out yesterday. And I did not get a summary of your daily events. I told you that I needed a summary of your day and that I need you to be here on time.

"Now, the students are expecting you to be here, and we have a special guest from the Sheriff's department here to talk about the *D.A.R.E.* program today and the importance of being drug free."

Defeated, with a blank stare Orenthal did not even attempt for a lame excuse, and followed Principal LaCosta down the hallway.

Entering the classroom, Orenthal was surprised to see a deputy with a canine standing at the front of the classroom.

Matt Martin stood up at the interruption and said, "Okay, class, here is Mr. James.

"Oh, yes," said Orenthal awkwardly as he walked up to the front of the room.

Shaking the deputy's hand, Orenthal said to the class, "Sorry I's late. I got stuck behind a school bus the whole way here." He reached down to pet the dog's head.

The deputy introduced the dog, saying, "This is *Zib*. He's used to detect drugs." Instantly the dog began sniffing Orenthal's hand.

"Hey, boy," Orenthal said. "You shaw is a good looking pup, isn't ya." The dog really seemed quite interested in the hand petting him, but Orenthal turned his nervous look from Zib to the kids.

Matt turned to Orenthal and suggested, "Maybe you'd like to say something to the kids about the importance of being drug free?"

Orenthal nodded slightly, turning towards the class. He sweated as he began his lecture. "Okay, kids, we all know that drugs are bad." Zib began sniffing Orenthal's pocket. Orenthal pushed the head of the dog away with his large mitt. Some of the students began chuckling. "But what you really need to understand is—" Orenthal continued, but Zib had unceremoniously smacked Orenthal's pocket with his paw.

Orenthal interrupted himself to say, "Down, boy." The dog began barking and growling curiously at Orenthal. The deputy eyed Orenthal curiously.

"Wow, he sure is a happy feller, isn't he," Orenthal commented as the dog pawed at his pocket, whining and barking. The whole class was now laughing out of control.

"Mr. James, what is it that you have in your pocket?" asked the deputy, aware that he was entering dangerous territory.

"Oh, nothing," said Orenthal. "I aint got nuthin' but a little money in my pocket." He pulled out a few dollar bills to prove it.

"Well, perhaps the dollars have a resin on them from the last person who had them," suggested the deputy. The dog continued to paw at the bottom of Orenthal's left pocket.

"Down, mutt!" growled Orenthal, clearly becoming upset. "These are a two-hundred dollar pair of slacks."

The deputy wondered if it was possible that Orenthal had brought drugs into the school. "Orenthal, is there anything else that you have in your pocket?"

"No, of course not. Just a little change that I got from the gas station this morning." As Orenthal's hand rummaged nervously through his pocket, a small piece of what looked like a folded magazine ad fell out and onto the floor.

The dog followed the folded piece of paper with his gaze. The kids were roaring in laughter at the dog.

Orenthal stepped forward subtly, putting his foot on top of the folded piece of paper. Zib scratched at Orenthal's foot.

The officer observed Orenthal's behavior very closely for a moment. Taking a closer look at Orenthal's sweaty face, he noticed that there was a white crust encircling Orenthal's nostrils.

Bending over to pick up the piece of paper, the deputy tapped Orenthal's black dress shoe with his expandable baton.

The dog began to whine and pant as if he had just found a prize.

Orenthal moved his foot, dragging the piece of paper with it. The deputy tapped on his foot again, looking at Orenthal bemusedly.

Realizing that he had no chance, Orenthal lifted his foot to surrender the folded piece of paper.

Opening the carefully folded magazine paper, the deputy saw a picture of a naked woman covered in a powdery white substance. In utter shock, the police officer stood there, hesitating for just a moment.

The officer had seen this before, and knew that this tactic was popular with the college crowd. A carefully cut page from a pornographic magazine can conceal the few grams of cocaine inconspicuously when folded properly. Also, the nature of the magazine added a nice treat and proved an ingenious way to market the illicit goods to predators like Orenthal.

"Busted," said one kid, sounding disappointed that Orenthal was stupid enough to get caught.

Understanding the enormous weight of this situation, the deputy announced, "Well, it seems that the dog has finally found our test!" Holding up the folded piece of paper, the deputy explained, "This was placed in Mr. James' pants to see if Zib would find it. And, sure enough, he did! See kids, even this amount of drugs can be found by a competent drug dog."

Orenthal, covered in sweat, looked confusedly at the deputy.

The deputy looked to the teacher and said, "Matt, I think it's time for Zib to take a break. He should go for a walk. Mr. James," he added , looking steadily at Orenthal, "Could you please assist me? Zib loves company."

Thinking quickly, Orenthal wondered if this could be some trick. Could the officer possibly be sympathizing with his plight, prepared to let him go? After a brief pause, Orenthal said, "Of course, officer. Lead the way."

The kids applauded loudly at the demonstration as they left the room.

The deputy placed his hand firmly on Orenthal's arm and said, "I think a visit to the principal would be prudent." They walked at a quick pace towards the front of the school.

Once the deputy had informed Principal LaCosta of what had happened, she asked Orenthal, "Are you kidding me? Did you bring drugs into my school? Please tell me that you are not this stupid! Tell me that you didn't bring cocaine into my school."

"Uh.... Honestly, Ms. LaCosta," Orenthal responded, looking to his left, "the kid at the gas station this morning must have given it to me with my change. I had no idea!"

"Well, I have no other alternative than to ask you to leave the school and to report this information to the judge. I cannot in good conscience have you here as a role model—a mentor to my students—bringing in drugs, even if it was on accident. I am going to have to ask you to leave." She pointed sternly towards the exit.

"Well, ma'am, I am telling you, this is just a misunderstatement," said Orenthal. "Miss LaCosta, I tell you, I can explain!" Orenthal smiled innocently. "I am here to help these kids get their education," he said, pronouncing the word perfectly.

She escorted Orenthal quickly towards the main entrance and then said, "Mr. James, I am going to have to ask you to leave at once. The possibility that you may have brought drugs into this school is beyond reproachable. I need you to leave, and I intend to file charges with the deputy if he finds it to be necessary."

"But I can explain!" Orenthal bellowed.

"You are despicable, Mr. James. If it weren't for the bad publicity this would bring my school, you would already be in handcuffs. Leave before I have you arrested."

Orenthal turned away from the principal and walked away slowly with a slight grin on his face. Thinking back over forty years ago, he remembered leaving the last public school he ever attended in exactly this fashion.

"You know, I could have arrested him on possession charges immediately," said the deputy.

"Could you imagine if this ever hit the papers?"

"I know. Still, what a degenerate!" Both the principal and the deputy laughed. "Did you see how scared he was?" The deputy paused his mockery to look down at Zib and say, "Good dog." He handed the dog a treat. The deputy placed the folded paper in an evidence bag. "This one, no one would believe."

## A Murder

It was 6:05 A.M. on a Wednesday morning. Orenthal's wife Clione was woken out of a deep sleep by the sound of heavy awkward footsteps clumsily climbing the stairs towards the master bedroom. Orenthal had not come home in the last three nights, and no one could have predicted the mood or temperament of the beastly drugged-up goliath.

For the rest of the world it was morning, but for the infamous Orenthal James, another three-day bender of booze, crack, and prostitutes was coming to an end.

The last three nights had been an absolute pleasure for Clione. Whenever Orenthal went missing for more than a day, she would sleep comfortably in the guest room of their home in her favorite clean white sheets, knowing that she did not have the burden of sharing her bed with the smelly, greasy has-been.

Clione had asked Orenthal for a divorce two years ago, and ever since then had been utter hell for her because he had promised that the only way that they would ever be separated, was in death and that he would kill her before he allowed her to disgrace his good name. This time, Orenthal managed to live up to his word.

Clione lived in fear for her life and the lives of everyone in her family because Orenthal had also threatened that he would kill anyone that she had ever loved. He told her that he could get away with murder, because he had friends and lawyers that would help him do it.

Hearing Orenthal climb the stairs made her heart pound, and she began to sweat. She prayed that he would just make his way into the master bedroom and fall asleep without incident.

Listening closely, she heard Orenthal's lumbering gait heading slowly down the hallway towards the master bedroom at the other end of the hall. Then there was silence. Clione sat there listening intently for any sound or noise, and she began to panic, wondering what Orenthal was doing.

The howl of a madman shattered the silence. Orenthal screamed, "Clione, where the fuck is you?"

"I'm in here, Orenthal," Clione said in a quiet panic, getting up and out of the bed as quickly as she could.

"Where the fuck is you, Clione?" Orenthal raged as he charged down the hallway towards the guest bedroom, kicking the door open in a fury.

Clione stood there in her nightgown, holding onto a sheet for comfort like a child would a security blanket. She tried to hide the look of terror on her face. "I am right here, Orenthal." She made a weak attempt to immediately defuse the situation by saying, "I'm glad you're home."

Standing in the entrance to the bedroom with his right hand holding the top of the door jam stood a psychotic, almost-rabid man of over six feet tall, weighing well over two hundred and fifty pounds; his clothes were sweat-through and there was white crust surrounding his lips and his nostrils. His eyes were a demonic black and confused. As if he were reading the exact words from her mind, Orenthal said, "You aint glad I'm home! *You wished I was dead!*"

"No, Orenthal. That's not true," she lied. "I have been worried sick wondering where you have been. And I am glad your home safely," she continued with a nervous smile.

"You spent all of my money, you whore!" Orenthal belted out violently with his head down and his eyes up as if he were a possessed bull about to charge.

"That's not true, Orenthal," Clione reasoned. "I haven't asked you for money in years."

"Lying whore!" Orenthal bellowed, taking a step towards her with drool running down his chin and spittle on his hands.

"Say you spent all of my money, Clione, and I will kill you quickly," Orenthal said demonically. "Otherwise, I'm gonna make it hurt."

Panic stricken like an animal in a corner, Clione had no idea what Orenthal was talking about. She was very successful on her own, and had never needed Orenthal's money. Four years ago, she even re-mortgaged their home in her name because Orenthal had over drawn all of his accounts and the mortgage was four months past due. Since then, all of the household bills have been Clione's sole responsibility. Orenthal had not contributed to a single bill, not even to groceries.

"Orenthal, do you need money? I can help you," Clione offered as if she were trying to negotiate the minutes left in her life.

"Too late, whore. I am going to kill you," Orenthal said. "You have embarrassed me for the last time." He was getting closer to her.

Clione recognized the rage in Orenthal's eyes that was focusing directly on her as he moved in closer. Trying to remain calm, Clione's fight-or-flight instinct kicked in when she noticed Orenthal's upper lip extending beyond the grimace of a madman. Knowing that he was about to strike, Clione ran as fast as she could towards the bathroom in the guest bedroom to escape her impending doom, hoping that she might be able to lock herself into safety.

Calculating the chances of survival while in mid-dash, she knew that she had no possible chances of escaping the clutches of this former athlete. As if surrendering, she did not even try to close the door to the bathroom, because she knew that he would only kick it in to get to her. Yielding to the control of this raging swine, Clione fell to the floor, raising her arms and legs to protect herself from the beating that she knew that she was about to take at the hands of her husband.

Like any predator, Orenthal pounced on his prey and allowed his instincts to take over. He grabbed Clione by her neck with one hand while simultaneously pounding her with the other. Orenthal delivered a series of brutal blows to Clione's small frame, furnishing her one of the most brutal attacks of their relationship. Clione hoped that she would die.

"What did you do with my money, whore?" Orenthal bellowed as he hovered over of her.

"Orenthal, no! I love you!" she screamed in desperation.

"Shut yo' mouf when I'm killing you," he said coldly.

"Orenthal, I want to help you! Do you need money?"

"Shut yo' mouf when I'm killing you!" Orenthal repeated as he beat her torso and her legs and back with unimaginable fury.

Clione succumbed to dying today at the hands of her abusive husband, and she welcomed the peace that death would bring her.

"You don't love me! You have never loved me!" Orenthal shouted as he pounded his prey. "My credit card is maxed out. My bank account is overdrawn. Where did you put my money?"

Mustering enough strength to make her final statement, she coughed, "You smoked it!"

The look in Orenthal's eye was a look of someone who had just heard a horrible truth that could never be taken back or ever be forgiven. This was the last thing that Clione remembered before everything went black.

Waking up a bruised mess and naked on the floor, Clione could barely breathe. Looking up she realized that she had been dragged into the master bedroom. It was evident that Orenthal had had his way with her. The three peaceful days without Orenthal had come with a certain price. She lay there nearly paralyzed with pain. It felt as if her eyes were swollen shut.

Clione recognized the snoring coming from the bed above her. She had no idea how much time had passed since the attack, but she knew that she had to move quickly to get herself cleaned up and out of the house to safety. She also knew that Orenthal could wake up at any moment to finish the job that he had started.

Limping into the guest bathroom slowly, Clione did not recognize the face that she saw in the mirror. It was a face that she had seen before, but this time Orenthal had gone too far.

Standing naked in the mirror, Clione took inventory of the attack. Both of her eyes were black. One pupil was completely red with blood. Her hair was falling out in clumps and her lips were swollen. Her arms and legs were bruised, and it appeared that her nose was broken. Opening her mouth, she witnessed that two of her front teeth were broken off. With all the other pain, she hadn't felt the tiny rough particles in her mouth.

Bursting into an emotional hell, Clione knew that this was the last time that she would ever allow Orenthal to hurt her again.

She limped back into the bedroom where Orenthal was sprawled out on his stomach. Orenthal slept much more like a hog than a human. His deep gargled inhales were followed by the sounds of a series of inconsistent choking and gagging. To hear him snore was enough to make most people nauseous, but to Clione, it was a sound that meant that she was safe for the moment.

Sliding the drawer of the night stand slowly open and reaching in to grab the loaded 357 Magnum handgun, Clione almost panicked at the surge of adrenalin that rushed through her body the moment that she realized that she now had the upper hand.

Standing at the edge of the bed, Clione aimed the gun directly at the back of Orenthal's head as she put her index finger on the trigger. Trying to persuade herself that this was the right thing to do, Clione let out a shriek of emotion and her eyes filled with tears.

The sound of her crying disturbed Orenthal's rhythm, and she panicked at the reality that Orenthal may wake up and find her pointing a gun at him. Clione did not know if the gun worked. Orenthal told her that he had a pistol permit and had bought the gun legally for self-protection.

As Orenthal's snores went silent, Clione was paralyzed with fear. Unable to focus through her tears and unable to pull the trigger, Clione was convinced that Orenthal was now awake. Did he know that she was standing there about to kill him? Paranoid, she darted quickly for the cover of the master bathroom.

Standing there, Clione heard the movements of what sounded like Orenthal getting out of bed. "Oh my God," she thought. "He's heading right for the bathroom."

As quickly and quietly as she could, Clione stepped into the shower and slowly pulled the shower curtain to cover herself. Leaning against the tiled wall, she raised the gun to eye level for her protection. A full ten minutes had passed as she waited for Orenthal to open the curtain and meet his demise, but the only sound that she could hear now was the pounding of her own heart.

Clione was driving herself mad with questions.

Had Orenthal seen her reflection in the mirror?

Had she closed the drawer to the night stand where the gun was?

Would she have the courage to pull the trigger?

Why did she marry this touchhole to begin with?

Suddenly, as if by a miracle, the sounds of Orenthal's snoring filled the room again. She couldn't stop herself from wondering if this could be a trap that Orenthal was using to get Clione to come out of her hiding spot.

More than a half an hour passed, and Clione sat in the bathtub too scared to move. Listening to the snores of the beast in the next room, she believed that she had the courage to finally kill the man that had abused her mentally, physically and sexually for years.

Walking slowly out of the bathroom and spying around the door, Clione was unsure of what she might see. It appeared that Orenthal had just rolled over to make himself comfortable and that he was still sleeping.

Seeing her own beaten and bruised reflection in the mirror, Clione's blood ran cold at the thought of her husband's savagery. Taking small steps in his direction, Clione was at peace with the idea of spending the next twenty years of her life in prison for killing the man that she had grown to hate so much.

Would she qualify for battered wife syndrome? The only thing that was certain in her mind was that Orenthal was about to breathe in his last snort.

As she pointed the cold piece of steel right at Orenthal's temple, Clione thought about the possibility of the bullet ricocheting off of Orenthal's hard head and possibly killing her also. Knowing that she had to pull the trigger now or never, Clione took the chance. Pointing the gun right at Orenthal's temple, she hoped that the bullet would enter his skull and kill him instantly.

Standing there, Clione's eyes filled with tears and she began to cry out loud again. Blinking her eyes clear, then blinded again by emotion, Clione realized that Orenthal had again stopped snoring.

Blinking her eyes closed tightly to clear the tears; Clione was shocked when she opened her eyes to the nightmare of seeing Orenthal laying there, now with his eyes wide open and looking right at her. He was awake and appeared stunned to see a gun pointed directly at his head.

"What the fu—" Orenthal began to yell as he surged out of bed, reaching for the gun. Clione pulled the trigger.

Clione fell backwards on the floor and dropped the gun. Blinded again by her tears, she was also deafened by the thunder of the gun. Clione's ears were filled with a sharp ringing from the gun blast. She could not believe that she had the courage to finally put that hog out of his misery. In a panic, something told her to open her eyes.

Clione hoped to witness the bloody corpse of her target, but there was Orenthal, sitting on the edge of the bed unscathed and reaching down to grab the gun off the floor. Confused and dazed, Clione could only read the words that were coming out of Orenthal's mouth: "What the fuck are you doing?"

Clione experienced another surge of adrenaline and kicked Orenthal as hard as she could right in the side of his face, planting her big toe into his eye socket. Grabbing her leg to control her movement, Orenthal was dazed from the boot to the head.

"You whore!" he shouted, and he prepared to pounce on her again.

Reaching for the gun and grabbing it off the floor, Clione grasped her only chance for survival. Aiming the gun right for Orenthal's center mass, she pulled the trigger of the gun furiously until it stopped firing. It seemed like an hour had passed, but in actual time it was less than two-seconds.

As Orenthal's eyes rolled into the back of his head, he fell forward in slow motion and landed directly on top of Clione, and much to her surprise, he was still breathing. His breaths were much like his snoring had been except for their obvious sound of desperation, as if he was choking on blood. His chest heaved up and down as he lay on her.

Trapped under the weight of the beast and completely drained of any strength, Clione thought that she might die under the deadweight of Orenthal as she tried to push him off.

Lying there completely devastated, Clione realized that Orenthal had stopped breathing. Realizing the fact that he was now probably dead, Clione was over come with emotion.

"I'm sorry, Orenthal! I am sorry!" Clione cried, mostly out of instinct.

Having heard that when people die, they can still maintain brain functions for up to ten minutes and can hear voices around them and understand what people are saying, Clione repeated guiltily "I am sorry, Orenthal!"

"I am sorry…!"

"I am sorry…*that I ever met you!"*

Just as she said this, Orenthal released his final breath and his entire body went limp.

Clione fell into an exhaustion that could only be brought on by such a traumatic incident, and she fell asleep wishing that she too were dead.

Waking up confused in a terrified panic, Clione did not know where she was for a second and had hoped that the memory that she had of the awful incident had just been a bad dream. A police officer was trying to get her attention by asking her, "Do you know who did this to you?"

Confused, Clione did not know how to respond to the question as she looked around the master bedroom.

"Did you know the person that attacked you and your husband?"

Now realizing that the police officer had mistaken the crime scene, Clione said, "No, Officer."

"How many men were there?" the police officer asked.

"No," she said, beginning to cry at the reality of the situation.

"Clione, how many men, and can you give us a description of the attackers? You are safe now. Please, try and think."

"Officer, I killed Orenthal. I am responsible for my husband's death," Clione said, holding back her emotion.

"You did this?" asked the officer, looking very concerned and almost confused.

"Yes, I am responsible for my husband's death."

"Did he beat you like this?" asked the officer.

"Yes, he did, and I killed him. I shot him," she said. The look on her face was a sadness that could not be described.

Speaking into his portable radio, the officer said, "Dispatch, I need you to expedite EMS to the James residence. I have a DOA and a badly beaten victim of a home invasion."

The officer turned back to Clione and said, "Okay, Misses James, you are in a safe place now. No one can hurt you like this ever again. Do you understand? I am Officer Thomas Robinson, and I am here to help you."

"Okay," Clione responded.

"I need you to describe to me the person or people that did this to you and your husband," the officer repeated slowly, raising his head up and down confidently. "And I need you to get this story straight before anyone else asks you these questions."

"I told you, officer, it was me that—"

Placing his index finger up as if directing her to stop talking. "Maybe I can help you Mrs. James. Perhaps, you are under too much stress to recall the incident due to the trauma that you suffered. It is possible that you do not remember anything about the attack or any description of the attacker," coached the experienced officer with his eyes wide open.

"Yes," said Clione very nervously, not quite understanding what the officer was suggesting or why. "That is possible."

"Let me explain to you, Mrs. James: It appears that you and your husband were the victims of a home invasion. We believe that perhaps a person or a group of people entered your home and killed your husband, and in the process, you tried to protect your husband and were also viciously attacked."

Clione stared inquisitively at the good officer.

"Do you have any idea who might have wanted to harm your husband?"

Just then, it was becoming clear to Clione what the detective was trying to achieve. Thinking back to all of the times that she had taken abuse at the hand of her husband, Clione said, "No, I have no idea who would do such a thing."

"So is it safe to say that you do not have any recollection of the attack?"

"Yes, officer. I do not remember anything."

Her entire world began to spin as she remained seated on the floor. Still in a daze, she could hear the sounds of sirens getting closer to the house. The room began to fill up with other police officers and emergency personnel who were tending to her and the body of her dead husband.

Officer Robinson said to the arriving EMTs, "Mrs. James has no recollection of the attack and needs to go to the emergency room immediately."

As Clione was lifted into the back of the ambulance, the coroner pulled up and parked in front of the house. She could also see dozens of men and women who appeared to be at the scene on official business buzzing around. Some men were taping off the crime scene, others stood guard, and still others were running in and out of the house as if wanting to be the first to see the blood. Some were whispering cautiously into their cell phones anxious to be the first to describe the murder scene to anyone who was not allowed past the police line.

The media was already setting up a perimeter across the street and down two houses, and a helicopter was flying overhead. As the back door to the ambulance closed, Clione heard one of the paramedics say, "Here, miss. We are going to administer a pain medication for your injuries." Clione again fell out of consciousness and into a deep sleep. She knew now that she would be safe.

## Three Hours Later

When Clione awoke, she could hear a television in the background. Her head felt as if it was encased in a wooden pallet. Raising her right eye slowly, Clione realized that she was in a hospital room.

Standing at the door was a uniformed police officer, and to her right her mother and her sister were sitting next to the bed. All eyes in the room were focused on the television hanging from the wall. No one realized that Clione had regained consciousness.

Turning her attention to the national news network, Clione could barely focus on the caption at the bottom of the screen. It appeared to read: [Orenthal James Murdered, Wife in Critical Condition.]

Above the caption was footage that appeared as if it were taken from a helicopter that was hovering over her house and neighborhood. Clione began to listen to the news anchor as she watched a stretcher being loaded into the back of an ambulance.

"...Again, you are watching file footage of Orenthal's wife Clione who was brutally attacked along with her husband in an apparent home invasion. It is now confirmed that the infamous Orenthal James is dead from multiple gun shot wounds. Police are saying that it is a gruesome scene. Again, police are looking for two armed men who were seen leaving the scene of the crime. A preliminary forensics report says that a weapon found at the scene had been used in other murders and robberies and was previously registered to a now deceased store owner who had lost the gun in a robbery in 1989..."

Clione knew that the information they were giving wasn't true. How did they have a description of two men who had fled the scene? And the gun, as far as she knew, was registered to her husband. Orenthal had told her that he had a permit for the weapon. Was that true? Could O.J. have committed the crimes attached to the gun?

Clione's head began to spin as she was trying to figure out what was going on. She sat there undetected and watched the scene on the news over and over of the ambulance driving up a ramp and onto the thruway with its red lights flashing. There was a parade of police cars escorting and following the ambulance. For whatever reason, the media played this scene over and over again.

"…Again, this is the ambulance that received Orenthal's wife, who is said to be in critical condition. Apparently, the death of Orenthal James was a result of a home invasion. Orenthal James was pronounced dead at the scene, apparently due to multiple gunshot wounds. In a few minutes, we are going to have Orenthal's estranged brother Rubin on the phone to tell us a little bit about Orenthal..."

Everyone in the room still had their eyes focused on the television screen. Clione's mother was holding a tissue in one hand and her daughter's hand in the other and appeared to be in complete shock as she watched the news on the television. She shook her head slowly as if rejecting the possibility of this nightmare.

Clione closed her eyes. Was she a murderer? No? Dazed at the impossibility of the events that had taken place, Clione fell back into a deep sleep.

Clione awoke gently to her mother asking, "Clione, can you hear me?" Clione opened her eyes, afraid to see what might be there. Was she about to be taken into custody? Was this nightmare just about to begin all over again?

"Honey, you and Orenthal were attacked. It was a home invasion. Honey, he was killed. They think that Orenthal may have owed a few people some money. And the police officer here needs to ask you a few questions," her mother said, grabbing hold of her daughter and hugging her desperately.

Her mother's grasp pressed painfully against her bruises, but she wanted to hug her mother before going to prison. Soon, everyone would know that she was responsible for her husband's death.

The police officer interrupted, "Ma'am, if you could please just step out of the room for a moment. I want to ask your daughter a few questions?"

"Of course, officer," she said politely. "Clione, I will be right in the hall, honey. I love you."

The plain-clothes detective wore his badge on his belt. He looked clean in a crisp white shirt and a dark blue tie. Stepping forward, he shut the television off and turned back to look at Clione.

"Mrs. James, I am sorry to inform you of this terrible tragedy, but your husband was killed today and you were brutally beaten. We need to get any information possible as to who may have done this to you; do you remember anything about the attack?"

"No, I'm sorry," she said. "I don't remember anything."

Just then the door to the room opened and a female doctor entered the room, closing the door behind her.

"Excuse me, ma'am, but I am in the middle of questioning a witness here. Would you mind stepping out of the room while I speak with her?"

Walking over to Clione with a pen light and ignoring the request, the doctor shined the light into Clione's eyes and said, "Officer, unlike you, I am bound by the law of patient confidentiality, and I'm am sorry to tell you that I just reviewed the results of Mrs. James CAT scan, and her medical condition is going to have to take precedence over your murder mystery." She walked over to the other side of the bed to review Clione's medical chart.

"Well, while we have her awake, do you mind if I ask her a few questions?" the detective asked.

"I am going to have to ask you to keep your questions to a minimum because Misses James is in a very fragile medical state."

"Okay," said the detective. "I will keep it brief. Now, Mrs. James, anything that you remember may be crucial to solving this murder. Can you tell us anything you remember?"

Clione slowly moved her head from left to right, not saying a word.

"Do you know of anybody who would want to see your husband dead?"

"No, everyone loved my husband," she said, swallowing hard. "There was nobody that I know who would do this to him."

"Okay. Mrs. James, because this is a high profile case, it is very important that we try and figure this out, so I am going to ask you a few questions about you and your husband's relationship, okay? Did you and your husband ever fight?"

"Fight?" asked Clione nervously.

"Yes, did you ever strike your husband in anyway, or did he ever hit you?"

Clione shook her head in affirmation to the question and was clearly shaken by the line of questioning.

The doctor stepped forward and said, "Excuse me, officer."

Stopping to look at the doctor, the man said, "I am a detective, doctor, not an officer, so please excuse me, I am in the middle of a murder investigation. Can you please keep your comments to yourself?"

The doctor replied with heavy sarcasm, "Oh, pardon me, civil servant. I regret that I am not up on the current chain of command within your little fantasy world of cops and robbers, but here, in the real world of life and death, my patient has been through a very traumatic incident and has suffered severe head trauma. It is entirely possible that she is suffering from amnesia. My client is entitled to her medical privacy, and I believe that I am acting in the best interest of my patient by telling you that she will no longer be answering any of your questions without the advice and consent of her attorney. So please, show yourself out the door."

"Doctor, have you ever heard of the police term obstruction of justice?" the detective asked.

"Oh, is a lawyer considered an obstruction these days? Besides, my client is in a heavily sedated state, which would probably lead a grand jury into doubting its veracity. Now, I admire your initiative at trying to solve this crime, but you must have the good sense to realize that my patient is very unstable, and I will not allow you to ruin any possibility of her immediate recovery. I am going to have to ask you to please leave. I would hate to have to pin Mrs. James decline in health on your overzealous police work."

Walking over to the doctor and handing her his business card, the detective said, "Please have her attorney contact me as soon as you feel that your patient is up to it, doctor…."

"Pinochet," said the doctor. "My name is Doctor Pinochet."

Having nothing further to say, he walked over to the door and held it open as Clione's family rushed back in to surround her bed.

## Five Years Later

It was now the fifth anniversary of the death of the infamous Orenthal James, and Clione was physically and mentally stronger than she had been in twenty years. As she was driving her SUV down the street on her way to teach a woman's Yoga class she heard the following news report on the talk radio station that she listens to frequently.

"...Today is the fifth anniversary of the Murder of the infamous Orenthal James. To this date, no person has come forward with any information and Misses James still has absolutely no recollection of the attack..."

Changing the station quickly from AM to FM, Clione couldn't help but smile when she looked at herself in the rearview mirror. She has never felt better in her life.

# POLICE REPORT
# HOME INVASION

INCIDENT NO. 101154-B

Victim # 1:

Clione James: Female, Age 42, Survived early morning home invasion. At the time of this report, Victim 1 does not recall anything of attack. Wife of Victim # 2

Victim #2

Orenthal James: Male Age 53, Died from brutal morning attack during a home invasion. Victim #2 was shot multiple times in the chest. Husband of Victim #1

**Narrative:**

After receiving a call of a smoke detector activation in the upstairs bedroom at the victims residence. Officer Thomas Robinson responded to the residence. Upon arriving at the scene, Officer Robinson entered the home through an opened garage door. Upon further investigation of the home Officer Robinson found Victim # 1 and Victim #2 brutally beaten and attacked in the master bedroom.

It was apparent that Victim #2 was DOA. Victim#1 was conscious and breathing and did not have any recollection of the attack. She only remembers hearing a loud verbal exchange before the attack.

**Suspects: An anonymous call to state police said that they witnessed two men who appeared to be armed leave the scene of the crime in a dark sedan.**

**NO FURTHER INFORMATION IS AVAILABLE AT THIS TIME.**

Page 6 Of 11

# Special Guest of Honor

## A Hogtale

Orenthal opened an envelope addressed to: The Honorable Orenthal James and was extremely excited to see that he and a guest were invited to the wedding reception of a completely unfamiliar couple. The hand written note attached to the beautiful stationary read:

*Dear Mr. James,*

*I understand that you are a very busy person, but we are having a wedding in your town and it would be an honor if you could join us as a special guest of honor.*

*I play college ball and it would be a great pleasure if you could please show up!*

*Your Biggest Fan,*
*Curtis Faraway and soon to be wife Jessica*

The wedding was going to be at one of the most prestigious and elite country clubs in the nation. Where else could he possibly go to hang out with people of this stature? Why shouldn't he go? He deserved it.

On the day of the wedding, Orenthal decided to wear an expensive pair of black dress shoes that were given to him by a sponsor. He chose this pair because they were comfortable. They weren't the most stylish pair of shoes that he owned, but he chose to wear them in case he decided to *cut-it-up* on the dance floor. These shoes were so comfortable on Orenthal's feet in fact, he felt that he would be able to run and jump hurdles in them.

Driving to the wedding, Orenthal wondered if he should stop off at a drug store to buy a wedding card for the newly married couple that he didn't know. Then he began to think, if he got a card; he would have to put cash in it. If he were to put a hundred dollar bill in the card, he would appear cheap; if he put five hundred dollars in the card, it would cramp his budget, and it wouldn't be appreciated besides. So, he decided that he would neither bring a card or gift and rested on the idea that his presence at the wedding reception was good enough, and besides, he *was* the guest of honor.

Orenthal was attending this function stag. For some reason his wife was just unable to make it. And he was unable to secure himself a date in time for the wedding. It seems his charm is just not what it used to be with the ladies.

Arriving at the gates of the country club, Orenthal witnessed the usual pomp and circumstance of a wealthy, elite wedding: the flowers, the limousines, the gorgeous setting—even the weather was picture perfect. The fanfare was quite welcoming to Orenthal.

Pulling his car up underneath a carriage house, he parked in a handicapped parking space marked with a sign that read RESERVED. Without hesitating, Orenthal put his SUV in park, checked his teeth in the rearview mirror, and adjusted his tie. He then walked comfortably towards the main entrance of the country club.

Walking across the amazing grounds, Orenthal felt that this was where he belonged. He witnessed groups of men smoking cigars, kids posturing as adults and the women were standing in circles, all were laughing with big white smiles. Everyone was dressed to the nines.

Walking into the main entrance of the country club, Mr. James was greeted by an attendant in a tuxedo who said, "Good evening, sir. Are you here for the Faraway wedding?"

Clearing his throat, Orenthal answered boastfully, "Yes, I am the…*uhh… special guest of honor."* Raising his chin and looking to the right, Orenthal waited to be recognized.

Unimpressed, the attendant said, "Sure. May I have your name please?"

Looking left quickly enough to tighten the muscles in his neck to cause a quick cramp; Orenthal looked back to the right, smiling through a grimace, and said, "Orenthal…Orenthal James."

Looking at him as if that were not possible, the attendant ran down the list with his index finger twice. "Okay, sir, I do not have you on my current list, but I am sure that it must be an error, so if you will please wait here I will check with the wedding planner." Without waiting for a response, he walked away.

Returning a few moments later, the attendant introduced a young lady, saying, "Mr. James, this is Melinda, the wedding planner."

Shaking Orenthal's hand politely, Melinda said, "Hello, Mr. James. We were not expecting you because we did not receive your RSVP, but I am sure that Curtis will be delighted that you came. The couple hasn't arrived yet; they are still at the chapel with the photographer, they should be here within the hour. If you wish to make your way into the reception area for a drink," she continued, looking over the seating chart, "I will find a spot for you at table number thirty-two. You will be sitting with a group of Curtis's college friends. They are all his teammates." She hesitated, inquiring tentatively, "If that is okay?"

Smiling, trying to not appear slighted, Orenthal joked, "Do they have girlfriends?"

"Yes, there are at least one or two females at that table, Mr. James," she said returning the smile.

"Good. I came to hang with the bridesmaids," Orenthal said, winking once slowly at Melinda, and then raising and lowering both of his arms as if doing the chicken dance. "If you know what I am saying," licking his lips and snorting. He said "Thirty-two will be just fine," and then walked away towards the bar.

Shuttering and shaking her head quickly as if she had just seen something that had repulsed her, Melinda thought to herself, "What a hog!"

Walking up to the beautiful and tastefully decorated mahogany bar, Orenthal announced his arrival to the bartender by roughly shouting, "Double scotch on the rocks, please!"

Surprised, the young bartender turned his head quickly like he had been caught doing something wrong and said, "Right away, sir! I am sorry. I didn't see you there."

Continuing as if he had been having a long conversation with the bartender, Orenthal commented, "So, hopefully there will be some beautiful bridesmaids here tonight." Grabbing his double scotch off the bar, he downed it as if he were a parched man drinking a small glass of cold water. "I'll take another," he added, slamming the glass onto the bar as if he were in a saloon.

Turned off, the bartender said, "Okay, sir," as he prepped the next drink, trying to take control of the situation. "We got all night, and there is plenty more where that came from." He nodded his head confidently towards Orenthal.

"That's the problem with kids your age," Orenthal said, looking at the bartender seriously but winking. "You got to live life to the fullest. You never know! Any second, some *scumbag* could come along and take your life away from you." Finishing his drink, Orenthal smashed his glass down on the bar carelessly, cutting his hand.

Confused, the bartender said slowly and cautiously assessing the situation, *"R-i-g-h-t,"* taking a damp cloth and wiping the ice and broken glass off of the bar, he then asked Orenthal, "Are you okay, sir?"

Orenthal didn't reply immediately but stared off into oblivion, holding a paper napkin to the superficial wound on his hand. At least fifteen seconds passed before Orenthal demanded, "Does it look like I'm okay?" He startled the young bartender. "Looks to me like I am in need of another drink," Orenthal said, looking mean.

Never having dealt with a situation like this before, the bartender stood in complete amazement at this man's behavior, afraid to turn his back on this unstable patron. He slowly prepared Orenthal another drink.

"So," asked Orenthal cockily, "who's got the coke?"

Handing Orenthal his third double in three minutes, the bartender asked, "I have several different types of cola, sir."

"No, you know!" Orenthal wrinkled up his nose repeatedly and snorted like a hog. "Coke!"

"Oh, sir, I think you're at the wrong party if you're looking for drugs."

"There's probably more drugs here than there are in all of South Central," Orenthal sneered, flashing an unknown gang sign with his two hands.

"Yeah," hesitated the bartender. "I don't think so."

"What are you, a fucking cop?" asked Orenthal sarcastically.

Just then a crowd of happy people approached the bar. The bartender, finally able to leave Orenthal, walked over to wait on them.

Walking away from the bar, Orenthal decided to mingle in the crowd, hoping that someone would recognize him. He grabbed two glasses of champagne from a tray and downed one as a young girl walked by smiling.

Distracted and daydreaming, a young Hispanic waiter approached Orenthal with a plate of shrimp cocktail.

"Shrimp sir," he asked politely?

"No, but you can find out where the coke is," said Orenthal, snorting and taking his index finger rubbing it furiously under his nose?

"Si' Sir," he said walking away.

Orenthal stood there to soak in the lavish surroundings.

A few minutes later a man wearing a heavy plastic apron, who looked like he had been washing dishes, waved Orenthal over to the entrance of the kitchen. Wasting no time Orenthal hurried over to him looking curious. "You are looking for coke?"

"Yeah," said Orenthal excited, "what you got?"

"I got crack," said the kitchen helper.

"You going to smoke it?" asked Orenthal impatiently.

"With you," he said, smiling proudly. "It would be an honor," waving Orenthal into the back room.

Walking through the large organized kitchen, and leaving through an exit door past a walk in freezer, the two men walked outside, around the corner and behind a dumpster where there was another person smoking a cigarette.

Shaking Orenthal's hand the man said, "I'm Jimmy," smiling greatly, missing two front teeth, "welcome to the smoking section!"

"Nice to meet you Jimmy," said Orenthal politely.

Wasting no time and lighting the stem of the used glass crack pipe, Jimmy inhaled quickly, handing off the pipe to Orenthal. Grabbing the pipe like a professional crack smoker, Orenthal simultaneously hit the end of the glass pipe with the butane lighter, and inhaled furiously. Like a drowning person would inhale fresh air, Orenthal did everything in his power to suck as much crack into his system as he possibly could with one inhale.

Holding his breath, and looking down as if he were in pain, Orenthal raised his head slowly. His eyes were fixed in rage, and he exhaled a green cloud of noxious chemicals. Choking and speaking at the same time Orenthal raged, "Yeah! That's good shit, I need to kill somebody," he announced unexpectedly.

Laughing innocently Jimmy said, "Yeah that will make you do it, I feel ya."

In a trance, grabbing Jimmy by his throat with both hands, Orenthal said, "I don't think you understand me," choking Jim the dishwasher furiously.

Judging by the look of fear in Jim's eyes, it was now clear to him exactly what Orenthal meant by his last comment. Being a life and death situation, Jim tried with all of his strength to break the clutches of this raving madman. His lips could move and his mouth was wide open, but he could not make a sound. No air could escape from his lungs, and there was no blood getting to his brain. The end of the hot glass crack pipe that was still in Orenthal's hand was now pressed tightly against Jim's jugular vein burning into his skin.

Lifting Jim by his neck like a rag doll, Orenthal launched him towards the steel refuse container, his head hitting first, then his body laid there in a crumbled mess on the ground.

The young man who was enjoying a cigarette who had just witnessed the assault said nervously, "Dude! What the fuck?"

Orenthal was looking around confused and dazed in a crack rage breathing heavily and snorting in and out. "He be all right," Orenthal said nonchalantly, then repeating, "he be all right."

Grabbing his cell phone, the young man said, "I'm calling the police!"

"Don't call the police," Jimmy yelled still choking and laying in front of the dumpster. "I'm on parole," he said desperately. "I will lose my job, I will go back to prison."

Understanding that he had probably just worn out his welcome at the country club, Orenthal decided that it was probably in his best interest to leave.

Entering the kitchen confused, walking past each of the staff preparing food, the bright lights and the noise from the busy kitchen caught him off guard. Like a rat caught in a cage, Orenthal was disoriented.

"Can I help you Sir?" asked a young kid.

Saying nothing, Orenthal marched furiously, almost in circles until the exit became clear to him. Entering the ball room, Orenthal barely noticed that the wedding reception had begun right in front of him.

Noticing the exit sign, Orenthal knew he had to walk straight across the room in front of at least 500 people to get himself out of this mess.

Walking in an apparent rage, his chest heaving, people began to notice the hulking man who appeared to be very angry. They were whispering and pointing as he carelessly pushed past hundreds of people.

Just before he got to the exit door, a man grabbed him by his elbow, snapping him out of his thoughts. He said, "Mr. James! You made it!"

Orenthal turned around quickly, remembering slightly where he was and why he was there, and said "Oh, yes, I did," he said smiling, "it is my pleasure, but I have to be going."

Surprised, the man said, "No, please Mr. James, could you please wait to meet my son Curtis? It's his wedding day, and he would love to meet you!"

"I would love to," Orenthal lied. "But I have to be going. I think I had an allergic reaction to the shrimp."

"Oh, wow," said the man genuinely concerned. "Are you going to be ok? Do you want me to have some-one drive you to the hospital, or at the least home?" the man asked.

"Oh nun'sense," Orenthal said. "That won't be ne-cessary."

"Here, let me take you to the VIP room where you can get a glass of water, and I will have my daughter who is an emergency room doctor take a look at you," offered the man. Taking Orenthal by his left arm and escorting him through a set of doors, they entered the Evergreen room. "Here, Mr. James. There is a full bar here, and you can relax. I will see if anyone has any Benadryl." Handing Orenthal a tall glass of water, he said, "You're not looking good at all Mr. James".

"I appreciate all that you're doing for me, Mr…."

"Faraway," he said, wondering to himself where his manners were. "I am sorry, James Faraway. It sure is a pleasure to meet you."

"Mr. Faraway, I really must be going… I'm just not feeling up to par," said Orenthal.

"Okay, but I would like you to meet my son and his new wife before you go," he said excitedly. "I will be right back," leaving the Evergreen room quickly.

Looking around the room, Orenthal spotted a table full of fresh fruit, pastries, cheese, and crackers. There was a small waterfall of chocolate. At the other end of the room was another bartender who seemed to be staring at him and a few bridesmaids who also seemed to be watching Orenthal as they whispered to each other.

Noticing a door with a sign that said BATHROOM on it, Orenthal got up from the comfortable couch and walked in a straight line towards the bathroom door. As Orenthal passed a small table, he noticed a beautiful lace basket containing a pile of unopened wedding cards. Unable to maintain his composure, he almost tripped on his own feet, and went cross eyed looking at the pile of loot. It was the look of a man who had just found something that he had spent a long time looking for.

Regaining his composure, Orenthal remembered the bathroom. Not noticing or caring, he walked right into the women's room. As he entered the bathroom, seeing his reflection in the large mirror, Orenthal noticed that his shirt was un-tucked, and stained. Staring into the mirror, Orenthal could barely recognize the monster that stared back at him.

Splashing cold water over his face three times, he patted his face gently with a thick cloth towel. Tucking in his shirt and fixing his tie, Orenthal knew he had to make a good impression if he were going to hang around.

Walking out of the women's bathroom, no one stated the obvious because they did not want to embarrass their special guest of honor.

"Mr. James," said Mr. Faraway proudly, returning with the young bride and groom, "this is my son Curtis and his new bride Jessica!" The new couple did seem very excited to see Orenthal.

"Hello," Orenthal announced. "I am so glad to finally meet you folks." He walked up to the bride and kissed her on the cheek, pausing to sniff her face. "You are beautiful," he said, looking her straight in the eyes awkwardly. "I say beautiful, just beautiful," he said licking his lips unable to compose himself.

Leaning over to shake the groom's hand, Orenthal said, "It is a real pleasure to meet you fine folks. I am so honored to be a guest here on your special day."

Looking a little uncertain about Orenthal's sincerity, the young groom shook Orenthal's hand and said, "Yes, we are glad to have you."

The bride nudged her new husband with her elbow and said, "Don't be shy, Curtis. He is your boyhood hero!" She looked at Orenthal excitedly!

"Do you know he is your number one fan, Mr. James? He said he would give up anything to have you here today, and here you are!" stammered the bride.

Embarrassed now, Curtis said, "Yeah, it's true. It sure is a pleasure to have you here." He smiled broadly. "I am honored!"

Orenthal nodded his head in agreement and replied, "And I want to thank you for thinking of me."

"Will you hang around, Mr. James? It's time for the toast," said Curtis. "Feel free to stay in here in the VIP room. Relax! We will be back," said the young man generously. Stopping quickly, he turned back towards Orenthal and asked, "Mr. James, did you bring a guest? Is your wife here?"

Orenthal replied awkwardly, "No, I am sorry. She wasn't able to make it."

"Oh, that's a shame," said Curtis disappointedly. "Well, if you can hang around for a few pictures I would really appreciate it." Curtis escorted his new bride out of the room.

Everyone in the VIP room emptied out into the ballroom. The bartender, knowing that this would be his only chance to catch a break, hurried into the restroom.

Checking to make sure that he was the only person in the room, Orenthal fixed his eyes on the basket full of cards. Walking over, certain that no one could see him for the moment, he grabbed more than half of them, tearing the button from the front of his blazer as he pulled it open to conceal them. Orenthal shoved the cards deep under his arm as he walked towards the exit.

Like a shoplifter, Orenthal headed straight for the nearest exit, which to his disappointment was the main entrance. He had to go through the ballroom, and he passed people with drinks in their hands, most of whom were aware of Orenthal's presence. Just as he was about to exit, Mr. Faraway grabbed him by his arm. "Orenthal, are you leaving? We would like to get a picture, if possible."

Making a half spin in an almost defensive mode, believing for a second that he had been caught, Orenthal said, "No, I am not leaving; I am heading to my SUV for my diabetes medication."

"Oh, okay, I will see you in the VIP room!" said the relieved man.

"Right oh," said Orenthal as he exited the country club and entered the parking area.

Darting towards his vehicle, Orenthal entered his cab and began immediately to open the cards. Tearing through the cards, he was looking for one thing and one thing only: cash! The first card had two hundred dollars cash in it. Tearing into the next card, there was a check for five hundred dollars. "Useless," he said out loud. He knew of a way to get rid of the checks, but they were never worth the trouble.

The next card had a check. The card after that had a check for one thousand dollars, made out to "the Bride and Groom." Orenthal only found check after check and for increasing amounts. "Shit," Orenthal said, throwing the checks into a pile with the opened envelopes.

Opening up the next envelope was a gift card for five hundred dollars. "What the fuck?" he said aggravated, putting the gift card above his visor. The next card had a hundred dollar bill in it. "Cheap fucks," he screamed putting the cash in a small pile. The next card had a check for twenty five hundred dollars.

Falling further into a fit of rage, Orenthal tore through each card faster than the last searching for green cash. Most of the cards had a check for the bride and groom. He had gone through all of this for a lousy three-hundred dollars in cash and a five hundred dollar gift card.

Absolutely enraged at the inconvenience that this had cost him, Orenthal did not know what to do with the evidence. Looking in the back seat of his car was a small black duffle bag. Orenthal opened the bag, stuffed the evidence into it, zipped it up, and leaned back, placing the bag neatly on the back seat as far as he could reach.

It was apparent to him now that he had to go back to get the rest of the cards in the VIP room. He reasoned that this was a first class wedding, so there must be thousands of dollars in cash in the other cards.

Getting out of the car and heading back towards the front entrance, he casually reentered the wedding reception. The noise of people clapping was perfect cover for him to head back towards the VIP room. Smiling broadly as he passed by jovial groups of people, Orenthal said, "Hello," a few times and smiled. "Hello everyone," he said pushing through a group of people.

Walking past the coat room and down the hall, he took a side entrance that he knew would lead him into the VIP room, but the door was locked. "Shit," Orenthal said, knowing that he would have to walk past the crowds again. Making his way back past the coat room and into an entrance of the reception area, Orenthal now darted towards the Evergreen room. As he entered the VIP room, he was surprised to see so many people.

Standing next to the lace basket was Mr. Faraway and the new bride and groom. Looking in Orenthal's direction to see who had just entered the room, they all stood there in a hushed urgency. Orenthal could tell by the look on their faces that there was a problem. Unable to help his initial reaction, he involuntarily frowned as if he knew he had been caught.

Knowing the importance of confidence to prove credibility in a situation like this, Orenthal quickly corrected his disposition and smiled, asking, "Why the long faces?" He stared at the small group innocently. "It's your wedding day! It's time to be happy!"

"Mr. James, did you happen to see anyone take the cards that were here in the basket?" asked Mr. Faraway with a look of disbelief on his face.

"No. What basket?" asked Orenthal guiltily. "I didn't even see a basket with cards in it. Where?"

"Right here," said the bride, pointing towards the empty basket. She was now holding the remainder of the cards in her other hand. Everyone was staring at Orenthal with a look of disbelief. The groom stood there looking more than suspicious.

"You have gots to be kiddin' me!" Orenthal blurted out. "Someone robbed the wedding? That's a crying shame. Anyone who would rob a wedding is a low life rotten degenerate," he offered the stunned group.

"Mr. James, when you were in the room, did you see anyone go near the basket?"

"No," said Orenthal. "The bartender left the room in a hurry, and I went out to get my asthma meds," he said.

"Oh yeah," said Mr. Faraway raising his right eye brow, as everyone else was now looking towards the bartender.

Shrugging his shoulders, the bartender said, "I didn't take them." For some reason, it appeared that everyone believed him.

"Well, this just doesn't make any sense," said Mr. Faraway. "Now we're going to have to call the police. This is just unbelievable."

"Well," said Orenthal, realizing his opportunity to throw off any suspicions. "Is my card in there? I put my card in the basket. There was cash in it."

"I thought you said you didn't even see a basket with cards in it," said the bartender to Orenthal, defending himself.

"I never said that," Orenthal snapped, pointing at the bartender. "I said, that I never seen anyone take em'. Don't go putting words in my mouth, boy. You'll get yourself in heap of trouble."

Looking through the envelopes, the bride began to cry. "How could someone do this?" she moaned.

Holding out a group of cards the new bride asked, "Do you recognize your envelope, Mr. James?"

"No, I don't see it," said Orenthal. "It was an orange envelope."

"Orange?" asked the surprised bride.

"Well, more of a mango color," said Orenthal, giving room for reasonable doubt. "I don't see it. They must have made off with it," he said, discouraged. "Well, this is a just a bummer." He shook his head.

Interrupting the silence in the room, Orenthal announced, "Hey, if you guys want to get a picture with me, we got to do it now, because I have another engagement to attend." He moved his tongue in his mouth and sucked as if he were clearing a piece of food from his teeth.

Everyone just looked at him in utter amazement. "No, Mr. James. If you need to go, please do," said the groom.

"I am really sorry about this," said Orenthal. "I have never seen such a thing. Well, I must be going. Congratulations on your wedding." He leaned forward to kiss the bride, who pulled her head away quickly. Dejected, Orenthal extended his hand to the groom, and said, "Good luck, y'all." Out of common decency, the groom shook Orenthal's hand. Orenthal made his way towards the exit.

Mr. Faraway escorted Orenthal through the crowd of people. Orenthal was talking, but Mr. Faraway was too preoccupied to pay any attention to what he was saying.

"Okay, I really gots to get going," said Orenthal, extending his hand towards Mr. Faraway. Orenthal noticed a police cruiser that pulled into the valet section and again repeated, "Okay. I gots to be going."

"Yeah, okay, Mr. James," said Mr. Faraway, walking away from him. "Thank you. Thank you for coming."

A group of people had gathered outside by the police car as Orenthal got into his vehicle. Driving past the crowd with his window down, Orenthal announced, "Good night, everybody! Thank you!" He hit his horn three times quickly. "Congratulations!"

It was obvious to Orenthal that his decision to leave had come not a moment too soon as he looked at the group of angry people watching as Orenthal drove away. One young girl who was too naïve to understand the situation blew him a kiss and waved as he drove by and said, "Bye, Mr. James!"

Looking at himself in the rear view mirror, Orenthal said, "What a fucking waste of time that was."

# Alligator Alley

## A Murder

Orenthal had been vacationing in Ft. Lauderdale for a week, and he was now rushing through the airport completely irritated that he, a very popular former athlete, had to wait in line amongst the commoners to book a flight. He had just brought back his rental car and argued for over twenty minutes with the attendant, and insisted that the front end damage to the vehicle was there when he originally picked up the car and was not his responsibility.

Orenthal had to be in Tampa by 7:00 P.M. to be a keynote speaker at a sports convention and had been offered one thousand dollars for appearing. It was noon, and he had plenty of time to make the one-hour flight.

Standing in line staring at his watch while holding his carry-on bag and exhaling impatiently, Orenthal wondered why the people in front of him had to take such a long time. Orenthal wondered why it seemed that everyone needed to be coddled through the simplest of tasks. Why couldn't people be more like him, prepared and hassle-free?

Stepping forward, it was finally his turn to book his flight. Being a *man-of-the-world*, Orenthal thought to himself how he would set an example of a speedy transaction for all of the people behind him to learn from. Because let's face it, the entire world was watching his every move; at least in *his mind* they were.

"Yes, sir. How may I help you?" asked the attendant politely.

"I need a ticket, preferably first class, to Tampa."

"Oh, I am sorry, sir, but because of spring break all of our flights to Tampa are booked solid."

"What? That be impossible!" Orenthal went cross-eyed and then looked up confusedly.

"No, sir. I am sorry: all flights, and even train service to Tampa, are completely booked, and it seems that your only option will be to rent a car. I am sorry," she said, almost looking amused.

"You have got's to be shitting me," Orenthal blurted out furiously. "I just brought back my *god-damned* rental car."

"Not my problem sir," said the woman mockingly. "Is there anything else I can do for you today?"

"Well, you're going to have to bump someone or something because I have to be at a sports banquet tonight. I am the keynote speaker."

"I'm sorry, sir, but perhaps you should have thought of that before today. There are over two hundred people on the cancellation list. If you would like me to—"

"You need to get me on one of those flights," Orenthal said loudly.

"I'm sorry, Mr. James, but—"

"Well, isn't this a *son-of-a-bitch,"* Orenthal cussed loudly. "Well, someone is going to have to pay for this one," he said looking around for an explanation from anyone.

The woman standing behind him seemed un amused as Orenthal turned towards her. "Can you believe this *booshit?*"

Refusing to look at Orenthal in the eye, the woman pressed her lips together and pushed a quick burst of air out of her mouth as if to say, "Too bad, loser. Step out of line."

"I'm going to have to get a pass or something. I can't drive five hours to Tampa."

"I'm sorry, sir, but there is no other choice."

"Oh, no. This is a major fuck up, and someone is going to have to pay for this one. This is not my problem. I don't have time to drive all over the god-damned country to make speeches for the *President* of the United States!" Orenthal said, raising his voice and placing both hands on the ticket counter.

Using everything in her power to maintain her composure, the woman had had enough dealing with ignorant people for one day. Carefully choosing her words and speaking just loudly enough that only Orenthal could hear her; the woman said with a polite smile, leaning forward, "Sir, *you're delusional.* Please step out of the line."

Looking around at hundreds of other passengers in different lines, Orenthal knew that he could not win this battle. Speaking quietly and bobbing his head with a psychotic smirk on his face, he said, "You know what? If you ever spoke to me like that on the streets, I would take a razor blade and cut your pretty face; from your eye to your mouth," he said using his index finger to show her where he would cut her.

Returning the psychotic look and using her pen to point to the right; as if showing Orenthal where he needed to walk to step out of line, the woman said, loud enough for everyone within a reasonable distance to hear, "If there's nothing else we can do for you today, sir, please step out of the line."

Looking at Orenthal as he turned, just about to walk away, she began to laugh out loud obnoxiously and said, "Thank you for choosing to fly with us today, sir." Taking her pen and pointing at the sign that said Rental Cars, the woman continued to laugh, adding additional insult to Orenthal's ignorance by saying, "Good luck finding a rental car today, and please drive safely." The woman was so amused at herself that she continued to laugh. "Next in line, please!" she called, still laughing as Orenthal just stood there in line staring at her.

Picking up his carry-on bag, Orenthal stepped slightly out of line and paused as he contemplated pummeling the sassy woman behind the counter. Standing there still staring at her, squinting his eyes in contempt, he hoped to intimidate her and said "Your lucky I'm a—"

"Get out of here, *you fucking mutt,*" she quickly retorted. Her tongue was sharp. *"Go!"* she commanded. "I don't have time to deal with your nonsense." Still smiling, she shook her head in disbelief. It seemed that no one heard the disgruntled exchange, and if they had, they were completely disinterested, or too busy with their own problems to care.

Orenthal walked away from the line intoxicated with spite. He could not believe how that woman had just antagonized him and gotten away with it. He didn't look back, but he could swear that he could still hear her laughing uncontrollably as he walked away.

Standing in line at the car rental company, Orenthal began to worry as he watched the clock ticking. Most of the people that were standing in line were desperate for transportation, and this rental car company was the only one left in the entire airport with any vehicles.

This whole process was beginning to be more hassle than it was worth, Orenthal thought to himself. He should have just stayed the extra day at his timeshare on the Intercoastal and saved himself the aggravation. But Orenthal was not a person to give up the opportunity for a public appearance so easily.

"Yes, sir. May I help you?" asked a polite middle-aged woman who was standing at the rental counter.

"Yeah, this is on the airline," Orenthal tried. "I need a luxury SUV for the day."

"I am sorry, sir, but we are all out of luxury. We have a four door sedan."

"Figures," said Orenthal. "Then I will take the next most expensive vehicle that you have available. And, can you rush the process here; I am in a bit of a hurry."

"Of course, sir. I will just have to ask you a few questions, and I will have you right on your way," she said smoothly, typing attentively on the keyboard. "How many days do you need the vehicle?"

"Just a day."

"When will you be returning it?"

"Tomorrow, first thing. I have a flight back to the west coast tomorrow."

"Do you have a major credit card and valid driver's license?"

"Yes." He handed them to her.

"How many miles do you plan on driving in the next day?"

"Oh just a few," he lied, thinking that his response might effect the price.

"Under 100 miles?" she asked nodding her head.

"Oh yes, way under 100."

"That will be $97, sir," she said.

"What- wait a minute? No, this is on the airline. They messed this one up, you see," Orenthal said, hoping for a miracle.

"Sir, we are not affiliated with any airline."

"I don't care. I have a conference that I need to be at, and the airline wasn't able to bring me to Tampa, and they told me that I would get a free rental car."

"Sir, that's impossible. We are not affiliated with whomever you were flying with."

"Are you fucking kidding me? This is a mess! I can't believe that *you people* cannot get your story straight!" fumed Orenthal, raising his voice madly.

"Excuse me sir, but I am going to have to ask you to watch your mouth when you are talking to me, or I am going to have you removed by security. This is the busiest travel time of the year, and you should have made a reservation months ago. Now, do you want a car from us or not?"

"Yeah, but I'm going to need the corporate rate or something. There is no way that I am going to pay full price."

Ignoring Orenthal, the woman said, "The total price today if you choose to go with us is going to be $97. If you're willing to sign the agreement, then you can be on your way."

"Listen. I have to be in Tampa in six-hours, and it is a five hour drive—"

"Wait! Whoa, did you just say you were going to Tampa?

"Yes."

"Today?"

"Yes."

"Tampa is over 200 miles from here."

"Yeah, so?" he asked casually.

Typing furiously into the computer, she said, "Well you just told me that you were going to drive less than 100 miles."

"So? What's the difference?" he asked cautiously.

"About $45 sir, the price is now $142. It will cost you more for unlimited miles. If you wish to add the additional insurance in the event of any damage to the car, the price will be $187.

"Are you fucking kidding me?" he hollered.

"Mr. James, I have just about had enough of your abuse. I have to ask you to leave this office. You are out of line, and you will not speak to me like that."

"Listen, bitch: I am the fucking customer," he hesitated, cocking his head left and right, before saying, "and I am always right. So, if I have offended you, then too bad. And if you think that I am going to get out of line, then you are surely suicidal because I have had enough bullshit standing in lines for a day. And if you don't want to hear my language, then you best be getting someone over here who will, like a manager, 'cuz I have had enough of your booshit, and I'm bout to slap da' shit outchyou."

Unimpressed at Orenthal's demands, the woman picked up the phone and dialed airport security. "Yes, this is Barbara at the rental counter. I need to have a customer escorted out of the airport for threatening me and using foul language. Yes, he threatened to slap me."

"Here we go," Orenthal said, spinning violently on his dress shoes with both hands in the air. "Must be the time of month where every bitch in the world came to work."

Disconnecting the line, and dialing a second number, the woman said, "Yes, Tim, I am sorry to bother you. Can you come out here, please? I have a customer threatening me. I just called the police, and they are on the way to throw him out."

"You're a liar… I never threatened to hit you, and I aint never hit a woman. 'cept for my wife," he said, licking his lips.

Coming out of the back room quickly was the manager, a kid who looked about nineteen and was at most twenty-three years old. "Yeah, Barb. What's the problem?"

Pointing at Orenthal, she said accusingly, "This guy threatened me."

"Sir, I am going to have to ask you to….. Wait a minute—are you Orenthal James?" asked the manager.

"Yes, I am," Orenthal replied, perking up and pretending as if he had been an innocent bystander.

"Well, what seems to be the problem here, sir?" he asked. It appeared that the young manager was eager to be speaking to a quasi-celebrity.

"See, *what had happened* was, I need a car to get to Tampa because the airline sold my seat, see. And she quotes me an original price for $97. Then she tells me I can't use my miles. And then she tacks on another hundred dollars because I need a car, and she is trying to take advantage of me. I think she is a racist."

"Tim, that's not at all how it happened," said Barbara.

"Barbara, this is Mr. James… *You know*, the infamous Orenthal James! He is an all time pro-baller, and the last thing he needs is us getting in the way of his business," he said as he was walking over to the other side of a service counter where there was a sign that said CLOSED.

Waving Orenthal over to the empty line, he said, "I'm sure sorry for that, Mr. James. Let me take you over here, sir. Now, what kind of a car do you need?"

"Luxury, of course," he said with a disgusting grin on his face.

"We are all out of luxury," he said. "Well, wait a minute," he pondered, winking as if he was going to pull some strings for him. "I can get you a luxury rental from someone who already has a reservation, and when they get here we will have to bump them down. You know, anything for you, sir, and I am sorry for the inconvenience!"

"Well, it's about time I ran into a competent professional today," said Orenthal, spinning his head around on his shoulders.

Entering the rental area were two police officers who both appeared to be out of breath from running. "Hey, Tim, you got someone giving you a problem?" one of them asked in a concerned tone.

"Oh, no, no. It was a simple misunderstanding," Tim answered with a smile. "We got it all under control. I am sorry we interrupted you. False alarm." Tim shrugged at them.

"Are ya sure?"

"Yeah, definitely," he said. "I am sure. No problems here."

"Okay, then. We got something going on down at the metal detector. We got to run," he said, and they both took off in the other direction, one of them speaking into a two-way radio.

"Okay, so sorry about that, Mr. James. I got you a luxury SUV, and all together that will be $209 on your credit card. If you will just sign and date the contract, you can be on your way."

The smile left Orenthal's face as he said, "Wait a minute! You're going to charge me $209 to be insulted by your company and expect that I will pay? You better do something with the price, or I will take my business elsewhere. And I will be filing a complaint with your headquarters, Mark."

Looking totally surprised, Tim said, "Well, I don't understand?"

"Mark, I didn't come here to be insulted by your employees," Orenthal said, pulling what appeared to be a silver card out of his wallet and placing it on the counter pushing it towards the young man.

"It's Tim, Mr. James. My name is Tim," he said, smiling innocently at Orenthal.

"Yeah, whatever, boy. I didn't come here today to have the cops called because of your employees' incompetence and my race. Now, there must be something you can do with the price, like cut it in half, cuz that's booshit, the way I was treated," he said, tapping the card which now appeared to be gold on the counter.

"Race?" asked Tim. "No, no, Mr. James. I can assure you that Barbara is the same race as you and I. I don't think this is a race issue. We're all human," he said, pushing the card back towards Orenthal, smiling confidently. "We don't accept that card here."

"You think you is funny, boy, don'tcha? Really funny, boy," Orenthal taunted.

"Well, I can give you a government discount, plus the triple A discount, and that will bring your cost to $155. How does that sound, Mr. James? I can't possibly subsidize your travels any more than this."

"It sounds like you isn't hearing me, Mark," Orenthal said, looking left and then right in a threatening manner before pushing the card which now appeared to be platinum back at the manager. "I want the car, and I want it to be complimentary, gratis, on the house, or I will be filing charges with my *attorney*— against not only Barbara but you and your company. And I'll hold everyone in this room liable for your behavior—"

"Oh, I see," said the young manager, defeated. "Just one moment, please." He picked up the phone and dialed. "Hello. Yeah, it's Tim in Ft. Lauderdale. Yeah, I just had a customer come in—Mr. Orenthal James; you know, the athlete—and, ummm, our customer service rep was unprofessional with him, and Mr. James is demanding a free rental car for the day or he is going to file charges with his attorney."

Tim then listened intently to whoever was on the other end.

"Yes, he believes it is a race issue. Very good. Thank you," he said, hanging up the phone smiling weakly at Orenthal.

"Okay, Mr. James, I think we are all set," he said pushing the card back towards Orenthal. "That card is really losing its luster with you, sir," he said before handing Orenthal the keys to the luxury SUV. "I am really sorry for the inconvenience. I really am. Follow me," he said, taking Orenthal's bag and walking with him. "Yeah, this is probably going to be Barbara's last day."

"That sounds good," Orenthal said, indignantly.

Opening the door to the SUV for Orenthal and putting his bag in the back seat for him, the young manager said, "You have a safe trip, sir, and again, I am very sorry."

Looking disgusted, Orenthal said, "Not as sorry as me, boy. Not *as sorry as me.*" He pulled the door closed on the SUV and drove away.

### Four Hours Later

Arriving at the convention center in Tampa, Orenthal learned that no one was expecting his arrival for tonight's sports banquet because he had not responded to the letter that they had sent him. Orenthal was standing there in complete distress while talking to the event planner.

"I'm almost sure I mailed in my confirmation!" Orenthal retorted.

"Mr. James, you were invited, but you never responded. So we assumed that you were unavailable, and unfortunately, we did have to get another keynote speaker. But you are more than welcome to attend the show tonight."

"Yeah, okay. That sounds good," said Orenthal, trying to hide his disappointment. "Well—Yeah, I was in town anyways, so I thought I would check with you," he lied lamely.

Walking away, Orenthal was infuriated that he had gone through so much trouble to attend this function only to have some female tennis player replace him. Orenthal was so ashamed that he had lost out on the opportunity to speak at this great awards dinner that he decided that, rather than be a spectator, he would prefer to just not go. Instead, he decided to scope out the area's nightlife. He planned to hit a few strip clubs, perhaps a bar or two, maybe a massage parlor, find a prostitute, smoke a little crack, and then drive back to Ft. Lauderdale.

Orenthal, being a piker and an experienced hustler, knew just how to handle this evening. Going into any bar or strip club, he would go through the process of getting noticed, hanging around only long enough for people to buy him drinks, and then, wanting to portray an existence of spontaneity and importance, leaving the place in a hurry before it came his turn to buy a round of drinks or even pay for anything.

Moving from bar to strip club to poker room to strip club to massage parlor, Orenthal had this game down cold. Orenthal is a loner and has mastered the skills of appearing to be otherwise. He was living on his past, and he was unable and unwilling to pull his own weight.

Every drink he had this evening was a gift; every lap dance was free for Orenthal. Tonight, even the crack was free. This was some really special treatment that Orenthal hadn't received for many years. Orenthal has worn out his welcome in every other city that he had ever visited more than once.

Finishing up the night, Orenthal knew he had no chance in finding a room and decided that he had had enough fun. He decided that he should head back to Ft. Lauderdale before this good evening turned ugly. Besides, he had an early flight out of Ft. Lauderdale in the morning, and did not want to take the chance of missing it.

"Well, ladies, I's gots to gets back to where I be going," he was heard saying as he walked out of the final strip club of the evening without leaving a tip. And just as quickly as he had entered Tampa, Orenthal was leaving.

Intoxicated on free alcohol and high on free crack and coke, Orenthal decided that his quick day trip had turned out to be not so bad after all. The VIP treatment that he felt he was entitled to made him feel right at home, and he did not want to wear out his welcome because he was sure he would return to this town real soon.

Orenthal got into his rented SUV and headed back towards Alligator Alley. The trip west driving through the Everglades from Ft. Lauderdale earlier had not been bad at all because it was daylight and the weather was perfect. The trip back seemed like it might prove to be a little more of a challenge. It was 3:30 A.M., and it began to pour down heavy rains. The winds were enough to rock the large SUV dangerously as it sped east. Crocodiles, native to the area and loving the weather, could be seen just beyond the fence in the twilight offered by the vehicle's headlights.

The skies lit up furiously with lightning, accentuating every dangerous detail. The chemicals in Orenthal's blood stream were now beginning to peak, making Orenthal tense, and he began to wonder if he should just get out of the rental car and run the two-hundred-plus miles back to Ft. Lauderdale.

Speeding in excess of ninety-five miles per hour in the pouring rain, Orenthal knew that he was making great time. The wind was blowing so hard against the vehicle along with the rain that it was almost impossible to see anything, so he slowed down to about eighty-five miles per hour. The lightning moved across the sky mysteriously like a slow electrical show. The thunder was terrifying.

Orenthal reached into his pocket for his cell phone when the SUV lurched as if it had been hit. Wiping out sideways, Orenthal had expected to hear the signature screeching of the tires, but the crash was completely silent. The car glided on a sheet of water and was completely out of control. The SUV turned on its wheels multiple times spinning in circles.

Looking forward, Orenthal could see the light of the headlights heading towards him and then the red of the taillights moving away as the vehicle spun out of control. Orenthal was completely disoriented when the car came to a complete stop, and it was a moment before he realized that his rental was now pointing in the wrong direction. His heart was pounding because he had just escaped certain death, but the headlights of oncoming cars (the ones that he had passed so recklessly moments before) were now flying past him, blowing their horns furiously. Pushing the accelerator to the floor, Orenthal spun the SUV recklessly back in the direction of traffic.

Orenthal noticed immediately that the vehicle was not handling properly, and the front wheel thudded as if it were flat. He pulled over and got out of the car. Through the pouring rain, Orenthal saw that both tires on the drivers' side of the rental were flat.

Standing in the rain, Orenthal waved hysterically for help as car after car passed him carelessly. People were flashing their lights, putting on their four-way flashers, or blowing their horns. It seemed like a hundred cars passed him when finally a car slowed down, a large blue luxury sedan. The man pulled up alongside of Orenthal and rolled his passenger window down and yelled out, "I will call the police emergency line when I get into cell phone range." He began to roll forwards.

Running to keep up with the four-door sedan, Orenthal screamed desperately, "Hey, buddy! It's a rental car with bad tires. Can I get a lift? I have a plane to catch!"

Pulling away and quickly rolling his window up, the man impulsively responded, "No, sorry. I don't have any room for you."

Orenthal stood there soaked to the bone, knowing that there had been enough room for him in that man's car. Why hadn't this guy helped him, he wondered? Why did people have to lie?

Standing there as the next car slowly pulled up alongside him, the driver rolled the passenger window down and yelled, "Get back in your car before a croc gets you." The person then accelerated quickly, offering no other help.

Standing in the middle of Alligator Alley in the pouring rain, Orenthal felt all alone as he looked around. Every flash of lightning revealed more sets of eyes along the chain link fence lining I-75.

Convinced that there was nobody on the road that was going to help him, Orenthal decided to get back into the SUV where at least it was dry and to drive the debilitated vehicle as far as he could on the flat tires while he looked for someone to help him.

Orenthal did not seem to care that he was damaging the vehicle recklessly by driving on the rims. Moving along at around twenty miles per hour, the screeching of the now bare rims on the pavement and the movement of the windshield wipers maddened Orenthal, and he turned up the radio to drown out the noise.

Ten minutes had passed, and Orenthal's cell phone was still out of service. Looking into the rearview mirror, Orenthal could see flashing lights in the distance coming up behind him. "It's about fucking time," Orenthal yelled as he pulled the vehicle to the side of the road.

Getting out of the SUV, Orenthal ran up to the side of the tow truck. Knocking impatiently on the window,

Orenthal noticed the name of the business on the side of the door: Recovery Experts Inc.

Rolling down the window, the unshaven and clearly disinterested truck driver said, "Sir, get back in your vehicle before somebody runs you over or a croc gets a hold of you and drags you into the swamp."

"Hey, buddy, listen: this is a rental. A tractor-trailer ran me off the road. I need to get back to Ft. Lauderdale to catch a plane. I need your help!"

"Get back in your vehicle, sir. We will call for help," the driver said.

Looking at the guy in the passenger seat of the tow truck, Orenthal said, "Don't you guys know who I am?"

"Do you think we give a fuck who you are? Get back in your vehicle before you get killed!" the passenger ordered Orenthal, nodding his head once in complete confidence. "The police are on their way."

"Unbelievable," Orenthal scoffed, walking back to the vehicle. Getting in, it occurred to him that he was still intoxicated and coming off of a coke high and that it was probably not such a good thing if the cops did show up.

A few minutes passed and Orenthal watched the rearview mirror in anticipation as he noticed another set of flashing lights pull up behind the tow truck. Getting out of the SUV, Orenthal thought that whoever it is must be there to help him. The rain poured down, and the thunder and lightning were constant.

Passing the tow truck, Orenthal saw that the new arrival was a marked police cruiser, and he was flustered when he heard the officer yell, "Sir, get back in your car."

Ignoring the police officer, Orenthal walked up to the police cruiser and leaned down right into the window, saying, "Hey, buddy, you sho' is a site for sow' eyes. I need your help." He leaned into the front window further.

The police officer was pulling paperwork away from a clip board and looked completely disinterested in Orenthal's plea, refusing to look him in the eye. "Sir, get back in your vehicle."

Knowing that this officer was bound by law to help him, Orenthal knew the exact words to use to get him the attention that he deserved: "I was in a bad accident; I think I am hurt. I need an ambulance. And I need to catch a flight in Ft. Lauderdale. You got to help me, officer."

The disinterested police officer just looked at him with a cold look on his face.

"Well, buddy, aint you going to help me or what?" Orenthal asked in frustrated desperation.

The silence grew; the officer just sat there staring at Orenthal as if he were waiting for something to happen.

Orenthal looked at the officer confused. Why wasn't this officer performing his civic duties and helping? The loudest clap of thunder he had ever heard startled him, followed by an eerie silence.

Still smiling, Orenthal fell to his knees and then slumped alongside the police cruiser. Orenthal never saw the passenger of the tow truck walk up behind him clenching a wooden baseball bat with both fists.

Smashing Orenthal's skull once more violently with the baseball bat as the police officer got out of the car, the two men moved quickly to remove Orenthal's corpse off of the roadway. In the meantime, the tow truck driver pulled forward and was preparing to pull the rented SUV onto the truck's flatbed.

Walking over to the chain link fence, the police officer used a sharp thick knife to remove the plastic quick-ties that held a section of the chain link fence together.

Pulling the section of the fence open like a gate, the two men dragged Orenthal's body over to near where six large crocodiles were waiting patiently. The tow truck driver, who was now wearing a pair of green wading pants, pulled Orenthal by his arms and dragged his floating corpse into the murky waters of the Everglades.

The man stepped past the nocturnal creatures, evidently comfortable with, though wary of their presence. The crocodiles watched the man clear away from the corpse. Walking swiftly back to the fence line, the man turned to watch as the crocodiles surrounded Orenthal's corpse like sharks to a bleeding hog.

Laughing at their process, as if they had practiced this a hundred times, the two men wasted not a second as they pushed the fence back into place, using plastic quick-ties to connect the fence back together.

"Wow, my hands still hurt," said the man to the police officer.

"Yeah, you clobbered that one good," said the trooper, laughing grimly. "Hell, if his head was a baseball, I think you would have whacked it out of the Everglades!" he laughed, handing the man the baseball bat in the rain.

The SUV was now loaded onto the flat bed. As the two men worked on the fence, the tow truck driver removed the vehicle's identification numbers and dislocated the battery in case there was a satellite-tracking device attached.

Less than five minutes had passed since the baseball bat cracked Orenthal's thick skull. Departing, the three men shook hands casually and everyone went on their way.

Anyone passing by on this dark rainy night would have surmised that it was business as usual for a person in a disabled motor vehicle in the most inopportune of places, and no one would have ever suspected that the infamous Orenthal James had just been killed by a sophisticated ring of car thieves who prey on unsuspecting victims. The automobile was now just another statistic, another missing rental car.

## 86 Days Later

Sitting in the living room of the James' house, Orenthal's son King answered the phone: "Yeah. No. He's not here right now. No, I told you! I have no idea. I haven't seen him in weeks. Sorry, I'll let him know you called." He hung up the phone.

"Where do you think he is?" King asked his sister Raleigh as she sat on the couch watching the television, disinterested.

"I don't know, and I don't care," she replied.

"Well, don't you think we should find him?" He dialed his father's cell phone before she could answer. He received the message, "...The number you have reached has been disconnected…."

"Well, he must have run off with some *ho*, or he's living in a crack house again, King. And I am not about to start acting like I give a shit, either."

"Well, maybe we ought to call him in as missing or tell the police," King suggested to his sister. "When was the last time we saw him?"

"I don't know. It must have been two to three weeks ago," she said.

"No, it was *way* longer than that," King said.

"Well, like I said, I don't really care," his sister quipped unsympathetically.

"I am going to call the police and make a missing persons report."

"I wouldn't. He's going to be pissed," said his sister.

"I don't care. What if he's in trouble?"

"I said I don't really care if I ever see him again," she shot at King before turning up the volume to the television.

Dialing 911 on his cell phone and looking nervous, the young man said, "Yes, hello. My name is King James, and I would like to report a missing person. My father, Orenthal, Orenthal James."

# Missing Person Report

## FILE # 7715454-

NAME: Orenthal James- ***Violent Criminal History***

PRIORITY: LOW

SEX: M AGE: 55 RACE: W HEIGHT 6.2 WEIGHT: 260

NARRATIVE:
Caller states that he has not seen his father Orenthal James in at least two- three weeks. Caller- (King James) states that it is not unlike his father to go this long without checking in. According to DMV files Mr. James is wanted for the theft of a missing motor vehicle which was registered to him from a rental agency out of Ft. Lauderdale 86 Days ago. Son states that his father has a drug problem and may or may not be in the area. No further information is available at this time
END OF REPORT-

Report Sightings at www.OrenthalJames.com

**NOTES: Missing Person Orenthal James has a large criminal history. He is known to use drugs. He has multiple outstanding warrants from Las Vegas, and New York. He is wanted for questioning in a homicide in Miami Florida.**

**WARNING: Violent Predicate Felon- Most Likely Eluding Law Enforcement.**
**Extreme Caution Advised*** KNOWN LIAR*****
**File # 7715484-**

# Engagement Ring

## A Hogtale

Walking into a local jewelry store, Orenthal startled the middle aged man who was sitting behind the counter about to eat his meal, a chicken Caesar wrap with a side of potato chips that he had just had delivered from the deli next door.

Standing up, the jeweler wiped his hands on a paper towel. "Good evening, sir. Can I help you with something?"

Orenthal stood there looking down into the glass case at the first thing that caught his eye, as if to portray that he had the means and impulse to buy anything in the store. Not recognizing the infamous Orenthal James, the owner of the store was convinced that this man was there to rob him.

Never looking up to acknowledge the shopkeeper, Orenthal just walked around the store looking into the glass cases. The owner reached for his portable phone so that he would have it when it was time to dial 911.

Trying to feel him out, the jeweler asked, "Sir, is there anything in particular that you are looking for?" He asked quietly so as not to hurry the process of an armed robbery.

Orenthal looked up. "No, nothing at all really. I am looking to get my girl an engagement ring."

"Oh, really," said the owner, convinced that this was a ruse to gain his trust. "How long have you known her?"

"About eleven months" answered Orenthal.

"Tell me a little about her," the owner slowly suggested. He, not being a stranger to the risk of a robbery from any customer, was well aware that some thieves walk into an unsuspecting jewelry store and ask to see an expensive diamond so that once in possession of it they can either switch it with a cheap look-alike ring or just boldly run out of the store with it.

"She has small hands," offered Orenthal.

"Ok," replied the owner. "What other kinds of jewelry does she wear?" He paused to wait for an answer and then offered, "Gold? Platinum? Diamonds? Does she have a favorite watch?" he asked.

Orenthal just stood there staring at the owner, sweating under the bright lights of the store looking confused. "Let me see that one there," he said, pointing at a two-carat diamond in a platinum setting worth about twenty-five thousand dollars.

"Now, sir, let me just tell you that that ring there costs about thirty thousand dollars. Is it in the price range you are looking for?" he asked cautiously.

"Oh, hell no!" responded Orenthal. "I am looking more in the range of five thousand. If that! But I want *bling,"* he said seriously.

"Ok. Let me take you over here," he said, walking over to the other side of the jewelry cases in direct line of two surveillance cameras. "Do you see anything that you like here in this section?"

"Let me see that one," Orenthal said, pointing at a ring outside of the section that the jeweler was moving towards.

"Ok, that ring there is going to run you about fifteen thousand dollars, so it is a little out of your price range," the owner said, pulling out a phony ring made to hand to a suspecting thief in case he decided to run with it.

"Now, Mr—?" the owner began. Orenthal just stood there like a donkey. "I am sorry, I didn't get your name," said the jeweler, verbally prompting Orenthal.

"Orenthal, Orenthal James," he said.

The storeowner was a bit surprised because he recognized the name but did not recognize the face. Looking a little closer at Orenthal, he thought to himself, "Wow, Orenthal James. Now a junkie?"

"Mr. James, I am sorry. I didn't recognize you!" The owner handed him the dummy ring. "This ring is around ten thousand dollars," he said. "If you will excuse me just a second, I will be right back." He walked over to another counter, appearing to be busy for a moment, and he even disappeared into the back room, giving Orenthal a chance to flee with the loot if that was his intention. When he returned, Orenthal was still there, staring into the fake ring.

"Wow, this is ten grand?" he asked.

"Yes, sir." He was now a little more confident that Orenthal was not there to rob him but still not totally convinced. Looking confused, the jeweler asked, "Aren't you already married, Mr. James?"

"Uh, yeah."

"Oh," said the jeweler. "What's going on with that? I mean, if you don't mind me asking."

"Well, my wife," Orenthal began, but he hesitated. "Well, my former wife, I should say…." Orenthal was stumbling on his thoughts and words. "My wife is no longer with me. I don't want to talk about it," he said, aggravated.

"Okay, no problem. I am sorry that I pried," apologized the jeweler. "So, your new girl, tell me about her?"

"Well, you see, I am not so sure that she is not a gold digger," said Orenthal. The storeowner looked confused, pulling his head back on his shoulders and thinking to himself, "Wow. That's a first."

"Okay," said the jeweler, at a loss for words.

"Well, you know how girls are these days: they are always looking to get a boost up, always trying to appear like they are everything, until you got them and you know what there all about and they run off with your money and your ring, and, you know, I's left standing there with my hands in my pocket," Orenthal said.

"Okay," repeated the store owner, looking unconvinced. "Well, maybe *now* is not the time to be shopping for a ring," he suggested reasonably.

"Well, no," said Orenthal. "And let me tell you why. If she is half as genuine as she pretends to be, then she is the girl I want to be wiff, and I don't want to take the chance that I don't do the right thing to make it solid at this stage in the game, so I would like to present her with a ring, but I don't want it to cost me too much, see?" He raised one eyebrow and lifted his chin so that he almost looked intelligent.

"Mr. James, I am not quite sure I follow you."

"Ok," he said. "What if I just buy a really nice setting, for, let's say, fifteen-hundred dollars, and you put in a fake stone, and you make it look like a twenty-five thousand dollar ring. How does that sound?"

The storeowner laughed good-naturedly. "Mr. James, you aren't serious?"

"Well, yeah, I am serious! You see, a man in my position, I's gots to be careful, see? You must understand with a guy like me, a woman can put on the greatest of fronts. You know, 'til the wedding day, or until it comes time to sign a prenup. Then if she turns out to be a money-hungry bitch, she can walk and I am out the two-grand, instead of twenty-five, see?"

"Okay," responded the owner dumbly, amazed at Orenthal's thought process. "And, if it works out, then what do you do?" he asked, playing devils-advocate out of habit.

"Well, then I come to you, and we do the real thing, see?"

"Yeah, but, Mr. James, being in this business, I would have to advise you that we would not encourage any of our customers to be so dishonest, especially in something so…" He paused, testing his next word in his mind before he said it: "sacred. —Let's say that you *do* get married and she finds out. Then you'd have a real problem on—her hands."

"No, no no," said Orenthal ignorantly. "See, this ring is a test, for a year, and if she is still the person she is now—in a year—then I would say she probably aint gonna change. Because, see, my experience wit' women is dat they all change. You don't know em' 'til you live with em', and you don't really know em' 'til you start throwing money at em'. After a year or so, some only after a few months, they will start to display the kind of unacceptable behavior that would be a deal crusher, and—you see— then I throw her out. With the ring, she thinks she's a winner, and she goes to hock the jewels, and she's got a big zero on her hand, see? Haven't you seen this done before?"

"Mr. James, I have heard of everything, but I have never heard of that." The owner laughed, shaking his head. "And, I would never recommend that, Mr. James, not to anybody. You see, right now, if you are trying to ask this woman to marry you, you should be doing everything in your power to earn her trust. And trust will help you to build a solid foundation. And that foundation will help you to build a love. And the love that you build stands on the foundation of that trust. It should be able to get you guys through any troubled times. And if even for a second you compromise your foundation, the trust, then the love is not genuine… And then the only thing that you really have is an unstable foundation built on deception. And that is, my friend, the problem with our world today: No one is willing to sacrifice the time, the effort, and possibly to suffer the pain of betrayal, to build a solid foundation. And that is why so many relationships crumble under the simple storms, the winds and rains of everyday life: If you don't have that foundation, if you're not willing to stick your feet in the wet cement and say, 'This is the only person in my life, and I am willing to do anything for this person. I am willing to sacrifice everything!' then you are only setting yourself up for certain failure. Don't you understand?" the jeweler asked as if her were trying to explain physics to a pre-schooler.

Orenthal, oblivious to the point that the jeweler had been trying to make, asked, "So, how much is a two carat cubic zirconium?"

Astonished at the question, the jeweler fumbled an answer: "Well, Mr. James…." He paused, shaking his head in disbelief. "A two carat CZ is going to run you about four-hundred dollars."

"Ok, I would like the CZ. I want it to look like the real thing. I want the *best* CZ money can buy, and I want it in *that* setting right there." He pointed with his big sausage-like index finger, leaving behind a greasy smudge on the glass.

"Mr. James, that is a hand-carved platinum setting, and it runs about five-grand alone."

"Oh, no," said Orenthal quickly. "Then how about that one?" he asked, pointing to a section of about ten settings.

Frustrated, the jeweler said, "All of those settings are platinum, and they are all around five-grand."

"Ok, ok. Then let's get into a white gold—that looks like platinum," Orenthal said.

"Mr. James, are you sure you want to do this?"

"Oh, yeah, I am sure, but I just don't want to have to eat my words in the future, you know," he confided, nodding his head in a convinced manner.

"Well, like I said, I think it is very risky. Especially if she takes it to a jeweler to be appraised, and she will want it to be, for insurance purposes—"

Orenthal cut him off. "Believe me, all women want to know what they are worth, and she will have it appraised. So, what we will do is, we will have her come here," he said confidently, pointing at the glass counter. "And you give it the twenty-five grand appraisal, and she's happy, I'm happy, and we will begin the misery," he said, smiling like a butcher.

"Mr. James, I am sorry, but that is called *fraud*, and I will not be any part of it. Really, this is just ridiculous. I am sorry—"

"Ok, so I won't bring her here. I have a friend who can look at it. She's so fucking stupid, she'll believe anything." The jeweler's eyes were wide open in disbelief. "So, how much is this setting?"

"That is a white gold setting, and it runs around twenty-five hundred," said the jeweler, purposely adding one thousand dollars to the price, hoping the desperado would buy it. "But, if you're serious, I can put a two carat CZ in that setting for around twenty-five hundred cash, if you're serious."

"No," said Orenthal; as if he knew the jeweler was now bullshitting him. "I will pay two thousand and not a penny more."

The jeweler responded, "twenty-two fifty cash, and you walk out the door with it tonight!"

Orenthal said, "No, I aint buying tonight. I have to get some cash."

"We take checks," the owner offered, wanting the sale.

"No, I don't have a check book."

"Ok, there's an ATM in the mall. To order it, I am going to need at least a two-hundred and fifty dollar deposit today…"

"Yeah, no problem," said Orenthal. "Here, put it on this card." Orenthal handed him a bank card.

"If you are not paying cash for the sale I am going to have to get the full sale price of twenty-five hundred, Mr. James. Do you have cash to put it on hold?"

"No. No cash. But can you just take the credit card number, and I will bring you in the twenty-two fifty in cash in the next few days. Yeah, that sounds good," murmured Orenthal.

"You sure are a man who knows what he wants, aren't you?" asked the jeweler.

"Yup, don't we all," he said, oblivious to the jewelers' sarcasm.

The jeweler, taking Orenthal's credit card and swiping it to put a two hundred and fifty dollar hold on it, was not surprised when the card came back denied.

"The card came back 'Funds Unavailable,' Mr. James."

"Whoa! Whoa, whoa!" cried Orenthal in a panic. "I said just take the numbers, don't run the card!" he yelled, looking totally aggravated.

The jeweler, thinking to himself, "This guy is an full blown shyster, and he doesn't even have two-hundred and fifty dollars to his name." said aloud, "Well, Mr. James, in order for me to put the stone in the ring, I am going to have to get at least a two-hundred and fifty dollar deposit; otherwise, if you have to think about it, you can always come back tomorrow." He was trying to give Orenthal the graceful option of walking out.

"Ok," said Orenthal. "I will be right back with the two fifty. I will go to the ATM and be right back. What time do you close?"

"I will be here 'til nine o'clock," said the jeweler, walking back to his sandwich and grabbing a potato chip off of the wax paper.

Pushing through the glass door, leaving behind another greasy smudge and walking towards the parking lot, Orenthal announced "I'll be right back."

"Okay! Good luck to you," said the jeweler, knowing that it was unlikely that he would ever see this drifter again.

Two and a half hours later, as the Jeweler was about to lock up the store for the night, he still felt a little uneasy from his interaction with the infamous Orenthal James. He was never more sure in his life that he was about to be robbed. Shaking his head in disbelief while walking to his car, the jeweler said, "God have mercy on any woman that ever marries that desperado."

# Like a Zit'

## A Murder

Charging out of the house after his son Jarmaine, Orenthal shouted, "Don't you walk away from me when I be' talking to you, boy."

"I have nothing to say to you," replied his son clearly furious.

"Why you so mad at me? I tol' you, I didn't do nuffin' wrong."

"Jesus Christ, Dad! Can you for once not speak like a fucking idiot? Try pronouncing your words instead of just mumbling like a fool."

"Don't you talk to your daddy that way, boy. You gots to respect me."

"Respect what? You're a fucking pedophile," his son retorted. Just as he said the word pedophile, Jarmaine saw something snap in his father's eyes. It was a look that he had never seen before, but had read about many times.

Orenthal grabbed his son by the neck and harshly asked, "What'd you say to me, boy?" His manner threateningly dared his son to repeat his words. "Say it again. What did you just say to me?"

Jarmaine knew that he had crossed a line by calling his father a pedophile, but he was going to stand by his words, even if it cost him his life. Choking through the clamp on his throat, Jarmaine said, "Leave my girlfriend alone."

"Boy, I tol' you, I have nothing to do with your girls. They all approach me!"

"This is the third girl that I have brought here that you pissed off with your comments. And Lee Anna told me that while I was getting ready to take her out to dinner you touched her inappropriately, and that's fucked up, Dad."

Letting go of the clutch on his son's throat, Orenthal hollered, "I never did such a thing! I never touched her!"

"So, what? Is she lying to me, Dad?" his son asked.

"Let me fill you in on one thing about women, Jarmaine: They are *all* liars. They are all phonies and liars, and they will do anything to make a man look bad. Women are money hungry, and they only care about sucking a man dry.

"Believe me, boy: I wouldn't touch her. She's your girl. But you want to learn the hard way.... Besides," he continued nonchalantly, "she's a slut. You don't want to be around that slut."

"Dad, she's not a slut. I love her, and you..." He paused, allowing time to test his forthright daring. It failed. "What's the use in talking to you? You only care about yourself," he finished weakly.

"I care about you, son! Believe me when I tell you women are treacherous. A woman hates everything in the world, especially themselves. Think about it, boy: they can't even get up in the morning and look at themselves in the mirror. The first thing they do is put on makeup, a disguise for the rest of the world. Why do you think they call it makeup? It is a disguise, and they are their own characters. They are fake. Much like their face, they act different depending on who they talk to. They put on a show for the rest of the world of just how innocent and cute they are, and eventually, when she can no longer get away with her act with you, she'll show you the real her. And you wont ever know the real her until you marry them. And once you marry them, they become the women they have always hidden…" The look on Orenthal's face showed that he was impressed with his own pseudo-philosophic ranting.

"Jarmaine, look at me when I am talking to you, boy. This is important, and I got to get it off my chest.

"I'm telling you, women are treacherous, cunning, and selfish, and they can put on an act for years and years 'til they know they got the upper hand. Believe me, they are patient. And once they know they got the upper hand, after you have a few kids and a second mortgage in both of your names, then they start to show their true colors. Then they start taking care of *you* less, they start sniffing around for another man, and they make a move to replace you. Trust me."

"Dad, do you really think that's what all women are like?"

"Think!" bellowed Orenthal. "I know, Jarmaine. If all of a sudden she starts watching her weight, going to the gym, and hiding her cell phone, *believe you me*, it's over. She used to want to look good for you, now she wants to look good for the rest of the world. By then it's over. She will take her act on the road, and she will perfect her performance, learning from one to the next. She knows that you know the real her, and she will cast you aside like a used rag when she is done with you. Then she will concentrate all of her forces on perfecting her charade for the rest of the world," Orenthal adjusted his stance so that he could look his son in the eye.

"It doesn't matter how hard you try. This is all women, Jarmaine, and it happens to all men. She will eat you up and spit you out without a care in the world, knowing she can take her act on the road to the next unsuspecting soul—she can and will, Jarmaine. You're a good boy, and I don't want to see you get hurt," Orenthal cooed in finality, completely convinced and trying to show his son that the cruelty of the criticism was true.

Unimpressed by Orenthal's interpretation of life, Jarmaine crossed his arms and looked away from his father.

"Listen, Jarmaine. Women hate themselves, and they are only happy when they are lying, conniving or cheating. Now you better watch a girl like that one, who just lied to your face. Girls are tongue happy, and by that I mean that they aren't afraid to tell a lie. A woman who is tongue happy is not afraid to make you look and feel bad."

"Dad, shut up, I don't care."

"Don't you tell your daddy to shut up boy. Now god-damn it listen to me!" Orenthal screamed and then continued his rant. "You see, men are different from women. If a man has a problem with another man, they will usually handle it the only way they know how, and that is, the two men will beat the shit out each other, and in the end each of the men knows their role. But women, they can't beat a man physically, so they sit and cunn' and connive their way through life, thinking of any combination of words to beat their man.

"God Damn it Jarmaine, don't roll your eyes at me like that," Orenthal insisted. "Women will tell their friends one thing; they tell their mothers another thing, they tell their sisters another thing, each lie a little bit different, each one satisfying a personal internal agenda. And these women, they are good at it. Hell, they invented this game. They can keep their stories straight, lying to everyone and themselves, and making themselves out to be the victim, and you to be the monster.

"You know the old joke: How do you know if a woman is lying? Her mouth is moving," he said with the sincerest conviction, not even bothering to laugh. "Believe me, son. I don't want to break your heart; I want you to believe in fairy tales; I want you to believe 'til death do us part and love at first sight. I am just trying to make you the wiser. Most men don't find out the truth 'til its way too late."

Trying to regain Jarmaine's attention, Orenthal pushed his son on the shoulder and continued, "A woman is good for one thing and one thing only." He winked at his son with a despicable grin on his face. "And I hope you believe me. Besides," Orenthal continued casually, deliberately slowing the speed of his words, "I am almost sure that she is good at that one thing." He smiled and shook his head, wiping his lips with his wrist. He hooted wantonly before saying, "She is one fine ho."

"See, Dad, you're way out of line. I really *do* love her, and you shouldn't talk about her that way. I am leaving," he said completely calm and defeated.

Laughing, Orenthal said, "Son, don't walk away mad. I's just trying to fill in the blanks for a young man with questions."

"I don't remember asking you for your opinion, Dad."

"Well, one day, you be glad I tol' you what I did. I wish I had had a daddy to tell me these kinds of things, 'cuz it could have saved me a lot of agga-ra-vation and unnecessary liti-gation. Life aint fair, son; I hate to be the first to tell you."

"Well, thanks for the pep talk, Dad. I am leaving, and you'd better hope she talks to me again."

"Son, if she don't talk to you again, believe you me, you be much better off. Move on to the next girl; have fun. That's what life is all about!"

Jarmaine walked away from his father filled with great disgust. Getting into his car, he started the engine and picked up his cell phone, dialing Lee Anna's number. When the car started, a squeaky belt chirped very loudly. Orenthal walked over to the window and knocked on it.

Jarmaine rolled the window down, but he was already preparing to leave a message. "What?" he asked shortly, obviously pissed. "She's not answering her phone. Hold on; I'm going to leave a message. Hey, honey, it's me. I am on my way to your house. Please call me back. I love you." Jarmaine hung up the phone, clearly upset. "What?" he repeated to Orenthal irritated.

"Son, if it makes you feel any better, I am sorry for the way I talked to the girl. Please just tell her I was messing around…."

"Okay, Dad. I've got to go."

"Wait—why is the check engine light on?" Orenthal asked his son.

"I don't know, I think it needs oil."

"Well, son, when's the last time you had an oil change?"

"Never, not since I got it—"

"Shit, boy! You gotta take better care of this car," Orenthal chided. "You got this car last year when you was a junior, and you're about to gradg-iate high school."

"I know," he said. "They are going to do it at school in shop as a lesson. I have all of the stuff to do it in the trunk…."

"Shit, boy. Pop the hood."

"No, Dad. I have to go."

"Shut the car off, and pop the hood—"

"Fuck! Why can't you just let me go?"

"Because I pay for this car, and I aint about to let you seize the engine."

Exhaling, defeated, Jarmaine reached down and popped the hood, killing the engine.

"Now, where is the dipstick?" Orenthal asked, looking around under the hood. "Okay, here it is."

Checking the dipstick, Orenthal coyly mocked his son: "Boy, there aint no oil in this car! You is lucky it even started."

"I know, Dad. I am going to take care of it but not now."

"Bullshit; I got a jack in the garage. I will help you change the oil—it'll only take ten minutes." Orenthal turned and walked towards the garage.

"Dad, I've got to go!" Jarmaine hollered, completely aggravated. "Fuck," he added, getting out of the car. Jarmaine knew his father was right, that the car needed an oil change, but could he possibly be right about women?

Orenthal had worked as a grease monkey for a local mechanic when he was in his early teens. If there was one thing he did know, it was the importance of lubrication.

Pushing the jack under the car and pumping it up, he said to his son, "Now, bring me the oil and an oil filter." Orenthal climbed underneath the car. "Okay, I need an adjustable wrench. Get me the adjustable wrench," he ordered his son.

"Where?" asked Jarmaine.

Orenthal pulled himself out from underneath the car and walked back to the garage. "Boy, you are about fucking useless. You don't even know what an adjustable wrench is. When I was your age, I was already working two jobs. You don't know how lucky you got it."

Grabbing a few tools and climbing back underneath the car, he continued ordering his son about: "Get me the bucket over there." Jarmaine grabbed the bucket and slid it under the car. "Now get down here, boy, and I will show you a thing or two about a thing or two."

Jarmaine was more pissed now than ever. He had taken a break to try calling Lee Anna again, but her phone went right to voicemail. "Call me, baby. I love you," he cooed, leaving a second message.

"Now, boy! Stop all this pussy-whipped luvin' and come down here. I will show you how easy it is to change your oil."

"Dad, I really don't care. I will pay someone to do it."

"Just get down here and learn something from your old man."

Crawling under the car to watch his father change the oil, Jarmaine watched as Orenthal was loosening a bolt from the oil pan of the car. "Here is the bolt you remove to release all of the old oil. Now, there shouldn't be much oil in here." Orenthal was pulling so hard on the wrench that the entire car was shaking on the jack. Jarmaine worried that at any second the entire car could crash down on them.

As the oil drained out of the car and into the bucket, Orenthal said, "Okay! Now, you used to be able to remove an oil filter by hand, but they have a special tool for it nowadays." He took the oil filter in his hands and used all of the force he could to try to remove it. He was not successful. "Wow! It won't budge. Get me a straight screwdriver," he said. "I will show you the other way we used to do this."

Sliding out from under the car and walking into the garage, Jarmaine repeated, "Straight screwdriver," out loud while looking for it.

"C'mon! How hard is it to find a screwdriver?" Orenthal was still under the car, using all of his strength to try and remove the baked-on filter. "Jesus Christ, Jarmaine! Where is the fucking screwdriver?"

Jarmaine hurried back to the car once he found it. He handed his father a long Phillips head screwdriver.

Shaking his head in disgust and letting a large burst of air escape from his lips, Orenthal sighed, "Tits on a bull, boy."

"What?" Jarmaine asked.

"Useless as tits on a bull, you are." Still shaking his head, Orenthal commented, "This will work."

"Now, watch this!" Orenthal said as he took the Phillips head screwdriver that Jarmaine had given him and used his palm as a hammer on the handle end of the screwdriver to push it through both sides of the oil filter. "There!"

Oil started dripping everywhere, running down Orenthal's arms and onto his face as he continued the lesson. "Now, twist it counter clockwise. Always remember: righty tightey, lefty loosey. Just like magic," Orenthal concluded as he loosened the oil filter from the car. "See, you didn't think your daddy knew anything about this, did you? Your car can't run without oil."

As Orenthal was tightening the new oil filter onto the car, Jarmaine's phone rang. Reaching for his hip, he grabbed the phone and saw Lee Anna on the caller ID. "Hey, baby. What's going on?" he asked desperately.

Orenthal could hear the girl screaming through the phone.

"What's going on, Jarmaine, is that your father's a fucking scum-bag! That's what's going on!"

Jarmaine pulled himself out from underneath the car and walked away from his father. "What's the matter, baby?"

Orenthal yelled from underneath the car, "Remember, don't listen to a word that bitch says! Remember what I tole' you, boy: liars, every one of them!"

"What happened, baby?"

"When you were in the shower getting ready, your father asked me if I wanted to be with a real man, and then he licked the front of my shirt and grabbed my ass!"

"What? He licked your shirt?" asked Jarmaine, devastated.

"Yeah, and he tried to put one hand under my shirt! The other was already on my ass, and he told me that he would lick every inch of my body!" she screamed furiously. "He's such a pervert! And when I tried to walk away from him, he called me a slut and grabbed my arm; that's when you walked in the room. I couldn't believe it. I have a black and blue on my arm!"

Jarmaine's blood ran cold. He could not believe his ears.

"Please tell me that you're lying. Tell me this is a joke," Jarmaine pleaded, searching for an escape.

"Lying?" she screamed. "Jarmaine, who could make this shit up? It's not funny. If you think I will *ever* step foot in your house again, you're wrong. He tore my shirt. That man is a serial rapist."

Looking at the car, Jarmaine watched as his father was still underneath. His entire world began to spin.

"Jarmaine!" Orenthal shouted, trying to get his son's attention again. "I need the fucking wrench. Do you see it? Get off the phone and help your daddy, boy."

Lee Anna continued through the phone: "What are you going to do about this, Jarmaine?" His face was beet red, his pulse elevated. "Tell me: Is this behavior acceptable to you?"

"No, it's not," he replied immediately. "I will take care of it." He slammed the face of his phone shut, trying to control his rage he inhaled furiously and held his breath.

Reaching down and looking under the car at Orenthal, Jarmaine was sick with bloodlust.

"Is she still bellyaching?" asked Orenthal as Jarmaine looked under the car.

"Yeah, Dad, but you know women: just a bunch of lying bitches."

"Alright! That's my boy! Now you're learning!" he lauded, laughing under the car obliviously.

"Hey, Dad? You're forgetting one thing."

Orenthal was hand-tightening the new oil filter under the car. "What's that, son?"

"You forgot to teach me how to use the jack," he said, twisting the handle.

"NO, JARMAINE!" Orenthal screamed his last words.

The front end of the car crashed and bounced off the pavement, the front axle crushing Orenthal. There was a horrible popping sound like something had been squished.

Now, Jarmaine had heard some incredible things about adrenaline and strength, but he would have never believed it if he hadn't seen see it: Orenthal pushed with all of his might and lifted the front end of the car off of the ground, higher than the hydraulic jack had originally lifted it. For a second Jarmaine was convinced that his father was going to push the car off of himself and get up to beat the shit out of him.

Screaming and grunting, there was another squishing noise and an inexplicable *pop,* which to this day Jarmaine cannot get out of his head. As Orenthal's muscles gave out, the car came crashing down, crushing him beneath it a second time.

Jarmaine looked under the car: there was no sign of life, just what appeared to be guts and fecal matter spilling out of Orenthal's pants. Immediately, Jarmaine called 911.

"My dad, he just had an accident. The car fell on him. Help!"

Jarmaine was really upset. He was extremely disturbed by what he had just done and witnessed. Screaming and shaking, Jarmaine yelled into the phone, "Help! He's going to die! Come quick!"

Jarmaine paced furiously as he waited for EMS to arrive, and he was crying hysterically. Looking underneath the car to see if there was any sign of life, it appeared that Orenthal's eyes were actually popping out of his head from the pressure. There was a pink bubble full of veins coming out of his mouth. As if he was chewing bubble gum and blowing a large bubble.

When the first police officer arrived on the scene, Jarmaine cried, "Help, help! My dad, he is hurt!" The officer grabbed a hold of the jack, twisting the handle to the right and then pumping furiously. Jarmaine was watching underneath the car, searching for any signs of life, hoping and praying that this was all a horrible nightmare. Adrenaline silenced the boy's every word and muddled every move. He shook and was confused.

The officer raised the jack up as far as it would go. As the officer lifted the car off of Orenthal, Jarmaine watched the pressure leave Orenthal's torso. The eyes were still bleeding, but they slowly went back into his head. The large pink bubble seemed to go back into Orenthal's mouth. Besides that, there was no movement.

"Oh my god," said the officer grabbing his two-way radio. "Expedite EMS, expedite! I got a man, possible DOA, crushed by a car!" Moving a victim of such an accident goes against all protocol, but the officer did not want to chance the possibility of the car falling on the victim again. Grabbing Orenthal by his pant legs, the officer pulled Orenthal from underneath the car. This left an unsightly wet red and brown drag mark from Orenthal's intestines, which were now in his pants.

Jarmaine was now hysterical at the reality of what had just happened. The concept was nauseating: Moments ago, the man was so full of life and hate, and he was now reduced to a most grueling visual, his guts pushing out of his pants and his mouth full of displaced veins.

As EMS arrived, most of the experienced people looked at the corpse in confusion. Understanding the grave injuries, they wasted no time loading him into the ambulance.

Looking at Jarmaine, the police officer asked sympathetically, "What happened?"

Wiping the tears out of his eyes, Jarmaine said, "He asked me to make the jack higher, and I never used it before, and the car fell on him…."

The officer shook his head. "This is a terrible tragedy, son. Let's hope he makes it."

"Oh my God! Do you think he will die?"

"It doesn't look good, but we can hope for the best."

Bursting into a fit of emotion, Jarmaine called his girlfriend. "Baby, can you meet me at the hospital? You're not going to believe what just happened."

## Three Days Later

Standing in the parking lot of the funeral home was the crew of rescue workers who had worked furiously a few days ago to bring Orenthal back to life. They had all come to extend their condolences to the grief stricken family.

Because rescue workers routinely deal with unusual deaths, they cope by becoming immune to gruesome details. To most, it might seem that their conversations were out of line, but for them, it was just business as usual as they stood in a circle waiting for the rest of their group to arrive.

Smoking a cigarette, one EMT said, "Yeah, the force of the car's weight on Orenthal's chest forced his lower intestines to escape through the path of least resistance." Taking another drag from his cigarette and exhaling quickly, he added, "The path of least resistance just happened to be his anus." Laughing, he joked, "Talk about bowel movement." The crowd laughed at the sick joke.

Another person offered, "Yeah, he popped just like a zit," The girls turned away in disgust.

Another rescue worker said, "The autopsy results prove that the actual cause of death was suffocation. The pressure on his chest forced Orenthal's esophagus and lungs to push out of his mouth, cutting off his airway." He continued his description with steady detail: "Had Orenthal lived, he would have been most likely been bedridden with a catheter and a colostomy bag for the rest of his life." He shook his head, evidencing a slight involuntary shiver. "That's no way to live. I think he's better off. It's too bad."

Flicking his cigarette, the EMT said, "Well, we better get in there. Try and keep your comments to yourself: I am sure the family is distraught." They all made their way to the line at the front door.

Inside, Jarmaine stood next to Orenthal's casket, greeting people as they came to pay their last respects. Knowing the official story, most people felt horrible for Jarmaine being a witness to the accident that killed his father. Hundreds of faces filed through, and all of them said the same things.

"Your father was a great man."

Lee Anna stood next to Jarmaine, shaking her head up and down in agreement, "Yes, Mr. James *was* a great man. Everybody loved him," she said knowing the *real* truth about the despicable degenerate.

"It was a terrible tragedy. We are so sorry…."

"Yes, thank you."

"Sorry for your loss… My condolences."

"Thank you."

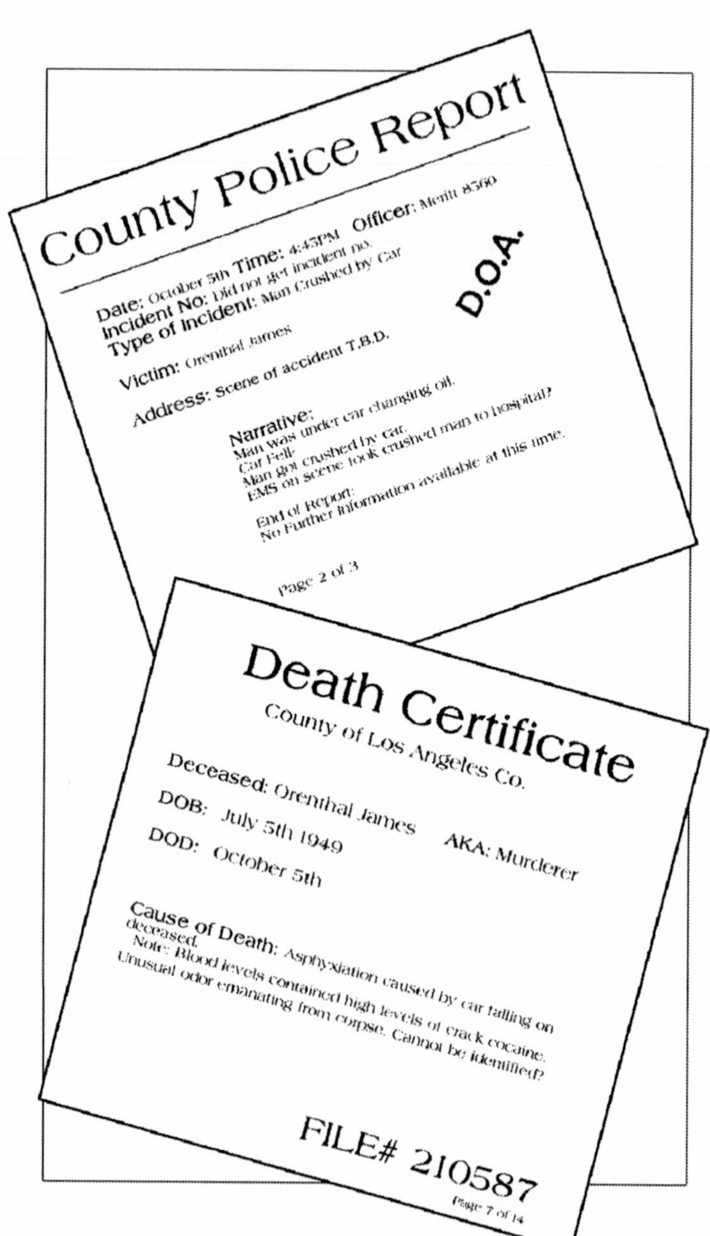

County Police Report

**Date:** October 5th **Time:** 4:43PM **Officer:** Meritt 8560
**Incident No:** Did not get incident no.
**Type of Incident:** Man Crushed by Car

**Victim:** Orenthal James

**Address:** Scene of accident T.B.D.

D.O.A.

**Narrative:**
Man was under car changing oil.
Car Fell-
Man got crushed by car.
EMS on scene took crushed man to hospital?

End of Report:
No Further Information available at this time.

Page 2 of 3

Death Certificate
County of Los Angeles Co.

**Deceased:** Orenthal James **AKA:** Murderer
**DOB:** July 5th 1949
**DOD:** October 5th

**Cause of Death:** Asphyxiation caused by car falling on deceased.
Note: Blood levels contained high levels of crack cocaine.
Unusual odor emanating from corpse. Cannot be identified?

FILE# 210587
Page 7 of 14

# Pig Pen'

## A Hogtale

Arriving at the local jail, under arrest, beaten, and abused, Orenthal would not settle down. This is Orenthal's fifth time in the county jail in the last five years.

It seems that once a year Orenthal loses control after overindulging on alcohol and drugs, and he ends up getting arrested and sent to the drunk-tank 'til he sobers up. He is then usually released into the custody of his attorney.

Having a high-profile inmate arrive at the county jail is never any fun for the staff. Orenthal was never an exception to this rule.

It took five officers five minutes to drag Orenthal from the police cruiser and then into a glass observation cell in the booking department. Orenthal was belligerent, incoherent, and combative towards the staff.

Wrestling Orenthal into the observation cell and closing the bullet proof glass slider, Orenthal would make this ten-foot by ten-foot, cement and bullet proof glass pen his home for at least the next forty-eight hours. It was Friday night at 1:30 A.M.

Usually a judge orders a drunken violator to be released in the morning with an appearance ticket once they have sobered up, but Orenthal was so unruly that the judge ordered him to be held on ten thousand dollars bail.

Orenthal was being charged with assault in the third degree, obstruction of justice, and disorderly conduct. He had punched and slapped a woman and her boyfriend at a local bar.

Being the infamous Orenthal James, he was usually able to walk away from incidents like this without charges, but the police had no choice when they entered the bar: the woman was standing there crying with a black eye, holding an ice pack to her face and clearly upset by the violent and unprovoked attack. The bar owner had demanded that Orenthal be arrested. This was his second time in a month beating up a woman in this bar, and the owner had just about had enough of Orenthal's criminal behavior. Orenthal had also threatened to kill the young girl.

As the steel frame of the observation cell door closed, Orenthal jumped up, attempting to escape. It was too late. He had stood there, pounding the glass door demanding to be released. There was nothing the officers could do for Orenthal. He was out of control. If he was not bailed out, he would sit in the holding cell until Monday morning. This would prove to be a long few days for the good people at the county jail.

As the five officers stood outside of the observation cell, they were all out of breath after wrestling with Orenthal. The sergeant, looking concerned for his officers, said, "Okay, men. Good job. Did anybody get injured?"

The men shook their heads no. One said, "No Sir, but I think I sprained my hand."

The sergeant pointed to another officer and said, "Why don't you take him up to the ER for an x-ray, and let me know right away what it shows. Everyone else, I am going to need a report from you."

It is the protocol at this facility that all high-profile detainees be treated with kid gloves because of the potential for bad publicity and lawsuits. Had this been any other inmate, he would have been the one heading to the hospital, not the officer.

"Okay, I need Mr. James placed on twenty-four hour observation," said the sergeant. "Don't take your eyes off of him. If there is anything out of the ordinary, I want to know about it immediately."

"Yes, sir," said one diligent officer.

"Let's hope he's bailed out. Until then, he's our problem. I don't want anything but professional courtesy extended to this inmate, and I do not want his cell opened unless it is a medical emergency. He is in our custody, and we will not be the center of an internal affairs investigation because of this jackass. Do I make myself clear?"

"Yes, sir!" the officers said.

Orenthal seemed to be in a trance when the sergeant approached his cell. "Mr. James," said the sergeant. "I am Sergeant Smith; I am going to see to it that you get treated with the utmost respect while you are here. In the meantime, I am going to have my people try and contact your people and arrange for you to get bailed out. Do you understand me, Mr. James?"

Orenthal just stood there staring out of the cell.

"Mr. James, can we get a few contact numbers from you—your wife, lawyer, or anybody who will be able to come and bail you out?"

Orenthal tried to push the glass door open with his hands. When the door did not budge, Orenthal pushed harder.

"Mr. James, I understand your predicament, and I would like to try and get you bailed out as soon as possible to spare you and your family any further embarrassment. I would just like to—"

Punching the door with both fist and banging his head off of the glass, Orenthal began to rage in the cell. He barked, "Let me out now!"

"Sir, I am trying to help you to get bailed out," the sergeant told him with forced patience. "Can you please give me a few contact numbers so that we can—"

"Let me out!" Orenthal demanded. "I am going to kill the first person I get my hands on!" He banged his head on the door.

"Okay," the sergeant explained to his men. "We're going to have to run video on this because no one will believe that he is doing that to himself. Just to cover our asses, tell the control room to start a video log. He is too out of it, and I don't want to see anybody here getting jammed up. Let's leave him alone for an hour, and hopefully he will go to sleep. Don't anybody antagonize him. Understand?"

The officers shook their heads as if this was business as usual for a Friday night. All of the officers left the observation area except the one officer that was assigned to constantly watch Orenthal.

"Open this fucking door!" screamed Orenthal, kicking the glass. The officer read his newspaper, hoping that if he ignored Orenthal he would go to sleep.

Kicking harder and harder, Orenthal started to crack the bullet proof glass.

The officer looking over at Orenthal said, "Hey, buddy, why don't you try and get some sleep, and we we'll try and get you bailed out."

This only enraged Orenthal more. Orenthal now began to kick and punch all four large pieces of the glass in the observation cell.

Knowing that each piece of glass was costly to replace, the officer said, "Mr. James, please stop kicking the glass. I don't want to see you hurt yourself, and I don't want to see you have to pay for them."

"I own this fucking county," said Orenthal. "When I get out, I will kill you and get away with it," he said to the officer in a rage.

Picking up the radio the officer said, "Sergeant Smith, can you come to observation please?"

"Received. En route."

Two minutes later, the sergeant walked into observation and saw that the bulletproof glass had cracked in all four windows.

"Mr. James, could you please have a seat, and try to fall asleep? We will see about getting you out of here in the morning."

"Fuck you, sarge! I want out tonight so I can kill somebody," he said, licking his lips. Foam was coming out of his mouth.

The sergeant smiled at Orenthal's nonsense. "Okay, Orenthal. Enough out of you. Try to relax and go to sleep."

The sergeant shook his head and looked at the officer who was assigned to Orenthal. "Just make sure the video stays running and that you keep an eye on him. It looks like it's going to be a long night for you. If you need anything, let me know," he said as he walked out of the observation area.

Orenthal continued to kick and punch the door. After a complete hour, he finally became tired. Realizing that the noise was not getting the officer's attention, Orenthal threw an entire roll of toilet paper into the stainless steel toilet bowl in his cell.

Orenthal flushed and flushed the toilet over and over until he created a river of water flowing out of his cell. Walking over behind the cell, the officer turned a valve shutting the water flow off and walked back to his newspaper, saying, "Lay down and go to sleep."

Kicking and punching the cell, Orenthal said, "Who the fuck is you, telling me to lay down? I ain't no fucking dog. I will fucking kill you. Tell me to lay down again motherfucker and I will fucking kill you!"

Realizing that that was a poor choice of words, the officer offered a truce, "Okay, sir, I am sorry. Please, if you can, try and go to sleep."

Orenthal stood there banging his fists, his head, his arms, and his hands off of the glass. "Let me out. I want to kill tonight," he kept screaming. "Turn my fucking water on."

After four hours of screaming, kicking, and banging, Orenthal finally sat on the bunk and fell asleep. The sound of Orenthal's snoring and gasps for air meant that the officer could finally relax. As long as he could hear Orenthal breathing, he knew he would be alright.

At 6:30 A.M., Orenthal woke up out of a sound sleep, appearing a bit confused and said to the officer, "I am starving. I need food." The officer walked over and slid two ready to eat bowls of puffed rice under his door. It was the only thing he had.

"What the fuck? No milk? How am I going to eat these without milk?"

Laughing, the officers said, "You'll be just fine."

Sitting there staring off into space, Orenthal said, "I have to see the nurse," as he sat on the toilet. "I have the shits, and I can't flush my toilet."

Most crack heads and dope fiends go through bouts of diarrhea after major binges or overdoses as a means of detoxification. It seemed that Orenthal sat on the toilet for an hour straight, having forceful gas and splattering diarrhea. The officer sat there disgusted.

"Man, I can't flush my toilet!" Orenthal said in desperation. "Turn on the water." Orenthal was still very belligerent and sweating profusely.

The officer, knowing that Orenthal clogged the toilet with a full roll of toilet paper, refused to turn the water back on because there would then be a flood of feces and urine onto the floor. Most people do not realize that these are the types of situations that a correctional officer deals with on a daily basis.

Trying to talk, the officer said, "Orenthal, I can't turn the water on. I need the captain's permission. You made a safety risk by clogging the toilet."

"Just great," Orenthal yelled while clutching his stomach and rocking back and forth in discomfort on the stainless steel commode. "What day is it?" Orenthal asked looking at the clock on the wall.

"It's Saturday."

"Is it 8 P.M. or A.M.?" asked Orenthal.

"It's A.M.," said the officer.

"This is bullshit! I need to flush my toilet!" Orenthal yelled. "I want a fucking supervisor. Bring in the sergeant."

"Sorry, Orenthal. It is shift change, and he is busy."

Standing up from the commode, Orenthal began kicking and punching the glass again, screaming, "If you think I am going to sit in here 'til Monday, you are wrong! I want to call my attorney; I want to call my wife! I will sue you, each and every one of you. You don't have any idea how powerful I am! I will have your fucking jobs! I am friends with the mayor...."

The officer just sat there. He had seen this a hundred times before. The most belligerent drunks that come in are usually the nicest people once they sober up.

"Is that all you're going to do is sit there and read your fucking book?" asked Orenthal.

"Yeah, pretty much."

"You lazy fuck. I need to flush my toilet."

"Mr. James, please lie down and go to sleep. The Captain is trying to reach your attorney, and he's trying to get you bailed out. In the meantime, I am going to have to ask you to be patient."

Lying back on his bunk, obviously forgetting where he was for the moment, Orenthal hit his head on the steel bench, and screamed, "This is bullshit!" Within a few minutes he was back to sleep.

Waking up to what seemed to be a full day later, Orenthal sat up and noticed that the clock read 10:30. The same officer was sitting there, so Orenthal asked, "Is it day or night?"

"Its morning," said the officer casually.

"Is it Sunday?"

"No, I just told you that it's Saturday," said the officer annoyed. "Go back to sleep."

Orenthal got off of the bunk and sat back on the toilet. His bowels attempted to excrete every bad chemical he had devoured in the last three days. "I am dying in here!" he whined. "I am dope sick. I need a doctor! Please help. The toilet is full of shit and piss, and I need to get out of this cell," he said. "I need food."

The officer said, "I just gave you puffed rice earlier and you didn't eat them."

"I can't eat them without milk… and a spoon…. I am starving and I am dope sick. I need food or I will die!" Orenthal cried in desperation.

The officer just sat there reading his book and ignoring Orenthal. Enraged again, Orenthal started kicking and screaming until he finally sat back down on the bunk and fell asleep.

When he woke up, Orenthal thought that another day had passed. The clock read 12:30, There was another officer sitting there reading a newspaper. "Hey, buddy, what day is it?"

"It's Saturday," he said, disinterested and not looking at Orenthal.

"Is it day or night?"

"It's afternoon."

"I need to flush my toilet."

"Sorry sir, I can't help you."

"Do you have any idea who I am?" asked Orenthal.

"Yeah, you're the infamous Orenthal James," said the officer. "The last time you were here, you almost broke my arm."

"That's bullshit," said Orenthal standing up, looking at the officer and wondering why he would lie like that. "Officer, I am still wasted, but I am a human being," he said. "My toilet is disgusting. Can you help me, please?"

"I can smell it," said the officer. "But I can't turn the water on because you flooded your cell."

"Man, can't you be a little humane? It's full of shit. I need to flush it, and I am starving."

"Eat your puffed rice," the officer said.

"Fuck this welfare food. I need a sandwich!" He opened the packages of puffed rice and poured them into the toilet. "That's what I think of your cereal," he said. "Wait 'til I get out of here, buddy. Wait till I see you on the streets," said Orenthal. After punching the glass, he lay back on the steel bunk, eventually falling back to sleep.

Waking up, the clock on the wall now read 3:30. Orenthal asked, "Is it Sunday yet?"

"Nope, still Saturday."

Falling off of his bunk onto his hands and knees, Orenthal crawled over to the sliding door and looked out through the cracked glass in a daze. It was apparent to the officer that Orenthal was suffering from withdrawal tremors. His whole body was shaking, and he was trying to open the glass door by pulling on it. After about fifteen minutes, Orenthal pushed his face against the glass door and started licking the glass. For over an hour, Orenthal sat on his hands and knees and licked the cracked glass door, staring out in a daze. Finally the officer walked over to the window and said, "Hey! What are you doing?"

Orenthal was dazed and confused and did not respond. He just licked the glass over and over from his sitting position. The officer said, "I hope you know that you're on video, and this doesn't look so good for you."

Staring off into space, Orenthal revolved around slowly on his hands and knees and crawled over towards the toilet bowl. Putting his face into the toilet bowl, the officer believed that Orenthal was going to get sick. At first, it was the sound of dry heaving, but Orenthal was actually eating the pile of human waste in the stainless steel bowl. What the officer believed were the sounds of Orenthal dry heaving was actually him eating so fast that he was choking. Like a starving dog eating canned wet food, Orenthal stood there on his hands and knees devouring his own feces and urine.

Horrified, the officer kicked the glass door and screamed, "Hey, hey! Don't eat that shit!" He picked up his two-way radio and said, "Sarge, I need you in observation immediately."

"Received. En route," the radio crackled back.

Two minutes later, as the sergeant and two other officers walked into observation, the officer was now puking into a garbage can wiping his mouth off with a paper towel. "What's the matter with you?" asked the Sergeant.

"He's eating his own shit," said the officer, holding onto the rim of the garbage can with both hands, nodding his head in the direction of Orenthal and then dry heaving. "Out of the toilet bowl," he continued, dry heaving again loudly over the can.

Surprised, the sergeant and the other officers walked over to the cell, and observed Orenthal, like a dog, eating and licking the toilet bowl clean…

"Oh, my god. That's fucking disgusting," commented the sergeant.

The officer, wiping his face, stumbled towards the cell with tears in his eyes from vomiting so hard. "He poured his puffed rice on his shit, and then he sat licking the window. Then he crawled over to the toilet and ate his own shit," he said walking quickly back to the garbage can again, dry heaving.

"What a fucking animal," said the other officer.

"And, sarge, the toilet was full of shit and piss."

"Stop," said the sergeant, "or I am going to puke." He stood there disgusted. "I don't know what to do," he said, kicking the cell. "Orenthal, stop eating your own shit! You're going to make yourself sick!" He looked away so as not to hurl at the sight.

Just like a rabid hog, Orenthal continued to eat and lick the shit out of the toilet bowl. He even ate chunks of the roll of toilet paper that he threw into the toilet bowl earlier. He ate the human stew until even the wet cardboard roll was gone.

"Working fifteen years in corrections, I have seen a lot of things," said the sergeant. "But I have never seen a man eat his own shit."

Picking up the phone, the Sergeant said, "Yeah, nurse, I am going to need to see you in observation immediately, please."

Ten minutes later, when the nurse arrived at Orenthal's cell, the entire stainless steel toilet bowl was completely licked clean—inside and out—and Orenthal was now lying on his bunk, on his back, sleeping with a look of satisfaction on his face, snoring loudly.

Orenthal looked as if he had gravy and oatmeal caked on his mouth and chin. The nurse refused to believe that he had just eaten his own fecal matter. "Is it safe?" asked the sergeant.

"No, you're not supposed to eat your own shit," said the nurse. "But more disgusting," she continued, "is to consider how many people must have used that toilet in the past month."

The entire group of people stood there completely grossed out. "What an animal," said the nurse. "Well, he looks okay to me. He's sleeping like a newborn baby with a full tummy," she said, shaking her head. "Let me know if he wakes up, and I will see him then," she said, walking out of the observation room.

From that point forward, Orenthal slept for an entire twenty-four hours straight. He had finally crashed after eating so much. The officers didn't have to keep an eye on him because his mouth was wide open and his snorts and grunts were loud beyond belief.

When he finally woke up, it was like a whole new world. Looking around the cell and out of the cracked glass, Orenthal knew exactly where he was, but he had no idea what he did to get there. "Hello," he announced. "Officer, why am I here?"

"I don't know," said the disinterested officer. "I think assault."

"What day is it?"

"It's Monday morning."

Standing up and walking towards the front of the cell, Orenthal asked, "Can I call my attorney?"

"Do you have his number?" asked the officer.

"No. Call my wife," said Orenthal.

"Give me her number," he said.

The officer tried the number multiple times, but there was no answer. "Sorry, Mr. James. There was no answer. Your wife is not there."

"Keep trying her," said Orenthal desperately.

For the next two hours, they tried calling every number for Orenthal's wife over and over, every five minutes. "Sorry, Mr. James. Your wife is just not there."

"Do I have bail?"

"Yeah, ten-thousand dollars" said the officer.

"If you check my pants pocket I got credit cards, and cash," he said convincingly.

Looking up at Orenthal, the officer could see a brown dried circle surrounding his lips, nose and chin and all over his hands. "Sorry, Mr. James. You had no money on you when you got here."

"That's impossible. I have more money than god," he replied. "Try my attorney again," he ordered. "This is bullshit; I will not be treated like an animal."

As the officer was trying the lawyer's phone number again, Orenthal said, "I am starving. Can I get something to eat?"

"Sure. Do you want some puffed rice?" asked the officer, half smiling and half gagging.

"Sure, I'll eat puffed rice. I'll eat anything," he said desperately.

"That's for sure," said the officer as he pushed two packs of puffed rice cereal under the cell door.

"Hey, buddy, do you got any milk?"

"Nope," said the officer. "You're going to have to eat them dry."

Tearing open the packs of puffed rice, Orenthal was forcing them with his hand into his mouth. "Hey officer, this cell is filthy, can you move me to another?"

"Nope."

"C'mon! Why aint my toilet flushing?"

"Long story," said the officer, shaking his head in disbelief. "Do you remember what you ate yesterday?" he asked Orenthal.

"No. Why?" asked Orenthal, concerned.

"Just wondering," said the officer, turning his head back to his newspaper. Shaking his head, the officer spared Orenthal the embarrassing details of his past twenty-four hours. He thought to himself how humiliating it would be to anybody if they knew that they had been caught on video eating their own shit.

"Sometimes, when I get really bad, I do things I don't remember," said Orenthal. "And then when people tell me what I did, I still can't remember," he said proudly. "Momentary lapse of memory, they call it." He smiled at the officer. "Hell, I could kill a whole room full of people, and probably wouldn't remember a thing about it," he continued speaking to the officer, who appeared not to be listening. "At least that would be my story, and I'm sticking to it," he said, winking his right eye and smiling, amused.

Walking over to the stainless steel mirror attached above the commode, Orenthal said, "Hey, buddy, can I get a toothbrush? And toothpaste? My mouth tastes like somebody took a shit in it."

The officer laughed to himself while reading the newspaper and said "Really, Mr. James? Well that's not too far from the truth."

45 Minutes Later

When Orenthal's attorney finally walked into the observation area, Orenthal announced loudly, "Well, it's about time!"

"Hey, Orenthal. I got here as soon as I heard."

"Get me out of here," Orenthal said in desperation. The door to his observation cell began to open.

Walking over to shake his attorney's hand, Orenthal said, "You sho' is a sight for sow' eyes."

Not wanting to offend his high-profile client, the attorney extended his hand as a simple courtesy. He then noticed that Orenthal had a dried crust all over his face, hair, and hands.

"What the hell happened to you, Orenthal? What is all over your hands and your face and in your hair?"

Looking down at his hands, Orenthal said, "Oh, I don't know. I don't remember anything."

"Jesus Christ, Orenthal! You're covered in shit! It's all over you! What happened? Why didn't you call me sooner? I would have come immediately," the attorney asked Orenthal.

"I tried to contact my wife all weekend and she did not answer the phone. I have no idea where she could be. It's almost as if she has fallen off the face of the earth."

Walking out of the secure section of the jail with his attorney, Orenthal said, "I don't know why the fuck nobody is answering at my house? I don't know where my wife is."

"Huh," said the attorney. "That's not like her is it?"

"No, I have no idea where she could be."

Let's get you out of here, Orenthal, before anybody else sees you in this condition."

"Yeah, take me home, I got to get cleaned up, look at me—*I am full of shit,"* he said shaking his head, smiling obliviously.

"You sure are," said his attorney. "You sure are."

## A Murder

Walking into his court ordered twelve-step drug and alcohol program, Orenthal was forty-five minutes late for the one hour meeting. Being a quasi-celebrity and all, Orenthal believed that he was above the law, and also believed that he was better than the nine other people who were also sentenced to this bi-weekly meeting.

"Mr. James, you are late again, but I am glad to see that you made it," said the drug counselor looking up at the clock on the wall, it was 8:45 P.M.

Sitting down, Orenthal tightened his lips and shook his head quickly, completely ignoring the woman's greeting.

"Is everything okay Orenthal?" the woman asked concernedly.

Sitting there without responding, Orenthal shook his head aggravated appearing that at any moment he could explode.

"Are you using?" the woman asked gently.

"No, I'm not using," Orenthal hollered, "and I'm not talking about it. I don't know how many times I gotta tell you people that I don't use drugs, and I rarely drink and drive. I'm not like you people. This program is not for me!"

"You know Orenthal, admitting that you have a—"

"Admitting what? That I'm a murderer?" Orenthal shouted, standing up quickly and inadvertently launching the folding metal chair that he was sitting on. "Is that what everybody comes to this meeting for? Hoping to hear me confess that I am a murderer? Well I'm not going to say it," Orenthal said to the confused group.

"Mr. James," the counselor said appalled, "I am very concerned for your mental health. You have been acting very—"

"Bla, bla, bla," said Orenthal walking towards the exit and then kicking the door open, "I have heard enough booshit from you for one night lady. I'm outta here."

"Well, I hope your not driving," the counselor said indignantly.

The group of people sat there and appeared disgusted with what they had just witnessed. "What an asshole," one of the ladies in the group said.

"Well, I am very sorry for that," said the counselor, "I will contact the court and tell them that he is no longer welcome in this program."

Getting back to where they had left off before the interruption, the group was about to wrap up their meeting when one of the women let out a horrifying scream while pointing towards the window.

"What?" asked the counselor.

"He's staring in the window!"

"Oh my god!" another woman screamed.

Focusing their eyes out into the darkness, they could see the eeriest shadow of a dark face staring into the window at them.

"What the fuck is wrong with that asshole?" one of the men in the group asked.

"Entitlement schema," the counselor answered matter-of-factly, standing up and walking over towards the window, opening it slowly. "Why are you sitting out here Orenthal?" she asked.

Orenthal just sat there catatonic; not moving a muscle, not blinking. His apparent state of mind made the drug counselor fear for the lives of everyone in the room.

Closing the window slowly, the counselor whispered urgently, "Somebody call 911," as she walked back towards her seat where she fumbled nervously in her pocketbook looking for her keys so that she could lock the door. "He's lost his mind."

Walking quickly towards the door the counselor panicked when one of the women in the classroom screamed, "He's not at the window anymore!"

Trying to put the key in the lock, the counselors hands were shaking and she dropped the keys to the floor. As she bent over to pick them up, the door swung open wildly. Everyone in the room acted in disbelief at the sight of Orenthal standing there; with his nostrils flared, eyes wide open with rage, and foam coming out of his mouth.

Grabbing the counselor by her hair and dragging her outside, Orenthal snatched the terrified woman up and carried her quickly to his vehicle as she screamed and flailed her arms and legs, trying to fight off her abductor. No one in the group could believe their eyes as they watched the scene unfold before them.

Throwing the woman into the back seat of his SUV and slamming the door, the woman begged Orenthal to let her go. It was as if Orenthal was on autopilot as he got into the drivers seat and looked into his rear view mirror and smiled.

Trying desperately to open the back doors, the woman realized that the child safety locks were on, disabling her escape. Slapping and punching the windows desperately, the woman begged for her life as Orenthal pushed his foot on the accelerator and said in a mocking voice, "Put your safety belt on!"

Screeching the tires out of the parking lot and onto the main road, Orenthal laughed demonically and said, "How am I doing boss?" as he sped up the exit ramp of the thruway, heading in the wrong direction.

"Orenthal…Please, you're heading in the wrong direction," the woman cried. "Please slow down… I'm begging you!"

"It's not going to hurt," Orenthal said, "I promise," flooring the accelerator and swerving dangerously to avoid a vehicle that was coming straight at them. "Did you ever play chicken with a tractor trailer?" Orenthal asked.

The headlights of a tractor trailer were approaching them head-on, as the woman in the back seat screamed in terror. Swerving at the last second to avoid the truck, Orenthal slammed the breaks and lost control of the SUV crashing into a cement barrier, and then flipping the vehicle onto its side. The sounds of breaking glass and scraping steel were deafening as the SUV slid one-hundred and fifty yards before coming to a rest against the cement barrier.

Climbing out of the passenger window Orenthal could see that the woman in the backseat appeared to be unconscious, "How am I doing boss?" Orenthal taunted. "Did I do good?"

Jumping onto the thruway Orenthal was now standing like a madman in traffic swinging his arms violently at the vehicles as they passed by. Too afraid to stop, the vehicles accelerated when they got close enough to see the expression on Orenthal's face.

Arriving on the scene of the accident in a marked police car, Officer Taddler was unaware of the abduction that had taken place, but realized quickly enough that Orenthal was is a psychotic rage. The officer got out of his car and cautiously approached Orenthal, asking, "Are you okay, sir?" Orenthal turned his back on the officer and stood there without moving. "Sir, are you okay?" Maintaining a safe distance from Orenthal, the officer stepped around him to better assess the situation.

Now turning his head slowly towards the officer in a fit of rage with blood in his eyes, he roared, "Does it look like I'm okay, asshole?" Orenthal charged towards the officer, trying to get his gun.

Backing away quickly, the officer grabbed a can of pepper spray from his belt and doused Orenthal with the bright orange solution, but it seemed to have absolutely no effect on him. Coughing, Orenthal continued to charge towards the officer like a bull. The officer took cover behind his vehicle and spun around quickly to warn Orenthal, "Stop, or I will shoot you!"

This wasn't quite an empty threat: the officer was actually holding an electric stun gun. Orenthal, with blatant disregard for the law and his safety, charged closer. The officer pulled the trigger, sending two lines with hooks into the direction of the charging beast. The first hook attached itself to Orenthal's left shoulder and the other hook snagged Orenthal's chest, center mass. The electric current dropped Orenthal like a ton. He flopped like a fish on the ground in a puddle of antifreeze that had gathered from the crash. Fearing for his life, the officer activated multiple charges from the tazer.

There was now a traffic jam that went on as far as the eye could see. People were standing outside of their cars and watching the scene as it unfolded. The officer now had the opportunity to call on his portable radio, "Dispatch, this is 032, Officer Taddler. Be advised, I am out on Pembrook and Fifth. Code-one! Code-one!"

Code-one is police terminology for officer needs help. "I have a large male, 255 pounds. Stun gun activated. Call EMS," he said franticly into his radio. "I need back-up!"

"Dispatch received, 032. Units' enroute. Be advised 032, fits the description of the suspect wanted for the abduction of a woman that was reported less than five minutes ago. Should be considered armed and dangerous," the radio crackled back.

As the officer stood over the drooling monster, he activated a series of shocks into the beast, which goes against all protocol. The officer did not want to take the chance that Orenthal regained consciousness until back up arrived. Orenthal was foaming from the mouth, his eyes were rolled up into the back of his head, and his snorts were loud and hollow, seeming to indicate troubled breathing.

As the first back up officer arrived, his knee landed heavily on Orenthal's back and neck, stopping the blood flow into his brain. Officer Taddler again activated a series of shocks into Orenthal as he lay flopping uncontrollably on the pavement.

As the next officer arrived on the scene, he pulled the trigger to a second stun gun, believing that Orenthal was resisting arrest, as another officer piled onto Orenthal's overloaded body.

Using leg shackles for Orenthal's arms and legs, the officers' hog tied him into submission, and continued to trigger both tazers'.

Orenthal's eyes were glazed over and red as he laid there motionless. One officer, holding a nightstick stood over Orenthal, hoping to be given the opportunity to strike him if he moved. Orenthal let out a gasp of air so powerful it moved the gravel from under his flaring nostrils. This was enough to relieve the nervous officers.

As paramedics arrived on the scene, they were tending to the counselor who had been abducted. She was hysterical as she described the attack. Nearly five minutes had passed as the officers were assessing the situation.

"He's not breathing!" one officer announced nervously trying to feel for a pulse in Orenthal's carotid artery, "No pulse! We need to unshackle him!"

Hesitant, to remove the shackles, the officers knew it was now a matter of life and death as they scrambled to un-cuff the hog tied Orenthal.

Rolling his lifeless corpse onto his back, the officers made room for the paramedics who worked cautiously as they were attaching electrodes to Orenthal's chest. "He's flat lined," one paramedic screamed. "We need the paddles!" A rush of emergency medical personnel now surrounded Orenthal's lifeless body.

Loading Orenthal into the ambulance, you could hear the crew working furiously to bring Orenthal back to life, "Clear!" they screamed multiple times, sending another series of shocks into Orenthal's body.

When they arrived at the hospital, they pulled the stretcher out of the ambulance slowly. One paramedic announced to the ER staff, "We have a DOA."

As they slowly pushed the corpse down the hallway towards the ER, "Yeah, the patient was involved in a serious automobile accident, and was tazered repeatedly by the police department. We did all we could do for this patient.

An attendant at the hospital asked innocently, "They electrocuted him?"

"Yeah, they juiced him when he was hogtied and pepper sprayed. He never had a chance."

12 Hours Later

Walking into the morgue at the local hospital, the Sheriff and two of his deputies met with the county coroner to investigate the death of the infamous Orenthal James. After a series of introductions, the sheriff asked the coroner, "Well, John, I am sure you're terribly busy, so we will only be a minute. Now, off the record, between us, what is the cause of this man's death?"

Understanding the Sheriff's approach, the coroner, shaking his head in disappointment, said, "Well, I am going to have to say that multiple unnecessary blasts from the stun guns were definitely a factor and probably the direct cause of this man's death."

The Sheriff, standing back with his arms crossed and looking concerned, said, "Yeah, well, doctor, that kind of talk is definitely not going to work in the best interest of this county. I don't have to explain to you that both of our positions are political in nature, and let's just say that we should work together on this one." He nodded his head confidently at the coroner and smiled. "So, is there any other diagnosis for this man's death?" he asked the coroner seriously.

"Well, of course, Sheriff," the coroner said walking around the corpse with his arms crossed holding his left hand to his chin. "If I am correct, this man was involved in a pretty serious car accident. That, added with the amount of drugs found in his system, would prompt me to list the cause of death as…" he said looking upwards as if searching for the answer, "disseminated intravascular coagulation; due to impact trauma, caused by the car accident, while in a hyper-excitable state, due to cocaine toxicity, causing cardiac arrest," he said, nodding his head confidently. "Anyone who wanted to argue with my findings would have to get a medical expert here to testify otherwise, and I don't think that that will happen under the circumstances."

"So my deputies are cleared of wrong doing?" asked the Sheriff.

"Sounds to me like natural causes, compounded by a series of events that no one could have predicted" said the coroner convinced.

"Yeah, that sounds more like it," said the Sheriff.

Addressing the deputies that had accompanied him; "Wrap up this investigation men, and get the corpse to the family. I want a report on my desk first thing in the morning."

"Thank you for your time, doctor," said the Sheriff as he and his staff walked towards the exit.

"My pleasure," responded the coroner as he covered-up the corpse with a white sheet, and then writing the words, "Natural Causes" as the official cause of death on the death certificate.

"My pleasure!"

# State Autopsy Report

County Coroner: Mitchell D. Heller

DEATH INVOLVING POLICE TAZER

Cause of Death of:

## Orenthal James-DECEASED
## FILE# 018642

CAUSE OF DEATH: Listed as disseminated intravascular coagulation due to blunt impact trauma while in a hyper-excitable state and cocaine toxicity.

"The application of the TASER was the trigger factor or the stressful event that caused the elevation of blood pressure, the elevation of heart rate which stressed an already damaged heart to the point that it went into cardiac arrest.

## DRUGS FOUND IN SYSTEM

Cocaine, Crack, Heroin, Marijuana, PCP's, Erectile Dysfunction Meds. Crystal Methamphetamine, ETOH,

NO-FAULT FOUND WITH STATE OR COUNTY AGENCIES
SEE ATTACHED

Page 2 of 3

# Birfday'

## A Hogtale

It was the afternoon of Orenthal's birthday, and still not one single person had called on him to wish him a happy birthday. Realizing that the possibility of someone throwing him a surprise birthday party was nearly zero, Orenthal took it upon himself to make some last minute plans.

Understanding that his popularity was dwindling more and more every year, Orenthal called as many people as he could and invited all of them to come and celebrate his birthday at a popular steakhouse. "C'mon, I got reservations to the greatest steakhouse in ten-states!" he bragged. "I would really love it if you could join me."

Orenthal told every person that he invited that dinner was going to be *on him.* He was buying, and if there was anything that anybody could do for him, it was to just show up for dinner, celebrate the meal, and have some drinks with him. Most people, after admitting that they had forgotten it was his birthday, agreed they would be there. Others refused to answer their phones or straight up lied to the infamous Orenthal James, regretting that they had had other plans.

Arriving alone at the front door of the well-known steak house at 5:15 P.M., Orenthal said to the hostess, "Yes, I have reservations here for fifteen people."

"Your name, sir?"

"James, Orenthal James," he lolled, using his tongue and sucking to remove something that was stuck in his teeth.

"No, sir. I'm sorry; we don't have a reservation for you. Who did you speak with?"

"I don't remember who I spoke with."

"Was it a man or a woman?"

"It was a woman," said Orenthal, pretending that he was just about to be furious.

"Well, let me see if I have a table for you," she said patiently, looking over a seating chart. "No, I am sorry, Mr. James; we are just too busy tonight."

"Well, you had better get the manager out here 'cuz this aint my problem," Orenthal said indignantly, "I got's fifteen peeple's headed here, and I don't need this *agga-ravation.* Not on my birfday."

"Yes, sir," said the woman, walking away nervously. "I will see what I can do for you."

A few moments later, the manager appeared and did not seem at all impressed. "Hello, Mr. James," he said curtly, "I'm sorry. When did you make your reservations?" he asked, shaking his head with his eyes closed.

"Ummm," Orenthal hesitated, looking up and then to the left. "Thursday—last Thursday. Or Wednesday. I can't remember," he lied.

"What name did you use to make this reservation?"

"Well, I believes I used Orenthal, Orenthal James," he said nodding in affirmation like a child who had just been asked his name.

"Well, Mr. James," began the manager, looking confused and doubtful, "I can tell you that we have been turning away reservations for the entire month of July for over a month now. Are you sure that you got the right restaurant?"

"Am I sure? Are you kidding me?" He changed tactics, trying to use flattery: "This is the greatest steakhouse in town! Where else would I have made reservations for my birfday?"

"Sorry, sir, but we don't have it," the manager said unsympathetically.

"It must have been one of the young kids that took my reservation," Orenthal suggested, leaving room for reasonable suspicion.

"No, sir. We have a strict reservation policy, and any reservations over eight people must be approved by me personally and nobody else. Are you sure that this is the right restaurant? Are you sure you have the right date?"

"Yes, I am sure," he said impatiently, "I know my birfdate! What am I going to do now? This is just great," he said, huffing in circles and throwing his arms up in apparent distress. Orenthal thought that if he appeared to be greatly affronted at the mix-up, that they would make an exception.

"Let me see what I can do, Mr. James. I will speak to the chef and ask him if he will make an exception." The manager turned and quickly walked away.

"Yeah, do dat! Tell 'em it's my birfday," Orenthal called after him, smiling like a victim.

Returning almost immediately, the manager said unsympathetically, "Mr. James, I am very sorry, but I am going to have to tell you no. We did not have a reservation for you this evening. I am sorry, you're going to have to take your party elsewhere. We're not serving you here."

Amazed, Orenthal said, "Did you talk to the chef? What did he say?"

"I talked to the owner," the manager said, "and he told me to tell you to… beat it!"

"Beat it?" repeated Orenthal flabbergasted. His eyes were wide open in disbelief.

"Yeah… Beat feet!... Keep it moving!... Get lost!... Whatever it is you want to call it. We're not serving you," said the manager plainly. "I was trying to be nice! But now, if you will—make like a murder charge, and *beat it,*" the manager said unsympathetically, turning his attention away from the slighted has-been.

Acting like he had not heard the manager, Orenthal continued slowly "Where, do you sah'pose…I beat it to… At this hour? I have people meeting me here in fifteen minutes!" whimpered Orenthal, genuinely concerned.

"Not my problem, buddy, but I don't have any more time to waste on you. Perhaps the commercial chain next door? They have decent food, and I am sure that they can accommodate your party of fifteen without a reservation."

"Wow, this is some shit on my birfday," cussed Orenthal as his son and his son's girlfriend walked into the restaurant. "Wait right here, son. We're going to move our party over to the next restaurant. These people say they don't *serve* our kind here," Orenthal said, trying unsuccessfully to insight some sort of racial overtone.

"What?" asked Orenthal's son, laughing? "I was here the other night with a large party, me and her and a bunch of our friends; you just got to make sure you have reservations. They have a strict policy."

"Wait right here. They're not serving us."

"Here we go—always a controversy wherever we go," said Orenthal's son disgusted. "And you wonder why nobody wants to go out with you. It's too much work, and… it get's old," he said, shaking his head sadly.

"Just wait right here," said Orenthal. "If anybody else comes, tell them that they are refusing to serve us here and that we are going to move the party next door."

Sweating, Orenthal ran out the door and hopped over a tall wooden fence to the restaurant next door. Walking up to the young girl at the hostess station, Orenthal passed right by an elderly couple that were waiting patiently to be seated. Orenthal interrupted, "I need to see the manager!"

"Here we go," said the young lady cynically. "What seems to be the problem?" she asked, ignoring his demand about the manager completely.

Orenthal rolled his eyes, attempting to explain: "Yeah, this place next door!" he whined, pointing with his fat index finger. "I had reservations for *fifteen* people to eat on my birfday and they messed up the *whole shabang*. They got the wrong day or something… Anyways, can we move the party here?" asked Orenthal in distress.

"Sure, that should be no problem," said the manager pointing. "I will push those three tables together, and we should be able to fit all fifteen people right there."

"Okay, great," said Orenthal, relieved. Just then, his mother was walking in the front door.

"Hey, Momma! It's over here now. We's gotta eat here tonight."

Her disappointment was evident. "I heard. Why? What happened to the restaurant?" she asked curiously shaking her head. "You know they won't serve anybody without a reservation, Orenthal."

"I made reservations!" Orenthal lied, acting as if he were scandalized. "They said they didn't get my reservations! They screwed it up somehow. Can you believe they did this to me on my birfday?" He leaned down so that his mother could kiss him on the cheek.

"Oh, Orenthal," she said, shaking her head sadly. "Happy birthday. Say birthday, will you please."

"Oh, Momma, let me help you," he said, walking her over to the table. "Hey, Momma, I hate to ask you this, but how much money do you got on you?"

Startled, pulling her head back and losing her smile, she said, "Why, Orenthal?"

"Because, you knows how it is, momma.... I got caught a little short this week, and I's got a bunch of friends coming, and I told them I will buy dinner tonight, and I need a little cash. *Jus' till next week*. I'll pay you back, I promise"

Shaking her head in disgust and opening her wallet, Mrs. James said, "Oh, Orenthal, I wouldn't have come if I knew you couldn't have afforded it. How much do you need?"

"How much you got?" he asked, biting down hard on his tongue.

"I got a few hundred," she sighed, pulling out a stack of hundred dollar bills.

"That's my girl!" said Orenthal. "I'll take eight hundred."

"That's all I got, Orenthal! I need some money 'til I get my check!" she said, begging for mercy.

"This is jus 'til next week, momma," he said, taking all the money out of her hand.

Mrs. James stood there shaking her head, nauseated, as if she had just been clobbered by a stranger. "I ought to just go home," she said frustrated. "This is ridiculous."

"Don't you want to be with your son on his birfday, Momma?"

"It's birthday, Orenthal, and no, I wouldn't have come if I knew I was going to get hijacked!" she fumed, smiling at the sight of her grandson walking towards them with a group of people.

It was now 6:15 P.M., and there were only nine people sitting there. Orenthal said, "Thank you. It is good to be surrounded by friends and family. When everybody gets here, we will order, and I want you to order anything you want, drinks included. I am paying for it all," he said, refusing to look his mother in the eye. He knew she was furious.

"I will call the other folks and see if they are on their way."

At 6:45, Orenthal looked at his watch concernedly. "Well, we can order some appetizers while we're waiting."

The two chipper waitresses were glad to finally take an order. "Is the rest of your party going to be here?" one of them asked.

"Well, I don't know. They should be. I don't know what happened. They were sup-posed to be here at 5:30. We can order," said Orenthal, disappointed.

Talking to himself out loud, Orenthal said, "Peoples be standing me up on my birfday. That aint right," he declared to no one listening.

No one else had shown up by 7:45, and everyone else was finally eating their dinner. The waitress walked up to Orenthal and asked, "Is there anything else we can get you folks tonight?"

Everyone at the table was chatting and enjoying small talk and seemed for the most part to be un-wanting.

"Well, I could go for another drink," said Orenthal. "Anybody else want a drink?" Orenthal asked excitedly.

No one responded.

"Yeah, everybody get another drink, and we will toast to me!" Orenthal suggested desperately.

Looking at his mother Orenthal asked, "You want another drink momma?"

"No, thank you," she said, unimpressed by his generosity.

Just then, a crowd of employees came out and surrounded the table, singing "Happy Birthday." One girl was holding a small birthday cake with a sparkler lit on top of it. *"Happy birthday, dear Orenthal. Happy birthday to you!"*

Orenthal sat there holding his chest as if he were holding back raw emotion. "Thank you all! Thank you all for being here for me tonight. And let's give my momma a great big round of applause for giving birth to me!" he cheered. Everyone clapped awkwardly.

"Thank you, Orenthal," said his mother, offering a diplomatic smile. "This was very nice."

Orenthal's mother was a woman of principle and class. There was no way that she was going to be anything but gracious, knowing that she was involuntarily paying for Orenthal's dinner and then some. She would have paid for the dinner happily, without question, but she allowed her son to give the rest of the world the impression that he was some sort of big shot. In reality, Orenthal was an opportunist, a fraud, always looking for a hand out. His mother knew that he was no good, but there was nothing she could do about it but smile gracefully.

Taking a sip out of his gin and tonic, Orenthal realized that there was something floating in his drink… "What the fu—?"

"What is that?" asked Orenthal's niece.

"It looks like a spider," said Orenthal. "It better be a gag for my birfday."

Taking a spoon and pulling a black, lifeless, real spider out of his drink, the whole table shuttered at the thought, as they all checked their drinks for bugs, pushing them away.

Orenthal turned and flagged down one of the waitresses. "Honey! You got to send me the manager! I got a poisonous spider in my drink!"

Looking around as if it was his lucky day, Orenthal said, "I ought to call the Department of Health! I have never seen this before."

Walking out and looking surprised at the find, the manager said, "Oh, wow! It's a spider. It was probably in the limes. I am so sorry, Mr. James," he continued flatly. "I will get you another one on the house." He reached forward to grab the glass off of the table.

"Whoa! Not so fast, buddy," said Orenthal. "I drank out of that, and I think I'm going to have the health department look into it," he said seriously. "I don't want to die of no *e-cole-eye* poisoning or anything."

"Mr. James," said the manager reassuredly, "I can assure you that the alcohol in the drink would have killed any bacteria. I am really sorry," said the manager reasonably.

"Well, that's okay," said Orenthal. We were having a nice meal 'til this happened. I think I am going to take the spider and the glass and turn them over to the Department of Health, unless there is something you can do for us right away."

It became apparent to everyone at the table what Orenthal was angling for.

"Okay, Mr. James. We will take the drinks off of the tab, how does that sound?"

"The drinks!" said Orenthal incensed. "We got people walking by laughing at us, and you want to take the drinks off the tab? You had better do a lot more than that!" he demanded in a violent tone. It was now apparent that Orenthal had had a few drinks.

Now, everybody at the table was incredibly embarrassed about the whole situation. Everyone agreed that the spider in the drink was definitely a minor set back for the evening, but no one other than Orenthal believed it was anybody's fault.

"If you will excuse me a moment," said the manager patiently, "I will be right back." He walked away towards the back of the restaurant. Unbeknownst to the manger, Orenthal had gotten up from the table and followed him across the room.

Pushing the swinging door open and walking into the kitchen area, the manager began to complain about Orenthal to the other staff, unaware that Orenthal had followed him and was standing outside of the door within earshot of the manager's voice.

"Like I give a fuck! This fucking *buffoon* thinks that I am going to give him more than a free drink because he found a bug in his cocktail!"

Finding the leverage he was looking for, Orenthal pushed the swinging door open and announced his presence by demanding, "Did you just call me a *baboon?"*

Spinning in a complete circle, the manager defensively responded, "No!" in complete shock. "I am not talking about you, Mr. James," he lied.

"Then who the fuck is you talkin bout'?" Orenthal asked furiously.

"Mr. James," said the horrified manager, "I was talking about something else completely. Not you."

"Yeah, tell that story to my lawyer," said Orenthal pointing at him. "I heard it with my own two ears. And if you think I came here on my birfday to be insulted by you, and have you loading our drinks with bugs, then you got another thing coming!" Orenthal turned his back to walk out of the kitchen, threatening, "This shit will be hitting the papers by tomorrow, and I will own this place."

Knowing the magnitude of the situation, the manager almost lost consciousness for a split second. Shaking his head, he shrieked, "No! Mr. James! I am sorry! It is not what you think—I never meant to—"

Turning to face the accused, Orenthal asked, "You never meant to what: put a spider in my drink or call me a *monkey*?"

"No, no! I never said that! Mr. James, please understand."

"No," said Orenthal, speaking loudly enough for other patrons to hear. "You understand this: We're leaving and I am calling my attorneys, and the health department. This is some boo-shit!"

"Mr. James, I am so sorry if I offended you," offered the manager sincerely. "I will comp the whole bill, everything, drinks included. If you please, just allow me to settle this informally to your satisfaction. Please give me a chance to make this right by you and your family, Mr. James," begged the manager, completely at Orenthal's mercy.

"Now you're speakin' my language!" replied Orenthal confidently.

The manager continued to plead: "I never meant to offend you, sir, and I am sorry if I did. I will comp the entire bill."

Turning towards the manager as if he had rehearsed this scene a hundred times, Orenthal said, "Well, then I want you to go out there, and apologize to my family for making a scene. And I want you to see if there is anything else that they want. And then, we're leaving. And I will go home and think about this siti-ation. But if we get anything other than superfluous service, from this point forward, I will blow this place right off the fucking map—me, and my lawyers. Are we clear?"

"Yes, sir," said the manager, following Orenthal back to the table.

"Okay, folks. I am so sorry for the little problem we had there. Does anybody else need anything?" the manager asked the table nervously.

Everyone sat there stunned, wondering what had just transpired in the back room. "Can I get anybody else a drink?—Mr. James, how about you?"

"I will have a scotch on the rocks," Orenthal said arrogantly, "and bring the rest of the table another round," he said smiling, reaching for a menu. "And hold the bugs," he said with a snigger.

"We's gonna eat good tonight!" Orenthal announced to the table.

Everyone seemed a bit confused because they had already eaten their food. What could Orenthal be talking about?

"We's eating good tonight!" he repeated. "Take a look at the menu again everybody, and see if there's anything else you'd like to order. We's eating good tonight!"

"Orenthal, what did he say?" asked his mother.

"He called me a monkey momma!"

"Oh… Orenthal, don't be ridiculous," she said. "Did you pay the bill?" she asked.

"Don't worry about the bill, Momma. I gots it under control. It's my birfday."

"Orenthal, that spider was nobody's fault," said his mother, clearly embarrassed on her son's behalf. "It was probably in with the limes like he said. It was an accident! This was in no way a malicious act. I hope you didn't make him take anything other than that drink off of the tab, Orenthal; otherwise, you are acting foolishly."

"Nope, Momma. I said, I's got it under control. Now let me handles it."

The two waitresses came over to the table, appearing overly hospitable and they handed out another round of drinks on the house. "Can I get anybody more drinks or food? No?"

"Yeah, put in another order of nachos," Orenthal ordered. "They was good. And I will take a chicken Caesar salad to go," said Orenthal. "Make it two chicken Caesar salads—they're small—to go, and I'll take another scotch on the rocks."

Everyone sitting at the table was clearly uncomfortable with what was happening. It appeared that Orenthal was intoxicated and that he was losing his rationale.

A few minutes later, the manager came out with the to-go orders wrapped in a large bag. "Okay, Mr. James. Here are your to-go orders, and here is your bill," he said, winking at him nervously.

Looking at the itemized bill, Orenthal went cross-eyed when he saw a total of $376.85 at the bottom of the receipt. Focusing, he then noticed the words underneath the total: COMP MEAL, NO CHARGE.

Leaning in, the manager said, "And, of course, you got the twenty percent gratuity to add to that, if you will, for the girls," the manager quietly pleaded on behalf of his employees, looking over his glasses into Orenthal's eyes.

Hiding the bill from the rest of the table, Orenthal said, "Don't worry about this here bill. I got it. If you guys want to get going, that's fine by me. I am just glad I could be with you all tonight for my birfday dinner. Does anybody else need anything? Coffee? Anything?"

Everyone just sat there shaking their heads in disbelief before getting up from the table and wishing Orenthal a good night.

At 8:30 P.M., Orenthal was polishing off his fifth scotch. Orenthal's daughter came up and kissed him on the cheek. "Good night, Daddy. Did you like the leather driving gloves that I got you?"

"Yes, honey. I think they were a little small."

"They were the biggest ones they had, Daddy."

"They'll work just fine, honey. They'll work just fine. Thank you!"

"Good night, Grandma," said his daughter, walking over to give her grandmother a hug and a kiss goodnight.

After her, the only people left at the table were Orenthal and his mother.

"Well, this was very nice, Orenthal. How much was the bill?"

"It's all set, momma."

"Orenthal, if they comped the bill, I want to know because I will not leave 'til every red cent is paid."

"Momma, I got it."

Orenthal's mother grabbed the attention of the manager as he walked by. "Excuse me, sir. Was that bill comped?" she asked concernedly.

"Momma! I said I got it!" squeaked Orenthal.

"Yes, miss. We took care of everything except the gratuity."

Appalled, the mother cried, "Orenthal! This is not acceptable! You need to pay the bill."

"Oh, no, Misses James. It is all set. I insist," the manager said sincerely.

"No, it's not all set. And it's definitely not acceptable!" crowed Orenthal's mother. "Too many freeloaders try to take advantage of social fear, and I won't allow it!" she declared. "Not on my watch! My boy was raised better than that," she announced, standing up.

"Momma! Let me walk you to your car," Orenthal said, devoid of any sincerity.

"No, Orenthal," she fumed. "Are you afraid I might get mugged?" she asked sarcastically.

"The streets are full of undesirables, Momma," Orenthal said honestly.

"As long as you're sitting here, Orenthal, I think I'll be alright," she sneered. Her sarcasm again went undetected.

Knowing that she would never see the eight hundred dollars that she had given Orenthal returned, she decided that she was going to do him a favor so that he didn't think that he was getting away with anything.

"Orenthal," she said graciously, "I want you to take the money that I gave you tonight, and pay the dinner bill, and be sure to leave a nice tip. And then, I want you to take the rest of the money and consider it a birthday present," she said smiling.

"I will, Momma; I will!" he wheezed like a scolded boy. "Thank you, Momma!"

As Misses James walked out of the restaurant into the parking lot, she must have been furious, but any passerby would have never guessed it. She wasn't so much mad because Orenthal had taken the eight hundred dollars from her, but she was incensed knowing that he would most likely leave the restaurant without paying the bill.

Back at the table, Orenthal was sitting with one of the young waitresses who had just brought him another scotch on the rocks. Opening the to-go order, Orenthal picked the chicken strips off of the first Caesar salad with his hands, eating them as if he were a primate. Pushing the lettuce aside, Orenthal opened up the second salad and picked just the chicken strips off again, devouring them like a mandrill eating grapes, discarding the vegetables as if it were just garnish for the chicken. Orenthal did not know that the Caesar salad dressing was dripping from his chin. The scene was one of absolute disgust.

Singing to himself as the waitress counted her tips, Orenthal looked like a sociopath as he stared straight ahead with gray eyes, stirring the ice in his drink.

*"Happy birfday to me. Happy birfday to me… Happy birf-day… Happy birfday, Happy birfday to me!"*

Chugging his scotch in one gulp, Orenthal reached into his wallet and pulled out a hundred-dollar bill and asked the waitress for change.

Placing a single twenty-dollar bill into the leather bill folder, Orenthal got up and headed towards the door. Stopping at the hostess station, the manager was standing there to wish Orenthal a good evening, "You have a good night now sir," he said smiling.

Pointing pompously towards the manager, Orenthal said, "You ought to be glad I was raised the way I was, or we would have had big problems here tonight." Hiccupping and burping at the same time, Orenthal finished, "It's a good thing I got some class."

Stumbling out the door, Orenthal walked towards his SUV. The manager knew it was his responsibility to not let Orenthal drive home drunk, but he couldn't find the heart to stop him.

Orenthal decided that he should head home early tonight to try and get some sleep. He has not been sleeping well at all. It seems that lately his dreams have been haunting him.

# Hog Hanging'

## A Suicide

Walking out onto the balcony of his hotel room, Orenthal knew that this would be the last night of his life. His despair had reached such a personal low: He was a fraud in every way possible, and he knew that he could not possibly go on. Not even the twenty-four hour sports network could distract him any longer from his failures. Looking longingly down, he estimated that it was about a one-hundred and forty foot drop to the cement patio below.

Orenthal was out of money and out of friends and had not worked a solid job in many years. The only lucrative occupation that he had had in ten years had been that of a professional victim. He sued anyone and anything that he could as a means of survival. Years of this tactic bred contempt in everyone including his lawyers.

A man of despicable means, Orenthal welshed on every bet he ever made. He always demanded more and gave less in every aspect of his disgraceful existence.

Orenthal had nowhere to turn. Earlier in the day, he had visited his estranged sister and told her that he was having some serious financial problems. Wishing him luck, she sent him on his way with two-hundred dollars in food stamps.

Sitting on the bed of the hotel room, Orenthal had cashed in his bonus points to pay for the room for the evening. If only he had the courage to stand on the rail of the balcony and jump to his death, he thought to himself, all of his misery would be over.

But he couldn't just walk out of this world a failure, a loser, a lost cause. He began to scheme how he would stage his own murder. This would allow his family to sue the hotel chain for money, and he could leave the world knowing that he was forever a victim.

As Orenthal lay there contemplating suicide, he called every person that he could think of in hopes that he could find a reason to live. In all, Orenthal had made seventeen calls to people who he considered to be his friends or close family members, and not one person answered his call. Was this a sign? he thought to himself. Running out of names and people to call, Orenthal sat there waiting for someone, anyone, to call him back.

Acting on his gut instinct, Orenthal knew what he had to do. Leaving a frantic message on his best friend's cell phone was the beginning of the end for Orenthal. He was about to leave his first clue for the detectives who he knew would eventually investigate his death.

"Hey, Ace. It's me, Orenthal. I am in big trouble, man," Orenthal bellowed into the phone with urgency. "I have people after me who say they are going to kill me. You need to call me back… right away. I need a ride out of town or a place to hide. If anything should happen to me, please tell my family that I love them…"

Closing the face to his flip cell phone, Orenthal knew that he had to begin to prepare the final scenes of his life by staging his faux murder. Standing up, Orenthal tore the shirt off of his back, blasting the buttons across the room.

Flipping the mattress off of the bed, Orenthal broke the lamp on the nightstand, sending the clock radio crashing onto the floor. Pushing the television off of the dresser, Orenthal was surprised that it was still working, tuned to the twenty-four-hour sports network; it was now on its side on the floor.

Sitting on the box spring, Orenthal took a razor penknife out of his pants pocket and began to cut himself on his hands. In his mind, these superficial wounds would prove to investigators that Orenthal tried to fight off his attackers. Taking the razor blade to his chest, Orenthal began to carefully cut the letters D, I, E, O, and J. These wounds would prove to the world, or at least leave room for reasonable doubt, that he had been the victim of a murder and probably a hate crime.

Running on pure adrenaline, Orenthal could not feel a thing as he was mutilating himself, but the smell of his own blood was making him high. Taking the penknife, Orenthal slowly pushed the sharp blade deep into his stomach until he began to feel a burning sensation. Pushing down hard, he pulled the razor out of his abdomen, leaving a five-inch diagonal slash.

Covered in blood, he stood up and began to destroy anything that he could in the room. The mirror on the wall next to the bed shattered into a hundred pieces when he punched it. Orenthal left a trail of bloody murder with every step that he took.

Walking into the bathroom, Orenthal tore the shower curtain down and used his hands to spread his bright red blood all over the tile floor, the sink, and the toilet. Looking at himself in the mirror, Orenthal did not recognize the monster that stared back at him. His face was pale and desperate. He placed his bloody palm onto the mirror and dragged it down to give the dramatic effect of a struggle. "Kill yourself," Orenthal repeated out loud as he stared into the mirror. This was the end for the infamous Orenthal James, and he was not proud of the man that he had become.

Orenthal went to the bedroom and pulled the phone cord out of the wall, throwing the phone across the room. He got on his hands and knees and then lay on his stomach and pulled himself forward on the rug, dragging himself towards the bed. Orenthal pulled the top sheet off the mattress that was flipped up on its side and pushed aside the large plush comforter. Taking the sheet from the bed, Orenthal finagled it craftily into what appeared to be a long narrow rope. Wrapping the long sheet around his neck, Orenthal tied the now makeshift rope into a half-Windsor knot as if he were putting a tie on.

Walking out onto the balcony and looking over the edge into the night sky, Orenthal knew that his time was limited. Taking the two ends of the sheet, Orenthal was able to tie a knot that he was sure would do the trick and would not loosen under his weight. Orenthal learned how to tie knots as a youth while camping with a state mandated group home for juveniles.

Tugging the knot and then raising his leg over the railing on the balcony. He now laid there on the rail in exhaustion, knowing he had already gone too far and had reached a point of no return.

Looking down over the rail, Orenthal again tugged the knot of the sheet as hard and as tight as he could around the rail of the balcony. He was now concerned that the sheet might tear under his weight. Orenthal could not take the chance that the sheet would tear; he wanted to be found hanging. Pulling again tightly on the knot, Orenthal finally convinced himself that the sheet *would* hold his weight.

As he lay there playing out the fantasy of his murder in his head, Orenthal leaned a little more over the side, displacing his weight unevenly over the edge of the balcony. If he could only lose consciousness, he thought, and let gravity do the rest; he would not have to muster the courage to finish the task.

He looked down over the edge. Orenthal's body was numb. Reflecting on what a horrible person he had become, and always was, he was just about to release the grip on his left leg and hurl himself the rest of the way over the rail when his cell phone rang.

As if waking-up out of a deep sleep, Orenthal wondered who it could be. Reaching into his right pants pocket, he pulled out his phone. The caller ID read ACE.

Should he answer?

No, he would let it go to voicemail. Orenthal gave Ace plenty of time earlier to call him back, but now Orenthal was ready to die.

Dropping his phone over the balcony, Orenthal did everything in his power to displace his weight and let gravity pull him over to his certain demise. Orenthal knew that he had to do this before someone witnessed the act.

Releasing the hold on his leg, Orenthal fell over the edge of the balcony where he hung in a gruesome, bloody fashion. The knot and the sheet both held perfectly.

Orenthal now had a strangle hold on the sheet that was tied around his neck as he hung helplessly over the balcony. Orenthal's hands, strategically placed in the knot prevented the knot from slipping and killing him instantly. Orenthal did not want to let go of the sheet as it was pulling itself tighter around his throat. If he were to let go, the knot would surely snap his neck or at the very least stop the flow of blood to his head. All of his weight was now pulling on his neck, and he refused to release his hands from the inside of the noose as he dangled one hundred and thirty-five feet above the cement.

Orenthal knew that as long as he held his hand within the noose part of the knot, he would be able to breathe. Looking up into the night sky and taking one final breath before releasing his grip, he panicked when he saw a surveillance camera at the corner of the building pointed directly at him.

Distraught at the possibility that he did all of this work to stage his own murder for nothing, Orenthal realized now that he did not want to die this way, and he began to ask himself a bunch of reasonable questions, that had come to him way too late. "What was the possibility of the camera recording his suicide? What would people think of him if they knew the truth? Who the fuck put that camera there anyway?"

Realizing now that Orenthal had to pull himself back onto the balcony, releasing his left hand from the noose, Orenthal was able to grab a hold of the rail at the top of the balcony.

When Orenthal had released his hand from the noose, the sheet pulled itself tighter around his windpipe and began to strangle him. Orenthal knew that if he could not pull himself over the railing within the next few seconds, that he would definitely lose consciousness and die.

Just then a light turned on from the balcony to the room to his right and the sliding glass door opened up.

"He's right there," a female voice said. "I think he is trying to kill himself."

A man about fifty years old in a security jacket appeared over the balcony. When he saw Orenthal hanging on for his life, he said very casually, "Sir, what, pray-tell, are you doing?"

Orenthal could barely choke out the word help as he dangled helplessly on the brink of death.

"What in the hell are you doing?" asked the man again with a grin, as if completely amazed. The security officer leaned forward informally against the rail of the next balcony to assess the situation closer.

With his eyes wide open, through his apparent distress Orenthal managed to choke out the word, "Help!"

"Alright," said the man walking away from the balcony slowly. "I'll be right over."

Orenthal knew now that he could sue the major hotel chain for incompetent security, if he could only pull himself over the balcony. In his mind, he had already figured out his new strategy: He would now say that he was attacked in his room while sleeping, and sue the hotel for damages.

As Orenthal hung there, he could hear the security guard entering his hotel room. "What in the blazes happened in here?" the man asked with a southern drawl, talking to himself. "It looks like bloody murder!" he exclaimed, still not making his way to the balcony.

"Help!" is all that Orenthal could gargle as he tried now with both hands to pull himself up over the balcony. Orenthal, still strong from his years as a professional athlete, pulled himself up onto the rail with all of his might, hoping that the security guard would be there to pull him the rest of the way over.

Orenthal was completely amazed when he seen the security guard still in the room placing the television back onto the dresser. "This is just a bloody mess," the security guard said. "You are definitely going to be charged for these damages," the man said, now walking out towards the balcony.

"Help!" Orenthal gasped as he felt the sensation of cold metal entering his stomach. Orenthal's abdominal wound was now caught on the decorative steel mesh of the balcony. He could feel the cold steel cutting through his intestines as he was trying to pull himself back over. His wound was now snagged like a fish hook onto the steel leafing.

In excruciating pain, Orenthal released his grip on the balcony, welcoming the snapping of his neck from the noose. The knot gave way, however, and his intestines were caught upon the balcony and shredded from the pull. Orenthal fell one hundred and forty feet.

Orenthal's body landed feet first half on the concrete and half on a very large cactus, spilling the rest of his blood all over the ground.

The security guard was now on the balcony, looking down. He said over a two-way radio calmly, "Call 911. Tell them he jumped."

Within minutes EMS and police had arrived on the gruesome scene. The sheet was still attached to Orenthal's neck. All of the rescue workers were looking up and pointing as they counted the floors.

As the coroner took pictures of Orenthal's corpse, another man reached into Orenthal's back pocket to recover his wallet. Opening the wallet, the man chuckled when he saw thirty-dollars worth of food stamps. "One less parasite sucking the American system dry," he joked.

The lead police officer said to the security guard, "This looks like he was attacked."

"Yes, I agree," he said, "but we have this man on video, and he clearly hurled himself over the balcony. I believe he attempted to make it look like a murder," the man said simply.

"We are going to have to review the cameras as soon as possible."

"Should we even bother trying CPR on this corpse?" asked one of the rescue workers.

"There's no use," said the coroner at the scene. "This man is dead. Shovel his corpse into a body bag. I'm tired," he said casually.

"Who's gonna clean up all of this blood?" asked the security guard. There were now bloody footprints everywhere from the emergency personnel.

No one answered him.

## Six Hours Later

Two security cameras had caught Orenthal jumping over the balcony, and the investigators were able to piece together what had actually happened.

"I have heard of people with demons," said the first investigator, "but this is remarkable. It appears that he is fighting an invisible man."

"And here is the hallway camera that shows that Orenthal is the only person to enter or exit the room in twelve hours."

"Thank god for video, or we would have definitely been under the assumption that this had been a murder."

The second investigator held a clear plastic bag marked EVIDENCE that held Orenthal's still-working phone. It rang.

"I still can't believe the phone didn't break from the fourteen-story fall. It landed right on a cactus."

"The phone says that the call is coming from Ace," said the detective, holding the bag in his hands to look at the evidence.

"Oh well, Ace," the other investigator sighed. "Your buddy Orenthal is dead. He killed himself. Too bad you weren't around to save him. You could have been his hero."

# CORONERS REPORT

File # 65469846-B

**Name of DECEASED:** Orenthal James A.K.A. - O.J.

AGE: Unknown at Time of Report

CAUSE OF DEATH:

Inmate did fall 140 feet to his death in apparent suicide.
Inmate did attempt to stage his own death as a homicide.

Multiple Blunt Force Trauma-
See Attached Report-

***Video Evidence on File***

UN-ASSISTED
**SUICIDE**

OFFICIAL BUSINESS-
Page 3 Of 6

# Maid-Man'

## A Hogtale

Viella Ortiz stood outside of Orenthal's house for over fifteen minutes. Ringing the doorbell, she waited patiently as she does every week, waiting for Orenthal to wake up and answer the door.

Viella was an established and professional housekeeper with references in Orenthal's affluent neighborhood. Most of Viella's clients are very wealthy and trust her with a key to their homes. This allows her to come and go at her convenience.

Viella always shows up on time and is always prepared to perform her duties to the best of her abilities, which was the reason why she had become somewhat of a celebrity in this wealthy community. It was very hard to find competent help in Orenthal's neighborhood.

Viella has worked hard cleaning houses ever since she was fourteen years old. She was married, earned a modest living, and paid her bills on time. She worked hard to send her children to school and had never once had a customer complaint in over twenty-two years of service. She had also never been subject to any claims of unprofessional behavior and had never been fired from any job. Her work ethic had always spoken for itself: she was a constant professional.

Waiting for Orenthal to answer the door on Thursday mornings had become somewhat of a ritual for Viella.

She had suggested once to Orenthal that perhaps she could get a key to the home so as not to disturb him in the morning, but Orenthal replied condescendingly, "Yeah, I give you a key one day, and the next day, *your people* come in while I'm out golfing and take everything including the kitchen sink."

From this day forward, Viella knew that she was dealing with a pompous ass.

"Good morning, Viella," said Orenthal when he finally opened the door.

She looked at her watch before replying in her Spanish accent, "Oh. Hello, Mr. James. Good morning." She continued firmly but politely, "I must get paid today for the last two weeks, Mr. James, plus today."

"I paid you for last week, didn't I?" Orenthal asked.

"No, last week you say you have not the money."

"I could have sworn I paid you, Viella. Don't make me fire your ass for cheating me," said Orenthal with a half a grin on his face.

"Oh, no, Mr. James. I work too hard. I not a thief," she replied, shaking her head seriously. "But, I do not work for free. I must get paid today." She remained firm as she walked into the house. "For today, one hundred dollars. Last week, one hundred dollars, and the same for the week before," she said, holding up three fingers. "I beg you please, Mr. James."

Orenthal just stood there, irritated.

"If you don't have, I must go," she said, looking around the pigpen.

Orenthal knew that the place would not get cleaned up unless Viella did her usual work. "Okay, I will look into it, Viella. It's too early in the morning for accounting."

"Well, I am just telling you, Mr. James, our agreement is that I get paid weekly, and in cash."

"I sure hope you got your green card, Viella. I'd hate to have to put in a call to Immigration officials, letting them know that you're out here working under the table," said Orenthal.

Clearly offended by Orenthal's attempt at intimidation, she said sternly, "Mr. James, I was born in the U.S. I am citizen for thirty-six years. Please don't patronize me. I treat you well. I work for fair price. The only thing that I ask is that you be fair and pay me as per our agreement. You pay me, or I go!"

"Okay, Viella, I will pay you," said Orenthal, smiling. "Jeez! I don't have a penny on me, so I am going to have to go to the ATM." He snorted and coughed as he walked away from her.

Viella knew by the look on that hog's face that she should just leave and cut her losses. But, she also knew she needed the money and did not want any negativity hurting her good reputation, so she began her work.

Orenthal's guest bathroom was a complete mess. The tub looked as if it had dried blood in it now for the third week in a row. "How could this place be so filthy?" she wondered to herself week after week. Without question, Orenthal's house was the most demanding as far as work load, and the most trouble as far as clients go.

Gathering all of the linens, the dirty towels, the sheets, the pillowcases, and the bathroom rugs, she carried four large loads of laundry down the stairs to the laundry room on the ground floor.

Sweating already, Viella loaded the first load of linens into the washing machine and prepared a bucket of cleaning supplies. She took off a small fanny pack, which contained her wallet, and placed it off to the side of the dryer on a small folding table. In her wallet, Viella kept her identification, money and credit cards, and pictures of her children.

Over the next few hours, Viella had a system of working through Orenthal's house. She cleaned the bathrooms: the sinks, the tubs, the shower, the windows, the mirrors, and all of the floors.

Heading into the kitchen she cleaned the sink, the counters, the stove, and the windows, loaded and ran the dishwasher, and wiped out the microwave.

In the living room and the den, she dusted the furniture and wall hangings, organized the various magazines, remote controls and other clutter, and vacuumed, and then headed up the stairs to work on the bedrooms.

Now Viella was replacing all of the bed sheets and making the beds in each of the bedrooms. She had now spent over three exhausting hours reorganizing Orenthal's pigpen. Walking past Orenthal's room, she saw him sprawled out on top of the bed sleeping face down and snoring loudly. Viella always thought that Orenthal must suffer from sleep apnea.

"Excuse me, Mr. James," she said, knocking gently on the door jam.

He stopped snorting.

"Mr. James?"

"What?" he yelled aggravated. "What?"

"I need to strip the bed down and replace the sheets."

"Do you have to do this now, Viella?" he asked.

"Yes, Mr. James. I am almost finished, and I need to get paid before I go."

Orenthal sat up, disoriented. "Jesus Christ, Viella. You are a pain in the ass. I think I am going to start using you every other week from now on. I am sick and tired of having to cater to you every time you're here."

Exhaling in disbelief and shaking her head Viella said "That's fine, Mr. James; my bi-weekly rate is $150. It is more work for me," she said.

"You've gots to be shitting me! And I am sure your paying taxes on that, Viella," he sneered sarcastically

"Mr. James, I pay."

Standing up and storming out of the room in his underwear Orenthal said, "Yeah, I'm sure you do."

Walking downstairs into the kitchen, Orenthal started slamming cupboards and doors, screaming something that Viella could not understand. Stopping for a moment to listen, she heard Orenthal scream, "Now, they come here, and they think they make the rules! What the fuck is going on with this country? Waking me up, like I don't need my sleep. Who the fuck does she think she is?" As she continued her work, she tried to tune him out.

"Viella," Orenthal screamed up the stairs.

"Viella…Where the fuck is the towel for the kitchen?"

Yelling back down the stairs looking puzzled, "It's in the wash Mr. James…"

"Oh, I thought you were ready to go?" Orenthal said mockingly. "There are no towels in the kitchen yet. What the fuck? I just spilled orange juice in the fucking kitchen; can you please clean it up…?"

Hurrying down the stairs into the kitchen, Viella said, "Mr. James I already mopped and cleaned the entire kitchen, I have no time to clean up after you again!"

There was orange juice all over the counter, juice all over the stove, juice running down the cabinets. There was a large puddle still dripping onto the floor, as Orenthal walked downstairs to the laundry room. Viella could see where he had walked through the puddles of Orange juice, tracking it all over the floor, leaving a distinct footprint.

Gasping in desperation, because she knew that this degenerate would not clean up the sticky mess, Viella ran downstairs for her cleaning bucket and supplies. Entering the laundry room, Orenthal was standing there, with a towel wrapped in his hand. Just standing there like a fool he said, "I need more towels."

Pushing passed him to grab the bucket and some rags, Viella ran back upstairs to the kitchen. Viella was exhausted and infuriated at Orenthal. She was so mad that she could feel the blood boiling in her face and in her ears.

Letting out a mutter just loud enough for herself to hear, she said, "Juice everywhere!" Getting a little louder she repeated, "Juice Everywhere!" As she was cleaning the counter she almost slipped on the wet floor and screamed, "JUICE EVERYWHERE!"

Orenthal screamed back from downstairs, "I didn't ask you to wake me up Viella; this is just as much you're fault as it is mine!"

Viella stopped to scream profanity in Spanish back at Orenthal, but she knew that she was a better person than him and refused to stoop to his level. After twenty minutes of cleaning rinsing and scrubbing, Viella was again finished cleaning the kitchen. Somehow there was even juice on the ceiling.

Walking through the house Viella announced, "Mr. James," she said a little louder, "Mr. James?" Walking back upstairs towards the bedrooms Viella could hear that

Orenthal was in the bathroom. Choosing not to disturb him, she took the opportunity to finish cleaning up his bedroom, changing the sheets.

When she had finished in the bedroom, Viella decided that she had had just about enough of Orenthal James for one day. She walked down the two flights of stairs to the laundry room, and she noticed that her fanny pack was unzipped and the contents were lying on the table. In horror, she dropped the laundry and subconsciously begged to God that the four hundred and fifty dollars that she had in her wallet was still there. "Oh, no!" she screamed. As she went through the bag, she saw her receipts, pictures of her family, and coupons, but no money. How could this happen? Starting to shake at the only possibility, she cried, "My money! No, no, no! My money!"

She walked frantically back upstairs towards Orenthal's room, holding the opened fanny pack out in front of her. Orenthal was still in the bathroom. Still frantic and shaking, she said loudly, "Mr. James?"

"Yeah," he answered.

"I need to—" she began, but the bathroom door opened and interrupted her.

"Viella, I got to go," he said as he marched out of the bathroom. Noticing that she was carrying the fanny pack, he turned quickly away from her, putting his belt on. "I am going to be late now," he said as he was buttoning his shirt.

"Mr. James," she said distraught. "My money?" she asked, looking for an explanation.

"Yes," he said, as he sat on his bed tying his shoes. "I will pay you your money—"

"No, Mr. James!" she cried, holding up the unzipped fanny pack. "My money is missing out of my bag. I had four hundred and fifty dollars, Mr. James! I need my money! My rent is due and my son—he is in trouble. Please!"

Reaching into his pants pocket, he said, "Here." He pulled out a large wad of cash and counted out the bills. "Here is money for last week, and here is money for this week. There, now we are all caught up."

Taking the money, Viella knew that these twenty dollar bills were the same ones that had been stolen out of her bag. Viella had carried that money around for over a week. She couldn't confirm the serial numbers, but she recognized the familiar crease in the center of the bills from the fold in her wallet.

"Mr. James, are you joking with me?"

"Joking? No, what are you talking about? What's wrong with you?" he asked.

Viella stood there with a bitter, disgusted panic on her face.

"No, Mr. James," Viella pleaded in desperation. "My bag was in the laundry, and I put it there, and it was zipped up, and I find it opened and ransacked, my money missing. Please, Mr. James!" she said with absolution. "I beg you mercy. I work too hard!" She began to cry, her hands shaking.

Unsympathetically, Orenthal said, "We all work hard, Viella. But some of us have real jobs," he continued. "And if it wasn't for people like me out there making real money and paying real taxes, then people like you wouldn't have a job. Now get out of my way. I have to go to work."

Lifting her head and speaking through her shaking hands, Viella issued one more plea: "But Mr. James, you owed me for three weeks," she begged, holding up three fingers.

"Well, I don't remember, and I don't think so, but we will talk about it next week," he said, walking out of the room. "What do you think, I'm made of money? Lock the door when you leave."

"Oh no," she cried, hitting the floor in exhaustion. "No. No. No! This can't be!" She lay there, shattered at the impossibility of the situation.

Getting up and running back downstairs to the laundry room, Viella went through every piece of laundry. She emptied the dryer and checked the lint trap. She looked under and behind the washer and the dryer to make sure that this was not a misunderstanding.

Folding each piece of laundry with the precision that only twenty years of experience could give a person, Viella cried, "No. No! No!"

Viella was defeated literally and figuratively. She did the math in her head though exhausted. When she walked into Orenthal's house earlier today, she had four hundred and fifty dollars of her own money. Orenthal had owed her two hundred dollars for the past two weeks, and she had expected to get an additional one hundred dollars for today's work.

In all actuality, Viella should have been walking out of the house with seven hundred and fifty dollars in cash. Instead, after a full day's work she had only two hundred dollars. She was robbed of five hundred and fifty dollars.

As she walked to the end of the street, she asked herself, "How could this be possible?" As she cried at the bus stop, she wondered to herself if she should call the police. This was not fair.

Getting on the bus and riding out of the neighborhood, she vowed to herself that she would never step foot in Orenthal's house again. How would she tell her son that he could not borrow the money? How would she pay the rent? What about groceries and the other bills? Viella was going to have to dip into her savings account and use the money that she was saving to buy Christmas presents with. She breathed in deeply and exhaled; she knew that she would somehow make it work. She clasped her strong hands together, closed her eyes, and said a prayer for the infamous Orenthal James.

Arriving home after a full days work, Viella started making dinner for her family. Pouring herself a large glass of iced lemonade, sitting down to relax, she pushed the message button on her answering machine: YOU HAVE ONE NEW MESSAGE.

"Yeah, Viella, this is Orenthal…Orenthal James- I have been looking for you for a couple of weeks, the place is getting pretty dirty, (he sniggered) We really need you over here… give me a call….or stop by…" (Click)

Viella had received another message on her answering machine when she arrived home after a hard day of work:

"Hey Viella, its Orenthal, hey listen, I would appreciate it if you would call me back and at least give me a little notice if you're going to quit… You could at least clean one more time so I can find a new maid… Call me…" (Click)

## Two Days Later

It was Thursday, and Viella was enjoying her new day off. Sitting on the balcony of her apartment drinking a cup of coffee, she was reading a Spanish newspaper when she heard her phone ring. The caller ID on the handset read "James, Orenthal."

Standing up to go inside so that she could hear the message he left, Viella now stood in anticipation in her immaculate kitchen.

After the answering machine beeped, Viella heard Orenthal say, "Hey Viella. You're never going to believe this! I had to do my own laundry, and I found some money in the dryer, and a picture of a girl that looks like your daughter. It's over two hundred dollars! I am assuming it was yours. Give me a call…"

Just as he was about to hang up, Viella picked up the phone and said, "Hello, Mr. James. This is Viella."

"Hey, Viella!" Orenthal cheered. "I knew if I mentioned money, you would pick up the phone."

"No, Mr. James, I picked up the phone to tell you that you can keep my money. Obviously, you need it more than I do."

"Wait, what's the matter?"

"Mr. James, I will not work for a thief. I work for only good people. I do not need your work. Please do not call me again."

"But wait, I have a picture of your daughter," he said innocently.

"Mr. James, I knew the last time that I left your house that you were a disgrace to anything decent in this world, but I had no idea just how depraved and immoral a man you must be. Why you grabbed a picture of my daughter when you stole my money is beyond me, but I can only assume that you are way more dangerous a predator than any person would ever imagine. It is clear that there is nothing sacred to you in this world and that you pose a threat to anyone and anything you come in contact with—"

"What are you talking about, Viella? I think your way out of line!"

"Wait, Mr. James. I'm not finished," she continued. "Judging by your behavior, I can only assume that you are not long for this world. You are hell-bent on self-destruction, and I can only pray for the people who are close to you. When He catches up to you Orenthal, may God have mercy on your soul." Having said her peace, Viella gently hung up the phone.

Pulling his head back on his shoulders, Orenthal stood there staring out unable to focus, appearing to be a bit confused. Almost as if he was convinced that he had no idea what Viella was just talking about.

"Oh well," said Orenthal out loud, "I guess I'll just have to get another slave. Who needs her?" he asked.

Just then, Orenthal's doorbell rang.

"*Oh, HELL,*" Orenthal yelled at the inconvenience. *"I'll be right there!"*

# And All God's Morn

## Revenge

Orenthal James had had an exhausting day on the golf course. He was a guest at an exclusive country club for the day and felt out of place because he no longer had the means or resources available to him to maintain such a lavish lifestyle. Orenthal barely ate or drank anything on this hot day, and the prescribed medication in his system was wreaking havoc with his equilibrium.

Heading home to his rented luxury condominium, Orenthal felt weak and light headed. Pulling into his parking spot, Orenthal knew that he could not afford to leave his brand new; two-thousand dollar set of custom golf clubs in the back of his vehicle, but he also knew that he would probably have a hard time carrying them up the stairs into his home. He was feeling weary and old. He could not wait to get upstairs so that he could take a nap before going to dinner.

Getting out of the vehicle, Orenthal felt that the heat from the sun was going to knock him out. Reaching into the back seat, he pulled his heavy golf bag out and rustled it onto his shoulder. Orenthal was sweating profusely.

Climbing each step, Orenthal felt as if he would collapse from exhaustion. Getting to the top of the stairs and around the corner, Orenthal dropped his golf clubs at his front door and fumbled with his keys.

Entering his house, Orenthal used the keypad on the wall to disable the alarm system. He struggled to remember the code, 0-6-1-2, though he should have remembered it because it is the same PIN that his bank had assigned him for his ATM card.

The air conditioning felt nice as he walked into his kitchen, reached into his refrigerator, and grabbed a glass pitcher that was filled with fresh lemonade. Orenthal loved lemonade.

Having retrieved a glass from the cupboard, Orenthal leaned into the freezer looking for ice, and a cloud of cool fog poured out onto his overheated body. He placed some ice in the glass.

Taking his cup and walking over to the kitchen sink, Orenthal slid open the drawer and pulled out a large wooden spoon that he used to stir the lemonade.

Pouring himself his first glass, Orenthal could barely catch his breath as he gulped the lemonade furiously, even swallowing a large ice cube. He was parched.

Pouring himself a second glass and setting it on the counter, Orenthal reached into a small basket and grabbed a paper napkin to wipe his brow and mouth with. As he looked out of the kitchen window into the pool area, Orenthal could have sworn that he saw a reflection in the glass, and he turned to see—

The sound was familiar. It was the stealthy sound of a golf club swung with conviction.

Smiling at the surprise, Orenthal never had the chance to realize that he had just been clubbed right between his left ear and eye with his own golf club. It was his titanium three driver; which, with the appropriate swing, can send a golf ball soaring at an incredible one hundred and fifty feet per second, with an unbelievable force of up to twenty-five thousand pounds per square inch.

Orenthal was dead before he hit the floor. This was a perfect swing. Large chunks of his skull were pushed into the cranial nerve responsible for sending information to Orenthal's heart. The sudden trauma interrupted the signals responsible for generating his heartbeat.

As Orenthal lay dead on his kitchen floor, the unknown intruder walked over to the keypad of the alarm system and sent an emergency panic signal to the alarm company by pressing the pound and the star buttons simultaneously.

Walking out of the door to the condo, the unknown intruder placed the golf club back in Orenthal's golf bag, walked down the stairs, and disappeared from the murder scene forever.

## Ten Minutes Later

When the police arrived at the scene, they were perplexed at the injury. One investigator took a monkey wrench as evidence, convinced that it was the tool used to terminate Orenthal's existence. Other not-so-convinced investigators believed that whatever was used as the murder weapon was taken from the scene of the crime by the perpetrator.

The barely melted ice cubes still in the glass of lemonade that was resting on the counter led them to believe that the crime scene was less than ten minutes old.

Investigators surmised almost immediately that due to the obviously brazen nature of the assailant that this was a crime of passion and must have been done by someone that Orenthal knew or was closely associated with.

## Six Weeks Later

Orenthal's family hired an agency to sell away anything of value in order to cover his legal bills and bad debts. Surprisingly, not too many people showed up at the sale. Walking over to a set of golf clubs, a young waiter who had stopped by the auction before heading into work asked, "How much for these clubs?"

"Three hundred dollars," said the auctioneer.

"I only have seventy-five," the young man said eagerly.

"Sold, to the man in the white polo shirt!"

Wiping some crud off of the titanium three driver, the young man said, "Hell, these are practically brand new. Someone would probably *kill* to buy these clubs at this price!"

Looking around the room, the young man realized that his comment was probably inappropriate under the circumstances and was almost embarrassed until the auctioneer began to laugh and said, "That's *exactly* what happened, my friend… One mans burden, another mans opportunity!"

## 12 Months Later

A year after the murder, Investigator Holcomb was closing out the case file that had been sitting open and unsolved on his desk even though he had examined every probable lead and questioned multiple potential witnesses.

With the lack of a murder weapon and no obvious suspects, the investigator slashed his pen across the log entries to the bottom of the sheet attached to the folder and wrote in red ink, "CASE CLOSED. NO FURTHER LEADS AT THIS TIME."

This act was unprecedented, especially due to the nature of the quasi-celebrity status of the victim. The controversy that had surrounded his life had finally come to a close.

But more than ten months had passed, and it seemed that no one, not even the media, cared about the disposition or status of the dead has-been.

The infamous Orenthal James was dead, and no one cared.

# UNSOLVED MURDER

## #1155438

### Narrative:

**MURDER: Orenthal James - DECEASED**
**It has been more than 1- Year since the murder of Orenthal James. He was found bludgeoned to death in his home.**

**No Leads, No Suspects, No Murder Weapon.**

CASE CLOSED
*Pending Further Evidence*

QUICK FACTS

Orenthal James was found bludgeoned to death in his home.

The case has yielded no leads, and no suspects to this murder.

A murder weapon has yet to be found.

Because of the nature of the crime it is believed that whomever is responsible for his death is some closely related.

**COLD CASE FILE**

Page 3 of 3
Inv. Holcomb #22